OTHER
MOTHERS

BOOKS BY M.M. CHOUINARD

M.M.CHOUINARD

THE
OTHER
MOTHERS

bookouture

Published by Bookouture in 2021

An imprint of Storyfire Ltd.
Carmelite House
50 Victoria Embankment
London EC4Y 0DZ

www.bookouture.com

ISBN: 978-1-80019-124-2
eBook ISBN: 978-1-80019-123-5

To Leo, for believing in Jo, and in me.

CHAPTER ONE

Stephanie Roden leapt from her desk and hurried out to the playground of Briar Ridge Elementary School, her cloud of curled black braids bouncing around her head. The end-of-recess bell had startled her out of her lesson planning, and sent an unsettling rush of adrenaline through her. Twenty-minute recesses were great for the kids but horrible for the teachers, giving just enough time to shift into a task, but nowhere near enough time to finish it. She shoved her arms into her black jacket, then gathered her composure as she pushed through the doors into the unseasonably cold spring air.

Several of her kindergarteners already waited on the strip of grass where the class gathered. She pulled out her whistle, gave three sharp tweets, and watched the little heads spin and run toward her. She smiled as they lined up, their faces cheerful and eager-to-please as she gently guided them into formation. Such little angels, all of them, even if they had moments where they acted like little devils. Lively spirits were important, she liked to remind the trainee teachers who occasionally worked with her—you want to channel their beautiful spirits, not break them.

She moved down the line, tapping each head playfully as she went. One, two, three… fourteen, fifteen, sixteen.

Sixteen—not seventeen, as there should be. Someone was missing.

She glanced back over the playground. Empty, except for Jim Karnegi, the third-grade teacher, and Karen Phelps, today's parent volunteer, each walking with lollygagging stragglers.

Everything was fine, she reminded herself. Someone had probably just gone to the outside bathroom without asking one of the two adults to take them.

She ran through her class roster in her head. *Nicole Marchand,* she realized, and a tendril of fear gripped her. Nicole was the missing child, and it wasn't like her to go missing. She was quiet, cooperative, and never a troublemaker; she'd never go to the bathroom alone without permission.

She looked back at her students, and kept her voice light. "Does anyone know where Nicole is?"

They looked at one another and shook their heads.

She waved Karen over. "I can't find Nicole. Do you know where she is?"

"No." Karen's huge blue eyes widened, and her blonde ponytail bobbed as her head whipped to scan the playground. "Are you sure she didn't already go in?"

"She might have," Stephanie said, but knew she hadn't. "Can you stay with them while I go check?"

"Of course." Karen turned to the children and started them singing 'The Hokey Pokey'.

Stephanie waited until she was out of the view of the other children to break into a sprint. She checked her classroom, but it was empty. She checked the 'big girl' and 'big boy' bathrooms, but they were empty, too.

She bolted back out to the yard, then slowed to a walk, shaking her head as she passed to let Karen know she hadn't found Nicole. With a practiced power walk, she surged down the midway of the playground calling Nicole's name, hoping to find her crouched behind something, lost in her own private game.

She followed the perimeter of the yard back toward the school building, bobbing and weaving to check behind the jungle gyms and the utility sheds. They were all abandoned and secured.

Her heart thumped in her chest. She slipped around the corner and down the ten-foot-wide space where the chain-link fence ran parallel to the school building, ending at the back entrance to the cafeteria. Her fear morphed into panic as she sprinted toward the dumpster enclosure near the door.

Because the brown gate that fronted the redbrick enclosure was ajar.

She called Nicole's name again as she yanked it fully open—and found nothing, except a few errant lettuce leaves on the pavement between the two dumpsters. She dashed to the side of the left dumpster, just to be thorough.

Nicole's crumpled body lay sprawled in the back corner, head covered by her puffy blue jacket.

*

At the principal's instruction, Karen Phelps led the kindergarteners into Ms. Roden's classroom. As the last one filed in, she glanced up and down the corridor. Once she confirmed it was empty, she reached into her jacket pocket and slipped out her phone.

"No phones allowed in the classroom!" one of the boys shrieked, and ran toward her.

She pushed it back into her pocket and stepped inside the room.

"She's a teacher, she's allowed!" one of the little girls called back.

"She's not a teacher, she's a mom," the boy answered scornfully.

"Well, it's nice to follow the rules, no matter who you are," Karen said. "I have an idea. Who wants to have an extra story time?"

Nearly all the hands shot up, as Karen hoped they would. She herded the children over to the carpeted area, snatched up a book from the shelf, and cast a frustrated glance back at the door.

CHAPTER TWO

Detective Josette Fournier surveyed the stacks of printouts and files dotting her home-office desk. She threw the final file onto what she hoped was the right stack, then pushed away from the cherry-wood desk and stretched her neck. She needed more coffee.

She smoothed her sweatshirt down over her pajama bottoms as she padded into the kitchen, then filled the bottom of her Bialetti Moka Express with Columbian roast. The little silver coffeemaker had been a gift from Matt Soltero, the man she was dating, after she'd become addicted to the espresso he made with his—or rather, after she'd become addicted to the *process* of making espresso with it. Purists would scream from the hilltops that it didn't make *true* espresso, she knew that. But with the right technique, low and slow and patient, the thick brown liquid that bubbled from the spout was surrounded by a rich, frothy crema just as luxurious as any she'd ever tasted. And there was a satisfaction—more like a soothing magic—in her control over the grounds and the timing and the modulation of the heat that her 'real' espresso machine just didn't deliver.

And control was something she was in desperate need of right now.

She frothed a cup of milk as she waited for the magical moment when the coffee would erupt and ran her mind over the work she'd just completed. Her therapist would probably argue that *working* from home wasn't quite the two-week respite she'd strongly suggested Jo take to grieve her miscarriage and get a handle on the 'cumulative PTSD' it had triggered from years ago. Double the cumulative post-traumatic stress actually, because she'd miscarried after a murder suspect shot her. But even if working wasn't the best thing for her, being home alone all day—no matter how much she loved her cozy little cottage—left her far too much time to spend in her own head. She needed something to focus her mind on instead of the endless cycling between pain and regret, futilely wondering if her baby had been a boy or a girl, blaming herself because she hadn't been certain she wanted the baby, feeling guilty because part of her was relieved she no longer had to make an impossible choice, and fighting the consuming terror that everyone and everything she loved would die as the result of her mistakes.

So, after failed attempts to distract herself with novels and binge-watching, she'd decided the healthiest outlet was her on-going obsession with the apparent suicide of Martin Scherer, a serial killer she'd hunted eight years earlier. The process of scour-ing and categorizing had allowed her to shift from something she couldn't control to something she could, and now nearly five hundred Golden Gate Bridge suicides were organized in a spreadsheet according to fifty variables, entered meticulously over her two weeks' leave. Nobody at the Oakhurst County State Police Detective Unit, not even her partner Bob Arnett, understood why Martin's death had sunk its claws so deeply into her. But what it came down to, at least for now, was her need for a sense of agency and the possibility of attaining closure, and this was a proactive way to work toward both.

She poured the milk into a mug, then rotated her wounded arm, ignoring the pain as she attempted to stave off stiffness. When the maker sputtered the final drops of espresso into the upper compartment, she flipped the lid closed, poured the contents into her mug, and topped it off with her steamed milk. She sipped, and closed her eyes to savor the warm, milky coffee. Rich, with not a hint of bitterness, and it made her feel human again. The purists could go to hell.

Anticipation pricked at her as she settled back in front of her laptop, now fully prepared to while away her last day off work in a blur of hierarchical variable searches. But as her fingers hit the keyboard, her phone rang. Tempted to ignore it, she took a quick glance at the screen just in case it was important, then answered it.

"Bob. Is everything okay?" After pushing her to take the leave, he'd never disturb her unless there was an important reason.

"Yep, I'm fine. But I just got called out to a homicide, and since you're coming back tomorrow, I thought you'd prefer to see the scene in real time rather than piece it together after the fact."

"I'm guessing this isn't some run-of-the-mill drive-by if you think I need to see it?" Jo cast a longing glance at her spreadsheet.

"No. I'll be honest with you—I tried to get Martinez to assign it to anybody else, but since I couldn't tell him why, he refused."

Her shoulders tightened. Their temporary lieutenant thought her leave was only because she'd been shot in the line of duty; nobody in the unit knew about her miscarriage. "What do you mean?"

"I'm torn about having you work it. The victim's a little girl. Very little."

A blinding pain flashed through Jo, and the vision she'd been seeing in her nightmares, of a young girl who called her mommy, appeared before her squeezed-shut eyes. She gripped the desk with her free hand, surprised by the intensity of the anguish that took her over. She forced herself to shift into slow, deep breaths.

This wasn't acceptable, she told herself. Of course she didn't expect to work everything out in two weeks, but she'd expected to have it under a functional amount of control. She'd taken time away to heal, and spent an hour nearly every day with her therapist talking it all through. The nightmares had finally stopped, and she was feeling almost normal again. Happy, even, excited about picking up a trail on a long-past case. But everyone had pain, everyone had bad things happen to them, and everyone had to find a way to deal with it all. The time for self-indulgence was over, and she couldn't let a case destroy her progress—this was her job, and she had to pull it together and do what needed to be done.

She took a deep breath, then pushed the anguish down and slammed her protective walls back up. A quiet numbness replaced the burning pain.

"How soon can you pick me up?" she asked.

*

Ten minutes later, Jo climbed into the undercover black Chevy Malibu and buckled in as Bob Arnett pulled out from the curb.

"You look like hell," he said. "Maybe I shouldn't have bothered you after all."

She glanced down briefly at her gray utility jacket, academy sweatshirt, jeans, and trainers, admittedly a far cry from the blazer and slacks she normally wore when working, then shot him a skeptical up-and-down look. His salt-and-pepper hair was scruffy, and his brown eyes peeped out from dark circles. "I'm gonna go ahead and ignore that coming from the man with the Louis Vuittons under his eyes and the marinara on his shirt."

He rested a hand on his small paunch. "Yeah, but that's my resting state. This isn't normal for you. In twenty years I've never seen your hair doing whatever you call that." He pointed at her head.

"Hey, if you surprise me on my day off, this is what you get." She laughed, but one hand shot up to smooth the messy bun of chestnut hair as the other pulled down her visor. She did look more tired than she should, her green eyes puffy and slightly red. But what else could you expect from someone who'd spent the last two weeks processing grief counseling and staying up till all hours compiling spreadsheets? "Don't worry, Bob, I'm fine. I promise."

He nodded, and swung on to the pike. "Good, because there's something I didn't mention on the phone."

She narrowed her eyes at him.

He avoided looking at her. "The reason I wasn't completely heartbroken when Martinez wouldn't let me hand this off is, the scene's in Harristown. At Briar Ridge Elementary."

Jo winced her eyes shut. Her sister Sophie lived in Harristown, and her two nieces went to Briar Ridge. "How old did you say Nicole was?"

"Five. She was a kindergartener."

Jo stared out at the forest lining the pike. Her niece Emily was in the first grade, while Isabelle was in the third. But even if Nicole wasn't in either of their classes, Sophie was sure to be freaked out by it all. "You did the right thing. She'll be calling me in hysterics either way."

"Yeah, that's what Laura said. She sends her love, by the way."

Jo smiled. "How is she?"

"Good. She decided to take a drawing class at Oakhurst Community College this summer. We'll see how long that lasts."

"Now, now. You're being supportive, remember?" Jo waved a finger at him and laughed. Laura, his wife, had struggled with becoming an empty nester, particularly in light of the long hours Bob worked. She'd had an affair and they'd almost divorced over it, until he'd agreed to give her more time and attention. That had translated into a string of new hobbies she wanted to try out, usually with Bob. "At least she doesn't want you to do this one with her."

"Truth. Even she can't deny my art skills begin and end with stick figures." Arnett pulled off the pike.

Jo caught sight of Briar Ridge Elementary in the distance. Harristown was the sort of quaint, quintessential New England town you found in movies, filled with redbrick and white clapboard, steepled churches and town halls, and abundant colonial architecture. Right in line with it all, Briar Ridge Elementary was a modern take on a classic schoolhouse, and in actual fact had started out that way. The original structure, built in the early 1700s, formed the center of the school, with newer redbrick wings extending out and around on either side, built up through the years as needs changed. One of two elementary schools in the small town, Briar Ridge was private, and part of the considerable tuition parents paid went to keep the original schoolhouse in pristine condition. It was quite a point of pride for Sophie, for whom those sorts of things mattered.

Arnett pulled into the U-shaped drop-off driveway that cut through the school's front yard and parked behind a squad car. Jo stepped out and pulled her jacket closer against the cold; despite a few warm days the week before, spring was refusing to give way to the promise of summer any faster than it had to. The tall, uniformed responding officer crossed over and introduced himself.

"Your team's already processing the scene." He pointed to the right side of the building. "Through there, then back where the dumpsters are. My partner's inside with the administrators."

He escorted them through the main entrance, out through the courtyard and playground, and around to a strip of tarmac that extended along the side of the building. The far end of the space was cordoned off with police tape, where two medicolegals in full kit worked the scene. Jo recognized Janet Marzillo, who oversaw the Oakhurst County SPDU's lab, and Hakeem Peterson, a relatively new hire, under all the personal protective equipment.

"Marzillo. Peterson." Arnett waved to them from across the tape. "We're suiting up."

Hakeem gave a two-finger air salute that he made sure didn't touch his face, then returned to work while Marzillo came over to talk with them. "Jo. I thought you weren't back until tomorrow?"

Jo slipped into coveralls. "My nieces go to school here, so Bob thought I'd want to be in it from the start."

"Gotcha," Marzillo said, carefully holding her hands away from her sides as Jo and Arnett finished slipping into their gear. Once they were done, she turned and led them to the girl. "There, to the left of the two dumpsters. Stephanie Roden, the teacher that found her after she went missing during recess, tried to resuscitate her." She gestured to a sky-blue puffer jacket. "She says that was over Nicole's head when she found her, but she had to move it."

Jo squatted down next to the little girl. Dressed in a sweet pink daisy-print dress with matching yellow tights, she looked like a doll that had been put through the washing machine, then tossed on the floor to dry. Her mop of midnight-brown curls were squashed and askew, and her eyes were closed; her mouth hung open in a small O-shape, and her skin was tinted a faint blueish-purple. The overall effect gave her an air of mild concentration, like she was trying to figure out the answer to a difficult puzzle.

Jo fought back a desperate wave of anger and helplessness as she stared into the tiny face, a precious life snuffed out before it began. Horrors like these, committed against the defenseless, were the ones that ripped at her soul. She forced herself through a series of deep breaths, and shoved the emotion down.

Shifting her weight to one heel, she surveyed the area from her current vantage point. Zero visibility from the playground, even with the enclosure open, unless you came around the side of the building. Same from the cafeteria door—someone could be standing there, looking out, and see nothing.

Jo turned back and pointed to several nasty red spots that marred the porcelain-skinned cheeks and throat. "I'm guessing she was suffocated?"

"The ME will have to make the final determination, but that's what it looks like to me." Marzillo's career as a medicolegal began in a medical examiner's office, and her opinions rarely turned out to be wrong—that was part of why she'd advanced to overseeing the lab. She pointed to a spray of tiny red dots. "Petechiae in both eyes, and here on both ears. Those marks on the neck have a strange shape and spacing, not what I'd predict from normal fingermarks, so my guess is the killer held her down and strangled her through the jacket, which would have distorted the contact to some degree."

Jo glanced up at Marzillo. "Can we test for touch DNA, then?"

"You read my mind. But don't get your hopes up too high, because on a day like this, it's very possible our killer wore gloves."

"And if they held her down, it wasn't just some sort of accident, or rough-housing with some other kids?"

Marzillo tilted her head. "No way. Someone knew what they were doing."

Arnett leaned over them. "Any other injuries?"

"We can't do a complete examination out here, but from a quick initial look, I don't have any reason to think she was sexually assaulted in any way."

"That's a blessing, at least," Jo said, fighting nausea.

Marzillo nodded. "There is some bruising on her chest, but that could have come from the resuscitation attempt."

"CPR's hard when they're that small," Arnett said.

"Have you had a chance to check the area?" Jo asked.

Marzillo straightened back up. "We've checked everything inside the dumpster enclosure, and around the perimeter. We did a quick look into the dumpsters themselves and didn't see anything unusual, but we'll have to go through the contents."

Jo scrunched up her face sympathetically. "So nothing to tell us how she might have ended up in here?"

Marzillo removed her gloves and tossed them in the biohazard container, put on a new pair, then carefully rolled Nicole onto her side. "Nothing conclusive, but my guess is she was alive when the killer brought her in here. You can see here, the asphalt scraped her dress, she has asphalt particles in her hair, and there are hairs and fibers from her dress on the ground. The teacher would have had to be pretty aggressive to cause all of that during CPR. It's possible she was killed on another similar surface, then dumped here, but—"

"But someone would have had to risk being seen walking with a dead child," Arnett said.

"Right. And Nicole was alive when recess began, twenty minutes before she was found dead, so nobody killed her earlier and dumped her."

"No," Jo agreed, standing up. "Nobody snatched her, killed her, then brought her back here all in twenty minutes. This is most likely our kill site."

Marzillo gestured toward the enclosure. "Whoever brought her here had to open the dumpster gate. We dusted for prints, and there's no shortage of them. We'll collect samples from all the cafeteria workers and the janitorial staff and start identifying people. But again, my guess is the killer wore gloves."

"So how did they get her back here?" Arnett said, staring out toward the playground.

Jo grimaced and pointed to the fence. "Maybe they stood by the end of the building and called over to her? Possibly the perp came through that gate?" She gestured to the fence near the cafeteria.

Arnett strode over and tried to lift the latch. "Locked." He gazed up at the eight-foot fence. "But you could climb this without too much skill."

"Wouldn't you hear it if someone climbed over a fence like that?" Jo asked.

Arnett looked skeptical. "Depends on where you were in the yard, and what you were doing. If some kid just fell and hurt themselves at the far end, you probably wouldn't even notice."

"So our killer waits for a distraction, snatches a kid, then brings her back here to suffocate her? That seems like a long wait for a tiny possibility," Jo said.

"Oh, one more thing." Marzillo pointed to an evidence bag. "We found that near the wall of the enclosure, a few inches away from Nicole."

Jo picked up the bag. A three-inch toy lay at the bottom, a figure of a pig dressed like a human, standing upright with one arm outstretched. "Do we know if this belonged to Nicole?"

"It's possible she had it with her when she was killed. Or someone may have just tried to throw it away, and missed the dumpster."

While Jo pulled out her phone to snap a picture of the toy, Arnett squatted down and peered under the dumpsters. "Nothing else lying around?"

"Nope, just Nicole, her jacket, a couple of lettuce leaves, and the toy." Marzillo shook her head.

"Do you know if the parents have been notified?" Jo asked, trying to push down the memory of her own reaction when she learned her baby was gone.

A matching cloud passed over Marzillo's face. "We sent an officer out as soon as we officially confirmed Nicole's identity. The parents should know by now."

"Then we'll go talk to the principal while you finish up." She put her hands on her hips, looked around again, and shook her head. "I'm getting two contradictory sets of cues from all this—some that point to a stranger, and some that make a stranger nearly impossible. I need some answers to make sense of them."

CHAPTER THREE

By the time Jo and Arnett pulled off their gloves, Marzillo was already refocused on the scene.

"Are you the detectives?"

The female voice behind them was strong, so much so that when Jo turned, she was surprised to find a slight five-foot-three woman in front of her. The woman's blue power suit matched her voice, as did her straight posture and grim expression.

"We are. I'm Detective Josette Fournier, and this is Detective Bob Arnett." Jo stripped the rest of her protective gear into the biohazard container before extending her arm.

The woman grasped it with one firm pump, then turned to shake Arnett's. "I'm Principal Eileen Pham. I'm sorry to interrupt, but I need to speak with you urgently. Our kindergarten parents will be here to pick up their children at one fifteen."

Jo checked the time. Eleven forty-five, so just over an hour before the class let out. But if the other mothers were anything like Sophie, they'd be here at least fifteen minutes ahead of that, carrying freshly baked cookies for the teachers. "Just the kindergarteners? You're not shutting down the whole school? Isn't that standard protocol?"

Pham shifted. "In situations like this, we go into a lockdown. We close the blinds so the students can't see what's happening, but keep them in their classrooms while we assess the situation; it's less traumatic to allow them to continue their normal day as much as possible. I've been waiting on your determination to decide if I need to contact the parents before the normal end of the school day. The kindergarteners get out earlier than the other classes, and we'll need to explain the situation to those parents."

Jo cringed mentally. "How many parents?"

"We have seven kindergarteners who ride the bus to school, and ten who are dropped off and picked up by their parents on site. Nicole was one of those ten, so now we have nine." Her voice wavered, betraying her stoic demeanor.

"Where are the children now?" Arnett asked.

"In class. Ms. Roden, the kindergarten teacher, and Karen Phelps, one of our volunteer mothers, are keeping them occupied."

"I'd like to keep the playground, including the courtyard, off-limits to everyone for now." Jo gestured to the officer waiting for them. "I'll have the responding officers secure the front of the building, to keep the parents outside. Then, when the bell rings, can you have Ms. Roden bring all the children out front?"

"Normally the parents wait in the front hall to pick up the children, so that should work well. However, I'm concerned that seeing two police officers will alarm them."

Jo chose her words carefully. Although she understood the logic behind Pham's delay in notifying the parents, word had probably already started to spread. "My suggestion is you contact the parents as soon as possible, so the presence of officers isn't a shock to them. Assure each that their child is okay, of course, but let them know you can't give further details for now. If they press you, cite student privacy."

Pham considered that, then pulled out her phone and punched in a text. "I'll get my assistant principal—Sally Lechliter—started on that right away. I'm sure you have questions you want to ask me."

A very slight smile tugged at the corner of Jo's mouth—she liked Eileen Pham. The principal was efficient and sharp as an ice pick, and most people probably found her cold and intimidating. But Jo saw the touch of puffy red around her tear ducts that matched the brief wobble in her voice. The principal cared deeply about the welfare of her students; she just chose to show it by maintaining the spine of steel that held everything together.

"We do, thank you," Jo said. "Since we can't speak with Ms. Roden until her students go home, can you give us an overview of what happened here?"

Pham gestured back toward the playground. "After morning recess, when Ms. Roden lined up the students to bring them back into class, she noticed Nicole was missing. She searched the grounds and found Nicole by the side of the dumpster. She checked for a pulse and tried to resuscitate her. When she couldn't, she called nine-one-one."

"Did she notice Nicole during recess at all?"

Pham shook her head. "She wasn't one of the supervisors out on the playground today."

"Who was?" Arnett asked.

"Our third-grade teacher, Jim Karnegi, and one of our parent volunteers, Karen Phelps. She's the one helping Ms. Roden as we speak."

"We'll need to talk to both of them before we go. Is that normal, to have parents monitoring the yard?" Jo asked.

"Briar Ridge requires volunteer hours from all our parents. We believe it fosters a sense of involvement and community that benefits everyone," Pham said with pride.

Jo vaguely remembered Sophie complaining about volunteer assignments; she hadn't paid much attention at the time. She turned toward the fence. "Someone grabbed Nicole or lured her off the main playground into this area back here. That means either someone already on school grounds did this, or someone managed to get onto the school grounds. Has that gate been locked all morning?"

"It should have been. It's only ever opened when we get deliveries, or when waste management comes to swap out the dumpsters. Neither happened today."

"Is there a camera back here that I'm not seeing?" Arnett asked.

Pham flushed. "No, there's no point since the cafeteria exit is key-carded. We have two cameras on the front of the building, the only public entrance, so anyone coming into the building is picked up on those."

Arnett pointed toward the buildings that jutted up against the school. "Unless someone came around the back here, and snuck along the property line."

"We always have at least two supervisors in the yard. They'd see and hear anyone climbing the fence."

Jo hurried to diffuse Pham's defensiveness. "Even the best system can't be one hundred percent foolproof, so we just need to figure out how our perpetrator manipulated yours. They either managed to get in somehow or someone already inside is responsible, so we need to look into both possibilities."

Pham's cheeks paled to a muddy gray at the implication, and she gave a single sharp nod. "I see. Besides the two cameras out front, there's an exit from the main building directly into the playground courtyard, and that has a camera, too. None of those entries are key-carded because children and parents routinely need to use them. We also have a door in each wing that opens out into the courtyard. They also have cameras, and no key-card locks."

"With you so far." Arnett jotted down notes as she spoke.

"We also have four exit-only doors. Two in the front of each wing on either side of the main building, one out the back of the cafeteria." She gestured to the door beyond the dumpsters. "And one in the multi-purpose room, in the opposite wing. I call them *exit-only doors* because with the key-card system, once you exit you need a badge to get back in. For that reason, those doors don't have cameras on them."

Jo mapped out the camera locations in her mind as she listened, and calculated the coverage. "So you have a record of everyone who comes into the buildings, but foot traffic inside isn't monitored."

"Correct. We have to be mindful of student privacy, and balance that with security. Our cameras record everything, and we cycle out the recordings every seventy-two hours." Pham tapped at her phone again. "I'll have Greg, our security guard, get the files onto a drive for you right away."

"Thank you," Jo said. "Another question. You have a record of every person who comes onto campus, then, but not necessarily when or if they leave? So they could visit their child's class, say, then go out into the yard without you knowing?"

Pham raised a finger, anticipating the question. "Yes, but we also have a mandatory sign-in system. If the parents come beyond the entry hall to drop off their kids, they're required to sign in at the front office and get a visitor's pass. Also, we have pictures of all authorized adults in our system, so everyone is verified before given a pass. Of course, we're a small enough school that within a month or so of each new school year beginning, all the teachers and staff know the authorized adults by sight."

"So by now a stranger would stick out?"

"Immediately." Pham's reply was emphatic.

Jo caught the grim glance Arnett threw at the building—she'd already reached the same conclusion, and tried to speak as matter-of-factly as possible. "We'll need a list of your faculty and staff. Everyone who works on school grounds. You do full background checks, criminal history, fingerprinting on everyone?"

Pham's eyes flicked between Jo and Arnett. "Of course. But nobody who works here would do something like this. A stranger must be behind this."

"Have there been any incidents recently? Anyone lurking around the school that shouldn't be? Any vandalism? Any disgruntled ex-employees?" Arnett asked.

Pham rubbed her neck. "Not that I'm aware of."

"Not even any disgruntled employees or parents?" Arnett pushed.

"I haven't had to fire anyone for years, Detective. And you always have parents with complaints, but nothing with the sort of rancor that leads to this." She snapped her wrist toward the dumpster.

Pushing farther wasn't going to help. "If anything comes to you, please let us know as soon as possible. Also, it's possible one of the children saw something that can help us, especially if we're dealing with a stranger. What's the best way to find out if any of them saw anything before they forget, in a way that won't cause concern?"

Pham considered for a minute. "Probably best to have each teacher ask their class, and if one of the students saw something, you can talk to them directly."

A brunette in an ill-fitting flowy dress and an awkward gait rounded the corner with a frantic expression, making a beeline for Principal Pham. "Eileen, one of the mothers is demanding to talk to you. I've tried everything, but…"

Jo anticipated Pham's response. "Please, go take care of it. Detective Arnett and I need to check the perimeter of the property before we go any further, and then we'll need to talk to the two individuals who were supervising the yard. I'm sure we'll have more questions after that."

*

Once Principal Pham hurried off, Jo and Arnett proceeded around the chain-link perimeter fence, inspecting it for gaps, holes, blind spots, and any sign of disturbance.

Jo stared up at the utility sheds. "These definitely provide enough cover for someone trying to climb the fence, but then our killer would have to cross a huge open distance between here and the east wing of the building."

They continued around. On the inside of the fence, the lawn was short, dense, and routinely trampled by a hundred and fifty children. On the outside, a paved sidewalk and a narrow residential street bordered the west side of campus. Private houses lined the back and east sides, with wooden fences that blocked visual access to their yards and left a two-foot dirt gap between them and the school's fence. On the east side the gap formed a channel similar to an alley, running between the houses and the school. The only potential evidence present was a few cigarette butts too ancient to be relevant and a solitary pile of desiccated cat feces in the alley. They bagged the cigarette butts, but left the scat.

Arnett tilted his head at the gap between the school and the houses. "I suppose someone could jump over from one of those yards."

"But we have the same issue with visibility. You could manage it if you timed it right, then ran and ducked behind the utility sheds. But to also snatch a kid and get her to the dumpster enclosure? That would take a miracle."

Arnett nodded. "And anybody hanging out on the sidewalk to the west would be visible to anyone in the playground, in the houses, or just driving down the street. Also not viable."

"So the only plausible cover is the portion of the alley by the dumpster, *if* our killer came from outside." Jo's fist punched her thigh. "To be thorough we should send Bader and his partner to canvas if anyone in any of the houses saw or heard anything suspicious."

Arnett gazed back toward the main building. "I'll have Marzillo send them out as soon as they aren't needed to secure the scene. Cafeteria next?"

They crossed through the east wing into the cafeteria, where the staff were finishing preparations on bag lunches. Jo introduced herself and Arnett to the workers, and asked to see the area that opened out to the dumpsters. The door was visible from the entire back area, even from the counter where children lined up to get their food.

"No sneaking in and out of that unseen," Arnett said.

"And we'll have a key-card access record for anyone who used it." Jo pulled out her phone. "For the sake of time, I'm going to ask Lopez to start on some of this while we finish the interviews."

Lopez answered nearly immediately. "Jo! You better not be calling to cancel for Fernando's tomorrow night. I haven't seen you in two weeks, and I swear I'll come to your house and chloroform you if that's what it takes."

Jo smiled. Christine Lopez had come into the department eight years before, during Jo's time as lieutenant on the force. She'd partnered temporarily with Arnett until Jo asked to return to detective and Arnett was repartnered with her. Then, about a year ago, Lopez's new partner had to go on long-term leave. Given her extensive cyber skills, she'd been temporarily assigned to the lab in a support role, and found she loved it so much she asked to make the change permanent. Since then, she'd worked with Jo and Arnett frequently, and had become one of Jo's few close friends.

"Somehow I have no problem envisioning a vat of chloroform in your basement right now. But no, I'm not calling to cancel." She caught her up quickly on the situation. "Do you have time to help us out?"

"I've got two cases I'm working, but I'm waiting for a slew of callbacks. What do you need?"

"Take your pick." She gave Lopez an overview of the situation. "We're going to put the two responding officers onto canvassing the area, but I'd like to be able to compare any information they bring us with a list of any known sex offenders in the area. And the principal is in the process of sending us an e-mail with a whole list of educators and staff we're gonna need to do deep dives on."

"I can knock out the sex offenders in fifteen minutes. And you know I love me a good background check—nothing better than a legal reason to snoop into people's lives." A can popped in the background, almost certainly a Rockstar, Lopez's preferred caffeine delivery system. "Send me everything and we'll see how far I get."

"I'll forward you the info asap. What would we do without you?" Jo sing-songed.

"What's that you say? Drinks are on you tomorrow night? Good, because I'm gonna need a lot of 'em, meeting Janet's new girlfriend. Anything else you need?"

"I'll let you know." Jo hung up, then checked her e-mail. Sure enough, Principal Pham's assistant had already sent the personnel information. As she forwarded it to Lopez, a loud bell clanged behind them, and Arnett jumped.

Jo gave him a you-have-to-be-kidding-me stare. "And everyone's worried about *me* having PTSD."

Arnett held up a hand. "Hey, those things are designed to be traumatic."

Jo checked the time on her phone. "One fifteen, so that must be the bell that lets the kindergarteners out. I say we go grab Roden and Phelps quickly, before they have the chance to talk to anyone."

*

They strode back to the central building, where two women were escorting a line of children out the front of the building. Some peeled off to parents with worried expressions who quickly scooped them up, while the rest filed onto the waiting school bus. Jo and Arnett dropped back, watching and waiting as inconspicuously as possible. One of the women wore a visitor pass on a lanyard around her neck—she had to be Karen Phelps, the volunteer mother, and that meant the other woman was Stephanie Roden. Medium height and middle-aged, Stephanie's raven-black braids framed dark skin tinged with gray, most likely the result of the day's trauma. Despite it, she had a quiet confidence and easy camaraderie with the children, who clearly adored her. She took time to talk briefly with each parent who approached her, and each walked away a little calmer for having spoken to her.

Karen, who Jo guessed was just past thirty, also seemed to have a good rapport with the children, but her interactions were slightly more distracted. Petite and curvy, with a ponytail of blonde curls, wide blue eyes lined with fake lashes, and a full face of makeup, Karen dressed like she'd just come from yoga class. Jo smiled as she flashed on her sister and her sister's stay-at-home-mother friends—they dressed the same way, and they usually had a Starbucks frappa-something in their hands as they complained about their carbs. Yoga moms, Jo had come to think of them, the new decade's upper-middle-class answer to soccer moms. Fit and fussy—but fierce.

Karen finished helping the children onto the school bus, then slipped her phone out of her pocket. After checking the time, she wrapped her arms around her waist and hurried back into the entrance hall.

Jo intercepted her. "Karen Phelps?"

Karen flinched slightly, as though someone had startled her. She looked up at Jo, then noticed Arnett next to her. "Hi, yes. I'm Karen."

Jo introduced herself and Arnett, then gestured back through the central hallway. "Can we speak to you for a moment?"

Her eyes flicked to the door, her expression wary. "Sure, of course."

Jo allowed her to take the lead. Karen pushed through the door to the playground courtyard with one hand, the other still wrapped around her midsection.

Once outside, she turned back to Jo and Arnett. "Have you found anything out? I can't believe something like this could happen. This is such a safe school, I just can't—" Her hand flew to her mouth as she fought back tears.

Jo reached out and placed a hand on her arm. "I can't imagine how horrible this has been for you. I'm sorry we have to talk to you right now, but we need to figure out what happened as soon as possible."

Karen nodded briskly, her hand still over her mouth. "No, I understand. It's just—Gia's my closest friend. Nicole's mother. Our children have grown up together and I just can't believe this is happening. I need to go check on her."

Pain stabbed Jo again as she imagined what Nicole's mother was going through. "Then let's get through this as quickly as possible so you can get to her. Principal Pham told us you're a volunteer?"

"Yes, I have two children here. My daughter Katie's in the fourth grade, and my son Willie's in the second."

"And you were one of the two yard supervisors during morning recess?"

She nodded quickly again, and her hand dropped back to her abdomen. Her words came out choppy and thick. "That's right. I was supposed to be keeping them safe. I should have stopped it. She's never going to forgive me."

"What should you have stopped?" Arnett asked.

She looked vaguely confused for a moment. "I should have seen whatever happened."

"You can't blame yourself. Whoever hurt Nicole made sure they weren't seen," Jo said. "How does yard surveillance work during recess?"

Karen's arms pulled tighter. "It depends how many people we have. Some days we have an extra volunteer, and then we can station one person in each of the back corners, and one in the courtyard. When we only have two, we do a sort of patrol. Walk around and scan everything. Today was just me and Mr. Karnegi, the third-grade teacher."

The formal use of Jim Karnegi's last name struck Jo as odd—
Principal Pham had been clear that the school was small enough
that parents and teachers knew each other well. "So you were
taking the patrolling approach today? Did you both cover the
whole yard, or divide it up, or…" Jo asked.

Karen's eyes flitted around the room. "Different teachers like
to do it different ways. Mostly you both just walk a big circle
around the yard, scanning, dealing with any incidents as you go."

The response felt strangely vague, yet strangely specific. "And
were there any incidents like that today?"

"I mean, nothing out of the ordinary…" Her eyes skimmed the
sky as she thought. "Daria Finley skinned her knee, and I had to
send her to the nurse to get it cleaned and bandaged. There was
a very brief argument over whose turn it was to play tetherball.
Mr. Karnegi took care of that."

"So when you were helping Daria, could you have missed
someone, say, jumping the fence?" Jo asked.

The tears sprang back into her eyes. "I—I don't think so,
I think I would have heard the fence. But I guess I must have
missed *something*."

"Did you see anybody out in the yard?" Jo asked.

Karen looked back and forth between Arnett and Jo. "No, I
would have dealt with it right away."

"I don't just mean strangers, I mean anybody. Teachers, staff."

Her eyes widened, and her voice went up an octave. "You think
someone from the school did this?"

Jo hurried to reassure her. "We don't think anything yet. But
if someone else happened to be out in the yard, they might have
seen something you weren't able to."

Karen looked slightly reassured. "Oh, I see. Yes, Ms. Madani
came out with a jacket for one of her students, right at the beginning of recess, but she went right back in."

"And do you remember seeing Nicole during recess at all?" Jo asked.

"No. She's not the sort of child you notice, really. She's quiet and she does what she's told, and she usually prefers to play by herself. Mostly she loves to draw with chalk on the ground. I'm pretty sure that's what she was doing today, right over there." She pointed to a series of chalk scribbles on the ground.

Jo followed her gesture. About fifty feet, maybe seventy-five, from the edge of the east wing. It would have only taken a few seconds to snatch Nicole from there and pull her back behind the building, especially if one or both of the yard monitors were looking in the other direction. "But you don't remember when during recess you saw her?"

"I can't even remember for sure *if* I saw her today. How am I going to explain that to Gia?" Her hand flew back to her mouth, covering a sob.

"This isn't your fault. Gia will understand that." But doubt tugged at Jo on Karen's behalf—bereaved people looked for someone to blame, and she couldn't honestly say *she'd* understand if her child had been murdered under a friend's watch.

Karen nodded into her hand for a moment, then took in a big breath. "Is there anything else I can tell you? If not, I'd really like to get over to her house. I don't like the thought of her being alone right now."

"One last question." Jo pulled out her phone, and showed her the toy Marzillo found near Nicole. "Do you know who this belongs to?"

Karen peered at the phone, brow creased. "No, should I?"

"Not necessarily, we just need to know if it belongs to any particular child or classroom that you're aware of?" Jo asked.

"Not that I can remember. But the kindergarteners have a couple of toy bins in their class, maybe that's where it's from?"

"Okay, thank you." Jo reached for one of her cards, but realized she wasn't wearing her normal blazer. She nodded to Arnett, who pulled out one of his and jotted something on the back, then handed it to Karen.

"Here's my card," he said. "I put Detective Fournier's number on the back. If you remember anything else, please let us know as soon as possible."

"And don't worry," Jo added. "The officers who contacted Gia would have made sure she had access to a grief counselor."

Karen inspected both sides of the card, then met Jo's eyes. "You don't know Gia. She doesn't trust strangers and she's extremely protective of her children. Something like this—I'm not sure she'll survive it."

CHAPTER FOUR

Karen power walked away from the detectives, fighting down both the urge to run, and the urge to check over her shoulder if they were watching. She took the shortcut across the front lawn to the parking lot, but couldn't remember exactly where she parked—she searched for the Tasmanian Devil sticker on her back window, then wove through the vehicles to her red Audi Q7. As she yanked open the door and dove in, she pulled her phone from the other pocket of her pink sports jacket. She tapped on a contact in WhatsApp, but then froze, staring down at it.

What if the police checked? Could they access her WhatsApp records? Recovered WhatsApp messages had been all over the news recently. She was probably just being paranoid, but it could happen, and if so, she couldn't have anything even vaguely incriminating on record.

Come on, Karen, she prodded herself. *Think.*

But decision-making had never been her strong point. She did best in life when she floated along and let the decisions make themselves. Her parents both went to Oakhurst U, so why not go there? Her high school art teacher was convinced she had talent and should pursue a career as an artist, so that's what she majored in. One of the most desirable boys on campus, a football player all of her friends thought was perfect, asked her out, so she went out with him. He was nice enough, handsome enough, mature enough, so she kept dating him. A year later, he asked her to marry him, and since that was about how long people waited before getting engaged, she said yes. Her mother advised her to get a wedding planner, so she did, and the planner ultimately made most of the decisions.

Not that she was a pushover—she wasn't. When she knew she wanted something, or that she didn't want it, she had no issue saying so. But the problem *there* was that her instincts were usually bad. Her never-at-home-anyway father called her *impulsive and naive*, while her mother's more generous interpretation was that she *led with her heart*. No matter what gloss you wanted to put on it, her decisions always backfired eventually.

Like today.

A woman standing next to a white news van glanced her way, and took a step forward for a closer look. Karen ducked her head and forced herself to focus.

When in doubt, do nothing. That had been the philosophy that had wreaked the least havoc in her life—wait until a clear course of action presented itself. If only she'd followed it when she found out Rick was cheating on her she'd still be married today, rather than struggling to make rent on her house and fighting to maintain a lifestyle that allowed her kids to still fit into Harristown's elite. So the best thing to do now was to say nothing, send no text, just pretend none of it ever happened. There was really no need for any of it to come to light, anyway. She was a trusted member of this community, and there was no reason to suspect her of anything, no reason even to talk to her about it again.

Unless one of the children had seen, and decided to tell someone.

She dropped her face in her hands and rubbed her eyes, as if pressing into them would bring back a clearer memory of the morning's recess. She was *almost* certain none of the children had seen. Because if one of them *had* seen, they'd have said something right then—no way they'd have let it pass.

But you could never tell with kids, especially the younger ones. Sometimes, when they were confused about something that happened, they'd just clam up and hide inside themselves while they tried to process it. And the police were sure to ask the teachers or parents to talk to the kids, and who knew what would come out then.

She sat upright and switched on the ignition. She had to pull herself together, not sit frozen in the car; the newswoman was already watching her too closely and she couldn't risk looking strange. She reversed out of the parking spot and forced herself to proceed slowly out of the lot.

What was it that expression said? Something about the wisdom to know which things you couldn't change? There was nothing about this she could change, so all she could do was wait. So she'd focus her energy on Gia, and deal with whatever came as it came.

She winced as her tires screeched around the corner. The next twenty-four hours would be nerve-wracking.

CHAPTER FIVE

Gia Marchand closed her front door behind the police officers, then stared down at the card they'd given her. The number for a grief counselor.

She or Anthony would have to go identify Nicole, they'd told her. Apparently, a teacher's positive identification didn't count. They'd call her once the unit finished processing the scene, and someone would have to go to the medical examiner's office.

No way would it be her. Anthony could deal with it.

They'd need to do an autopsy, because Nicole's death wasn't 'natural,' and they had no idea how long it would take. In the meantime: *it's horrible, you must be in shock, do you want us to stay with you, can we call someone, you should at least take the number for the grief counselor and call them as soon as possible.*

Like that would undo any of what had been done. Like that would bring her daughter back to life.

She stared at the little cardboard rectangle. The *yellow* cardboard rectangle. Had someone purposefully chosen the color of jaundice? Or was the card just old? Had it originally been white, pristine, but had languished in a squad car where cigarette smoke and exhaust fumes and God knew what else slowly transformed it into something dingy and disreputable? From a box of a thousand somewhere, each one waiting to be plucked out and slipped into the numb fingers of some victim whose life had been irrevocably altered? How long would it take to go through a box like that?

How many babies, women, human souls did the world go through each day?

She banished the ridiculous thoughts—she didn't have time for them. She had to figure out what she was going to do now, how she was going to handle this. There'd be an investigation, and the police would want to talk to her. People would want to come console her. It simply wouldn't be possible for her to keep them at arm's length for any period of time. What was she going to say? What was she going to do? All she knew was she'd have to be very, very careful.

At least Anthony was in the middle of 'debriefing' a client. He'd be at work the next few days during most of his waking hours, and that would make everything easier to navigate.

She needed to focus. First things first—she'd have to pick up Nicholas shortly from school. Her phone was already chiming with notifications, most likely several someones offering to bring him home for her. But that wouldn't do. They might try to talk to him, even ask him questions. She'd have to have a conversation with him, help him through it all, go over what to say and what not to say, what to do and what not to do. Where did she even start? She'd have to figure it out, because Anthony most certainly wouldn't handle that.

Her only other responsibility for the night was dinner. But no—most likely she wouldn't have to deal with that. She had no idea when Anthony would be home, but by the time he was, someone would have organized a sign-up circle and today's volunteer would arrive with a nourishing, comforting meal for the three of them, the first of a rotating roster that would magically appear every evening for the next two weeks. She'd been on plenty such circles herself, and delivered everything from lasagnas and salads to chicken soup to champagne and cake depending on whether the recipients were bereft, sick, or blessed with a new baby. Tomorrow she'd get away with putting up a sign asking that the family not be disturbed, a signal that the food should be left on the porch, but today she'd have to deal with whoever showed up. With a few careful texts, maybe she could make sure either Karen or Molly snapped up that first slot. Not that they'd be easier to deal with—they wouldn't—but she was going to have to face them anyway.

She took a deep breath and looked up from the card. That was decided, then. She'd text the girls, then go pick up Nicholas. She'd just have to figure out the rest from there.

She crossed the room to pick up her phone. As she passed, she threw the grief counselor's card into the fireplace.

CHAPTER SIX

By the time Jo and Arnett finished talking to Karen Phelps, Stephanie Roden had finished matching up her students with their parents.

"Did something about that chat with Karen strike you as odd?" Jo asked as they hurried after Stephanie down the east wing hall.

"You mean how she was picking out her words like hundred-dollar bills that'd plopped into manure?"

"The ones about her yard supervision, anyway," Jo said. "And, the more I see and hear, the less likely I think it is Nicole was killed by a stranger."

Arnett rubbed his chin. "For the most part, I agree. But we can't rule it out. All it takes is the right pervert to pass by at the right time."

Jo nodded. "We have two possibilities. Some random person saw an opportunity, or some not-so-random person associated with the school created an opportunity. So which is more likely? We're talking about a twenty-minute window for the killing, and that's generous."

"If Karen Phelps is right, Nicole was drawing with chalk right near the end of the east wing. Especially if she did it habitually, fairly simple to grab her and drag her behind the building, or lure her with the toy we found. But I admit it'd take balls of steel to jump the fence and hope nobody sees or that she doesn't cry out," Arnett said.

Jo scanned the colorful posters on the walls as they walked down the hall. "Either way, the killer would need a distraction, and the only one we've heard of so far is when Karen Phelps helped the fallen girl."

"But if a random killer hung out watching for any length of time, someone would have seen him," Arnett said.

"Exactly. And even if everyone was distracted, Nicole would have heard the fence rattle, and it would have startled her. They said she was quiet and obedient, but wouldn't she have called out?"

"Kids freeze up. Hell, adults sometimes freeze up," Arnett said. "You think that's what Phelps was covering up? That she heard the fence while she was helping the girl, but didn't do anything about it?"

"Maybe." Jo nodded. "We'll check with the responding officer and see what the canvassing turned up, and Lopez is widening the circle for sex offenders. Although I'm not sure how much help that'll be since there's no evidence of sexual assault."

Arnett shrugged. "Maybe Nicole fought him, and he had to kill her to keep her quiet before he was able to do anything to her."

"But if we're talking about what's more likely, the conditions all favor someone who had a reason to be here to start with. Someone the yard supervisors and kids know and trust, because you probably wouldn't even notice someone like that. And it would explain why Nicole didn't cry out."

"Hell, they could even get her jacket off without a fight."

Jo frowned. "Right. But normally if someone snatches a child, it's a relative or a pedophile, and in both cases, they want to get the child away from the scene, not just kill them where they are. Why do it this way?"

"Maybe it all went south fast and they had no choice. Or maybe it's just someone who hates kids."

"My guess is someone like that wouldn't be able to work on staff for long without acting on their impulses, so maybe we want to start our check with the newest hires and work our way back."

"Or maybe one of the teachers reached their limit," Arnett muttered under his breath as they caught up with Stephanie in front of her classroom. "Teachers can lose it, too. And children are fragile."

Jo introduced herself and Arnett while Stephanie unlocked the classroom door. Stephanie motioned them in and pointed toward the student desks. Jo and Arnett perched themselves on the top portion of the two closest to the large metal teacher's desk. As soon as Stephanie sat down in her roller chair, her controlled composure deteriorated—her shoulders sagged forward and she dropped her head into her hands.

"I'm sorry," she said. "I just need a moment. This is the first chance I've had to process any of it."

Jo spotted a box of tissues on the far corner of the desk and moved it closer to her. "I understand. It's the most draining thing you can do, burying your emotions for the sake of others. Take all the time you need."

She looked up and examined Jo's face. "You understand. It's like projecting some sort of hologram through sheer force of will, like you're watching yourself be some sort of robot. I feel like someone hit me with a truck and backed over me several times, and I'd really like to go throw up. But, what can I tell you?"

Jo asked her to recount how she'd noticed Nicole was missing, and how she discovered her in the dumpster enclosure. Her account matched up with what Principal Pham and Karen Phelps had already told them.

"Did you see anybody strange in the area? Maybe lurking around the fence?" Arnett asked.

She shook her head. "I was focused on looking for Nicole, and I was trying to hurry while not upsetting the children. But I'd have noticed if someone was around that shouldn't have been."

"Do you remember anybody besides Mr. Karnegi and Ms. Phelps who were around? Maybe someone who works here walking through the halls? Even any of the teachers?" Jo asked.

Her brow knit. "Not that I remember, but it's possible. I wouldn't have thought twice about something like that."

"Can you tell us a little bit about Nicole?"

Tears sprang up in her eyes. "She was a sweet little girl, never caused me a moment's trouble."

"So not the kind to go wandering off on her own?"

Ms. Roden was emphatic. "Absolutely not. If anything, she tended to hover near me."

"Karen Phelps thought she might have been drawing with chalk on the cement by the east wing, by herself. Was that something she did in that spot every day?"

"Not necessarily every day, but yes, she loved to draw often over there, and she usually played alone."

"Did she have difficulty getting along with the other children? Was she bullied?"

"Oh, no, nothing like that. The other children like her—liked her—she was very generous and always kind and helpful to others. She just preferred her own company."

"You said she hovered near you. Were there other adults she did that to? Anyone she was particularly attached to?"

Her brow knit. "No, not that I'm aware of. I've never really seen her interact with any of the other teachers or staff."

Jo pulled up the picture of the toy on her phone. "Do you recognize this?"

Stephanie looked carefully before answering. "Not specifically."

"So it's not from your class, or something you saw one of your students with?"

"No." She looked up at Jo. "Why?"

"One of our CSIs found it near Nicole, in the corner of the dumpster enclosure. Can you say whether it was there or not when you found Nicole?"

Stephanie closed her eyes to think. "When I looked around the corner of the dumpster, I saw her jacket, and her yellow tights sticking out. I tossed the jacket aside, then checked for a pulse and tried to resuscitate her." She opened her eyes and shook her head. "It's possible I threw the jacket on top of it without realizing, but I honestly can't even tell you which direction I tossed it."

Jo glanced at Arnett to see if he had more questions. He fished out another card, made another notation on it, and handed it to Stephanie. "If you remember anything else, please call us as soon as you can."

She set the card on her desk. "I will."

*

After leaving Stephanie Roden, Jo and Arnett pulled Jim Karnegi out of his classroom. He confirmed what Karen Phelps had already told them: the two had circled the yard, stopping where needed. He'd seen Karen deal with an injured girl, but hadn't noticed anything or anyone unusual in or around the playground.

As Jo and Arnett strode back to the central building, a text came through from Lopez:

> *Only one registered sex offender in Harristown, Ricky Arlo.*
> *Will branch into neighboring areas.*

Jo pulled up the e-mail containing Arlo's information, including a description and picture. Six-one, two hundred pounds, dark hair; not exactly the sort of stature that hides itself easily. She scrolled to the violation—two years ago he'd been arrested for exposing himself on his porch to his neighbor.

Arnett grimaced skeptically. "Not exactly a hardcore child molester."

"Not the typical path toward grooming, no, but I suppose you never know. Maybe this means he exposed himself to the neighbor's child?"

"Possible," Arnett said. "Should we pay him a little visit when we finish here?"

"I think we should, to be thorough."

"Yeah. The last thing we need is the PTA boycotting because we didn't put on a manhunt for Harristown's version of Slender Man."

They continued on to the principal's office, which was part of a large main office suite. The rectangular space was divided lengthwise by a white laminate-and-wood counter that came up to the middle of Jo's chest; the left-most section was broken by a door that swung open to let people in and out of the official side of the space. In front of the counter, several chairs lined the wall for parents or students who had to wait to be helped. Behind the counter several desks, cabinets and bookshelves, all in industrial medium-gray metal, scattered across the room. On the right side of the space were two doors, one marked with an 'Assistant Principal' placard, and the other with a unisex restroom symbol. The principal's office was on the left, next to what looked like a general-purpose photocopy and file storage room.

An earnest twenty-something man in a security-guard uniform and spiked black hair recognized them immediately.

"I have the information Principal Pham said you needed." He bent to pull a three-ring binder and a thumb drive out from a cubby behind the reception counter. "The footage from the surveillance videos, and our sign-in records. I have our IT guy putting together a list of all the key-card activity this morning. As far as the footage, I can watch with you if you like. I'm guessing you'll need help identifying everyone?"

Jo extended her hand. "I'm Detective Josette Fournier, and this is Detective Arnett. I'm sorry, I didn't catch your name?"

Bright red spots appeared on his cheeks, and he ran his finger through his spiky hair. "Oh, sorry, I'm Greg. Greg Chen. Stupid of me."

"Happens all the time. And yes, we'll definitely need someone to help us identify the people in the footage." Jo glanced around the office. "Is there somewhere quiet we can go?"

"The principal said to use her office, over here." Greg grabbed a laptop off a desk and led them into a roomy office with a large cherry desk, a meeting table, and an assortment of filing cabinets and bookcases. Everything was clean and organized; even the pile of folders on Pham's desk was meticulously stacked and centered. Greg graciously motioned Jo into Pham's large, ergonomic chair, and pulled two smaller chairs over next to the desk with a single hand. Struggling, he hurriedly set the computer on the surface of the desk, knocking over a container of noxious green liquid in the process.

"Dammit." He jumped to grab paper towels out of the principal's private bathroom, and Jo helped him mop up the sludge.

"What *is* that?" Arnett asked as he shoved a stack of files out of the way.

"Some all-natural smoothie deal that gives her energy. I asked once what was in it, but she lost me at wheatgrass." Greg faked a shudder.

Arnett took a step back, hands in the air. "It smells like someone dumped a compost pile into a riverbed."

"That must be the fish oil." Greg gathered the soiled paper towels. "I'll toss them outside."

Arnett stared down at the desk. "If that's what it takes to be healthy, I'm out."

Jo tried to unwrinkle her nose. "There has to be a midpoint somewhere between daily meatball subs and yard clippings soaked in petroleum."

Greg returned, free of paper towels, and set up the computer. He held out his hand for the drive, then plugged it in. He sat as it opened, and gestured Arnett to move his chair closer. "That'll be easiest for us all to see."

As they adjusted, he continued. "I try to monitor the camera streams as much as possible as I take care of my other responsibilities, so I have a view set up that captures all the cameras at once. I figure that would be the most efficient view to watch?"

"Makes sense," Jo said.

Arnett pulled out his notebook and flipped to a clean page as Greg began the video. Jo oriented herself to the views: the cameras labeled one and two pointed down at about a forty-five degree angle to capture the main entrance through the central building, camera three pointed from the courtyard door back through the main hall of the central building, and cameras four and five pointed almost directly down at the two wing doors that opened onto the courtyard.

Jo pointed with two fingers to those last views. "You can barely see into the courtyard from that angle, and you can't see into the playground at all."

Greg paused the video. "They aren't worried about capturing the playground since there are always supervisors present when the kids are out there. It's just to document who goes in and out."

Jo grimaced, her fledgling hope they'd catch something useful on those cameras gone.

Greg played the video at triple speed until the first people trickled in: cafeteria workers, janitorial staff, teachers. He slowed and paused for each individual, naming them as they went along.

"Do you have a night janitorial staff? Would they be here already when school opens?" Arnett asked.

"No, our staff works during the day, and does a final pass after the kids leave. Everyone's out of the building by ten at night, unless something very unusual is going on. And everyone left last night, I already checked."

Once Arnett nodded, he started up again, fast-forwarding through the relative quiet, until the drop-off began.

"You can't see me anymore, but I'm out at the top of the walkway, by the drop-off loop. I survey the area and make sure the kids go from the cars directly into the buildings. Most of the older children's parents use the drop-off loop, but some of the younger kids' parents like to park in the side lot and walk them all the way into class."

Sure enough, most of the parents never appeared, and instead single children or siblings walking together approached the front entrance camera, then disappeared from sight. Some continued directly to their classes, while some appeared on the inner-yard-door camera, running out to the playground for a last few minutes of freedom. But occasionally, parents did walk into the building with their children; Arnett jotted down each name, time of entry, and time of exit.

Jo simultaneously checked the sign-in sheets for the parents who came into the building. "Why are only some of these parents signed in?"

Greg shrugged. "They're supposed to sign in, but they forget. At least that's what they say, but I think a lot of them don't want to bother with the hassle if they're only going to be a few minutes. I'll bet anything you don't see most of those parents come back out, because they probably ducked out one of the exit-only doors. Those are closer to the parking lot and the side street than coming back through."

"What's the point of having a system if nobody bothers?" Arnett grumbled.

Greg was right—almost every parent who hadn't signed in also didn't reappear on camera.

"So for all we know, any one of those parents could be holed up in the restroom, or the dumpster enclosure?"

A skeptical shadow crossed Greg's face. "Well, technically, yes. But why would one of the parents do that? This is something a maniac would do. Isn't that what we're looking for?"

Jo didn't answer. In her experience, 'maniacs' came in all sorts of unexpected packages. She motioned for him to begin again.

About halfway through the influx of children, Jo recognized Nicole's puffer jacket and curls. "Who's that she's walking with?"

"That's her brother, Nicholas. I think he's in the fourth grade," Greg answered.

They continued on. Five minutes after the first bell rang, the trail of parents leaving campus trickled out. A few more children arrived late, but far fewer than Jo would have predicted based on her experience with human nature. After that, the viewing turned tedious and hypnotic. They watched the video as fast as they could without missing anything, but someone appeared just often enough to keep them from getting into a routine. Most often that happened on camera three, as a teacher or administrator passed from one wing to the other.

Then, twenty minutes before the bell rang for recess, a man hurried toward the building, entered, then turned past camera three toward the west wing.

Jo glanced down at the sheet in front of her. "Nobody else is signed in—who's that?"

Greg paused the recording and leaned toward it, brow knit. He played it in slow motion, and his expression cleared. "That's Anthony Marchand."

"Anthony Marchand?" Jo leaned forward for a better view. "Nicole's father? Are you sure?"

Greg let the tape run to where Marchand appeared on camera three, and paused it. "Yup. That's him."

"Let it run," Arnett said.

They watched the tape run up to recess, then through it. A trickle of kids came out past camera three, presumably after they'd used the restrooms. Then, about five minutes after recess ended, Stephanie Roden ran past camera three toward the main office, then back out with Principal Pham and Greg while the assistant principal raced out the front of the building toward the drop-off loop. Several minutes later, she escorted the paramedics in.

Anthony Marchand never reappeared.

CHAPTER SEVEN

After finishing with the surveillance footage, Jo and Arnett asked for copies of the sign-in sheets. Before leaving, they checked in with Marzillo and Peterson, who were knee-deep in trash and not looking at all happy about it. Nicole had been removed to the medical examiner's office, and Marzillo promised to text them as soon as they knew anything else.

"Who first? Ricky Arlo or Anthony Marchand?" Arnett said, back in the car.

"The more we see, the less I believe this could be some random sicko off the street." Jo tapped her fingers on her leg. "Most likely Anthony Marchand left work once he heard about Nicole, and Arlo's house is on the way to theirs. So I say call the Marchands on the way while we pay Arlo a visit," Jo answered.

As they made their way back out to the front, the bell rang. Jo braced herself, half-expecting a flood of children to fly past them. Instead, the teachers took turns walking their classes out in an emergency-drill formation. The children looked uncomfortable and confused—they knew something out of the ordinary was happening, but didn't know what.

"Aunty Josette!"

Jo turned toward the little voice—her niece Emily, walking amid the first graders, big green eyes worried and her fists clenched around handfuls of her blue dress. Jo smiled, but put a finger up to her lips. Emily put a matching finger up to her own mouth, but didn't smile back.

"Let's go," Jo whispered to Arnett, hoping to avoid being spotted by her other niece. But as they strode out among the lines of children, Jo noticed Sophie waiting on the lawn among a group of parents—scared and angry parents—and a camera crew from a local news station. Sophie's eyes widened as she caught sight of Jo. With a stern expression she lifted her hand and held it up to her ear—*you better call me.*

Jo nodded her assent, then turned away. When they reached the car, she climbed into the driver's seat, immediately started the car, and drove away.

Arnett paged through the information Principal Pham had given them. "I'll call Anthony Marchand while you drive."

But that was easier said than done. He didn't answer his cell phone, and Gia Marchand didn't answer hers. When Arnett called his business number, Marchand Operations, his assistant said he was out consulting all afternoon, and couldn't be disturbed.

"I'm with the Oakhurst County SPDU," Arnett said. "I believe someone already called today and told you there's an urgent matter we need to talk with him about?"

The man's voice softened slightly. "I assume you're talking about the situation with his daughter. I promise you, I put the message through to him. But when he does group team-building, he insists that nobody brings in their cell phones, and he leaves his behind as well, to set a good example. I doubt he'll get the message earlier than six this evening. Do you have his wife's contact information?"

Arnett's pause lasted a beat too long. "I'm sorry, did I lose you?" the assistant asked.

"I'm here. There must be someone you can call wherever he is. This is an emergency."

"I'm sorry, Detective, those are my instructions."

"Fine, tell me where he is, and we'll go there ourselves."

"I'm sorry, I can't give out that information."

Arnett squeezed his eyes shut incredulously. "You can't give out that information to the police, when his daughter's welfare is involved?"

"Many of the companies we work with don't want the public to know they've hired business analysts, and we have confidentiality clauses in our contract."

"You're telling me the people you work for wouldn't understand the need for us to reach him?" Arnett's voice rose an octave. "Do I need to get a warrant?"

"A warrant would be excellent, that would give us a legal exception to those contracts."

"Never mind, we'll track him down at home." He hung up and turned to Jo. "What kind of asshole doesn't have arrangements for emergency contact about his wife and kids?"

"The kind I wouldn't want to be married to, that's for sure." Jo turned onto Arlo's street. "But he has to go home, and I'm not sure it'd be a bad thing to talk with his wife before he gets there, anyway. It's always harder to get a read on individual parents when you have to talk to them as a pair."

He glanced over at her as they got out of the car. "Look at you, already back to finding silver linings everywhere."

"What can I say, it's my superpower." Jo shot him a look, then glanced at the house in front of them. Folk Victorian, moderately sized for the neighborhood, exterior well-kept. The yard and the landscaping, however, were another story—the lawn had morphed into something far closer to a jungle, and the bushes that lined the base of the house were raggedy and dying. Four warped Adirondack chairs surrounded a rusty lattice table on a porch dotted with dirt-filled pots.

"That grass makes my eye twitch," Arnett said as they passed.

They rang the bell, and Jo inspected the contents of a row of pots next to the door. "What do you think those dried stems used to be?"

Before Arnett could answer, the door yanked open. Ricky Arlo, dressed in jeans and a faded tee, glared at them. "Detectives this time. It never ends, does it?"

Jo introduced herself and Arnett. "We'd like to talk to you. Can we come in?"

His annoyance turned to anger. "Hell, no. Let me guess, some ex-husband kidnapped his toddler and there's been an amber alert, but you need to talk to me *just in case* it turns out the eyewitness report that identified him got it wrong?"

Jo kept her face blank. "A child was killed today at Briar Ridge Elementary School."

Arlo's face softened for a moment into a mix of horror and sadness before the annoyance returned. "I don't know how many times I have to tell this story. Maybe I should write up flyers and post them in the yard so people can just help themselves. I'm not that kind of sex offender. I'm not actually a sex offender at all, and I shouldn't be on that damned list." He pointed across the street to the woman who'd emerged from the facing house. "Mrs Moynahan over there? She hates me. She doesn't like that I don't keep my yard as pretty as everyone else does, and says I'm bringing the property value down. Had to make nasty remarks every time she saw me. But this is America, or at least I used to think it was, and I can keep my lawn however I want. So I stopped mowing it at all, stop trimming, stopped everything. *Figured she'd get the point and shut the hell up,*" he yelled the last part for the woman's benefit.

"You shut the hell up, you disgusting redneck pervert!" the woman called from across the street.

"Guess that didn't work?" Arnett asked.

"'Course it didn't. You can't make people like that see sense." He flipped her off.

"And I'm guessing there's more to the story," Jo said.

"Look, I'm not proud of it, okay? If I could go back and undo it, I would. I came out one morning to get my mail from the box, and she started poppin' off at me because I was wearing my robe. Said this wasn't a trailer park, and just because I didn't have a 'real job' didn't mean I didn't have to cover myself like everyone else. And something in my head just snapped, and I told her a robe *is* covered up, that's the whole damned point of a robe, and if she didn't understand that, I'd show her the damned difference. So I flung my robe open and waggled it at her, and like I said, I wish I hadn't, *but that look of horror on her face was perfect!*" he yelled again. "Of course she pressed charges, and even when the police told her she was being ridiculous, she insisted they prosecute. And, because of a bullshit technicality, because I did it technically in public, I'm on the sex offender registry and I have to pay for a stupid mistake for the rest of my life."

"You should be behind bars! You're a foul, disgusting disgrace of a human!" the woman cried out.

Jo turned to her. "Ma'am, please go back inside your home."

"This is my property, I can stand on my porch if I want," she called back.

"Until I arrest you for disturbing the peace," Arnett replied.

Arlo nearly squealed with joy. "Do it. Please do it. For the love of God, please do it."

The woman's mouth snapped shut, but she crossed her arms over her chest and refused to budge.

Arnett turned back to Arlo. "I'm going to need you to calm down, too."

Arlo slumped, chastened, and his voice dropped a notch. "The point is, I didn't hurt any kid. I'd never hurt a kid. I'd never hurt anyone, even an adult, I just had one stupid moment I wish I could take back. But I can't."

Arlo suddenly looked a decade older, his expression chagrined. Jo struggled with zero-tolerance policies on a good day—human behavior was far too complicated to reduce down to such judgments, and this wasn't the first time she'd seen the law applied in a way it obviously hadn't been intended. Still, that wasn't up to her, and she had her job to do. "We still have to ask where you were this morning."

"Here. I'm a software engineer, and I work from home. I live alone, so I can't confirm it for you. Days like this almost make me wish I had an ankle monitor, so you all wouldn't even have to ask."

Jo sighed internally and shot Arnett a look—this man hadn't gone anywhere near Nicole. Arnett's expression echoed her opinion.

"Well. We're sorry we had to bother you, and we appreciate your cooperation. We'll let you get back to your work," she said.

Her words deflated the last of his anger. "I'm sorry, too. I know you're just doing your job." He gave one sharp wave, then closed the door.

Jo shook her head as they walked back to the car, fingers tugging at her necklace.

*

Arnett's eyes widened ever so slightly as they pulled up in front of the Marchands' two-story, redbrick colonial-revival home. "This isn't a house, it's a museum."

The corner of Jo's mouth turned up. Why was he always surprised? He knew the rich cities and neighborhoods in the county as well as she did. Better in fact—he was born and bred in Oakhurst County, while she'd spent a large portion of her childhood in New Orleans. Her parents divorced when she was a teenager, and moved Jo and Sophie back to New England, where their mother was originally from. Western Mass managed to feel both oddly strange and like home at the same time to Jo, something she'd never managed to fully reconcile.

But she had to admit, this house was impressive: columned, gabled porch, manicured lawn and shrubs, and herringbone redbrick walkway. "You're probably not wrong. This has to be period, and I'm sure somebody famous lived in it at some point."

"What'd'you think, six bedrooms?" He gazed up at it as they got out of the Malibu.

"Probably not far off. My sister's is smaller than this, and she has five."

"I got into the wrong line of work." Arnett shook his head.

"How did I manage for two whole weeks without your house envy and tirades about the price of gas?" Jo laughed.

"Two-fifty a gallon when I filled up this weekend! I remember when it was—"

"Under a dollar a gallon!" she interrupted, her eyes wide in mock horror.

He glared at her. "You're not that much younger than me, you know."

"But I *am* younger, and don't you forget it," she said. "And I don't get the chance to say that very often anymore, from the wrong side of forty."

They stepped up onto the porch, and Jo rang the bell. Several voices murmured in the background, then soft footsteps approached. The door opened to reveal Karen Phelps.

"Detectives," she said, pulling the door open and stepping back. "Come in. Gia's in the living room."

She turned and led them to the left through a bright, broad hallway, past two open doors to the right and a grand staircase. The living room was a continuation of the hall, both painted in happy shades of lemon yellow and trimmed with white crown moldings and baseboards. Leather-bound books and family pictures, mostly of Nicole and Nicholas, filled two built-in bookshelves. A large, tooled mahogany fireplace dominated the room, surrounded by white couches—how in the world did she keep those clean with two children?—and yellow chairs with slate-blue accent pillows and drapes.

A tall, slim woman with Nicole's dark brown hair sat bolt upright on one of the couches, her expression calm, her hands wrapped around a handmade green ceramic mug with a delicate lace pattern around the top. Her tan blouse and brown slacks were perfectly tailored, designer, and flattered her in an understated way. A smaller, auburn-haired woman with green eyes perched on one of the armchairs, hunched toward Gia with a worried expression. Her ill-fitting forest-green sweater accentuated her slouched posture in a way that, for reasons Jo didn't quite understand, called up the old-fashioned stereotype of a spinster librarian.

Jo took in Gia's composure. After Karen's earlier pronouncement she'd expected Gia Marchand to be a quivering mess, but she looked almost as if she were hosting a luncheon. Both Karen and the other woman looked far more upset than she did, and looked confused to boot. People grieved in different ways, of course, and you never knew how people would respond to a tragedy. But Jo had witnessed far more forms of grief than she cared to remember, and something about the energy in the room was off.

"Gia, these are the detectives I was telling you about," Karen said, then turned back to address Jo. "That's Gia, Nicole's mother, and that's Molly Hayes, another friend of ours. Her daughter also goes to Briar Ridge, and the three of us have a boutique together downtown. She just closed up early so she could pick up her Shauna and hurry here to help."

Jo formally introduced herself and Arnett as Karen slid into the other armchair.

"Please, sit." Gia motioned to the couch across from her, her expression still neutral, and moved to get up. "Can I get you something to drink? Tea? Coffee? Water?"

"No, thank you. We're fine. We're so sorry for your loss."

Gia nodded once. "I'm not quite sure why you're here. Two officers already came to notify me. Have you caught the person who did this to my daughter?"

Jo carefully kept her face blank, trying to decipher Gia's tone. It wasn't exactly hostile, but there was a wariness to it that surprised her. "Not yet. We have some questions we'd like to ask you."

"Ah. Of course." She sipped from her tea, carefully holding back the tag that hung over the side.

"Has anything strange happened to Nicole at school recently?" Jo asked.

"I'm not sure I understand?" Gia's eyes flicked back and forth between Jo and Arnett.

"Just anything unusual. Anybody that paid her special attention recently, any strange occurrences in the playground, anything like that?" Jo asked.

"Nothing that I know of." She set her mug down, removed the tea bag onto a small plate, then met Jo's eyes again. "But she's a beautiful child. Strangers always stop me to tell me how adorable she is, and often offer her things. Do you think she caught someone's attention, and they broke into the schoolyard?"

Jo chose her words carefully. "We can't rule anything out at this point. So I know this is a sensitive question, but was there anyone at school who did those things? Was maybe more fond of her than they should have been? Or who did something that made you or her feel uncomfortable?"

"No, not that I can think of…" Gia's expression shifted slightly, as though she'd connected something. "Do you mean made me feel uncomfortable about Nicole, or just uncomfortable?"

"Anything."

She leaned forward slightly. "Well. Last year, my son Nicholas' teacher, Jim Karnegi, flirted with me. Not a big deal at first, but it started to get out of hand. I had to ask him to stop."

Molly shifted in her chair as Gia answered, and Jo noticed a movement from the corner of her eye as Karen's posture straightened.

"How did he react?" Jo asked.

"Well, he wasn't happy. He gave me the cold shoulder from that point on, and also gave Nicholas a hard time. But the worst was, he filed a complaint with the principal."

"What type of complaint?" Arnett asked.

"He claimed Nicholas wasn't paying attention in class, and was disruptive. He claimed to be worried about him, that he had ADHD or something."

"Disruptive how?" Arnett asked.

"I'm not fully sure. My husband took care of it. He put in a letter of rebuttal, and had Nicholas' other teachers all put in letters confirming they'd never had any sort of issue with him."

"So you think it was retaliatory?" Arnett asked.

"One hundred percent. The timing was too coincidental."

"And is there anyone else you can think of that might hold a grudge against you? Who'd want to cause you pain?" Jo asked.

Gia's eyes maintained their controlled stare. "Everyone has people who don't like them. But I can't begin to imagine what type of grudge you'd have to hold against someone to want to murder their child."

Jo held her gaze. "People can be unpredictable when they feel they've been wronged."

Gia lifted a hand in a *who knows* gesture. "It's possible I cut someone off in traffic and they followed me to Briar Ridge, something like that. If so, your guess is as good as mine."

Jo's eyes narrowed slightly—the words were cavalier, but the tone was flat, void of emotion. She glanced at Molly and Karen. "Do you know of anyone who might be holding a grudge?"

They looked at each other, and Gia. Karen shook her head.

"Not at all," Molly said, eyes wide with fear. "In fact, Briar Ridge has always been an excellent school. Something like this… You have to be completely insane to harm a child. Have you checked the area for pedophiles? Or vagrants? I just saw an episode of *60*

Minutes where they talked about how mental illness is a huge factor in the homeless problem."

Arnett's jaw clamped down, and Jo could read the sarcastic rejoinder on his face: *not a lot of homeless people in this swanky neighborhood, lady.*

"We have officers canvassing the area around the school right now. If anyone was in the area that shouldn't have been, we'll know by the end of the day," Jo said.

Molly nodded and sat back, but looked unconvinced.

"If anything occurs to you, please let us know as soon as possible." Jo shifted gears and turned back to Gia. "Is Nicholas here, by chance? We'd like to ask him if he saw anything strange on the playground today."

"He's upstairs with the other kids. But we haven't had the chance to tell them what happened to Nicole yet, so if you talk to him, I have to ask you to be very careful about what you say."

Jo took a deep breath—she wasn't quite sure how to navigate that, but she'd have to do the best she could. "That's fine. But before you get him, I have a couple more questions."

Gia, who'd started to rise to go get Nicholas, sat back down. "Alright."

"When we went over the security tapes this afternoon, we saw you drop off Nicole and Nicholas to school."

"That's right," she said.

"But then, just before recess, your husband appeared on campus. Why was he there?"

Her face paled slightly, and her knuckles tightened around the handle of her mug. "Oh, right, I forgot about that. He had to drop off the permission slip for Thursday's field trip. He accidentally put it with a stack of paperwork in his briefcase, and today was the deadline to return it if we wanted Nicholas to go. And it would have been deeply embarrassing for both of us if we didn't get it in on time, since I'm supposed to be one of the chaperones."

Jo watched her face closely. "He didn't sign in, and we didn't see him leave."

She gave an exaggerated, exasperated headshake. "He never does. I've told him time and again, but he doesn't listen. He says it's ridiculous because everybody knows him and it takes too long. And he always goes out the side door near my son's classroom, because he parks on the street."

"Actually, we didn't see you leave again, either," Arnett said.

The color returned to Gia's cheeks in a rush. "Didn't you? I must have gone out the side, too. Sometimes I do when I'm in a rush, and I had a long list of errands today."

"Ah. That makes sense." Jo nodded. "We weren't able to reach your husband at work. Do you know when he'll be home?"

"I don't. He owns a business analyst company, and he gets very intense about his job. When he's in the implementation stages of the process, he doesn't like to put 'limits on his time frames.'" She put air quotes around the words, and gave another exasperated shake. "I've left two messages for him, but I'm not sure when he'll get them."

Jo exchanged a glance with Arnett, who looked as incredulous as she felt. She pulled out her phone, and located the picture of the toy found with Nicole. "Do you recognize this?"

All three women leaned in to examine the picture. "No. I mean, I know what it is, but you're asking if it belonged to Nicole, right?" Gia asked.

"Yes," Jo said.

"No, it doesn't belong to either one of my kids." She glanced at Karen, then Molly. "Do you recognize it?"

They both shook their heads.

"Do you recognize it from anywhere else, maybe one of the classrooms? You also volunteer at the school, don't you?"

Gia sat back. "All three of us do. I don't remember seeing it anywhere, but then, I'm not sure how much that means. Why? Did you find this with Nicole?"

"We can't comment on that right now." Not completely true, but Jo didn't want to explain how Stephanie Roden's attempt to resuscitate Nicole had altered the crime scene.

"And I know this is a hard question, but we have to ask it, just for the sake of being thorough. But—"

Gia cut her off. "You need to know where I was at the time my daughter was being killed."

Molly gasped, and Karen made an indignant choking sound.

Gia waved them off. "No, stop. Of course they have to ask, or they wouldn't be doing their jobs. After I dropped the kids off at school, I stopped by our boutique, Earthly Delights. We sell our art there. I work in ceramics, Molly in blown glass, and Karen makes jewelry. Today was Molly's day at the shop, but I needed to drop off some bowls I made over the weekend." Gia paused, took a deep breath, and stared down at her mug, face still neutral. "After that I had a doctor's appointment. My ob/gyn, actually. To confirm I'm pregnant. Dr. Leslie Natale, office twenty minutes from here in West Haven, and the appointment was at ten this morning. So, yes, as my baby girl was being murdered, I was finding out I have another child on the way. Very ironic, since Nicole wanted a baby sister more than anything."

Stunned silence filled the room. A string of emotions flashed over Karen's and Molly's faces as they tried to figure out how to react to joyous news overshadowed by horrific tragedy. As Jo herself tried to settle on an appropriate response, tears sprang into both Karen's and Molly's eyes.

Jo struggled to push her own down, like beach balls determined to surface in a pool. She cleared her throat. "I'm so sorry that your wonderful news had to come at such a horrible time."

Gia nodded. "Would you like to talk to Nicholas now? Or maybe all the children? They were all on the playground today."

"Who else is here?"

"Karen's daughter Katie, and her son Willie, and Molly's daughter Shauna. Katie and Shauna are both in the fourth grade with Nicholas, which is how we all initially met and became friends. Willie's in the second grade, so just a little older than my Nicole," Gia answered.

Jo did a quick calculation. Interviews with children were tricky and required specific protocol, more so the younger they were. They were suggestible, their memories and focus were unpredictable, some were afraid to talk to strangers and others were so willing to please they'd tell you whatever they thought you wanted them to say. Depending on the sort of interview—if they suspected a child had been molested, for example—she'd bring in a specialist and be sure to tape everything. But, she decided, she'd received enough specialized training to approach this sort of an interview. And for Nicholas, who must realize by now something had happened to his sister, it would probably be best to talk to him alone. For the other children, the most important variable was to make them as comfortable as possible, so keeping them together and having their parents present would probably be the best approach.

"We'd like to speak with Nicholas alone first, then the rest together," Jo said.

Gia nodded. "Okay. Karen, would you wait with the other kids while we talk to Nicholas? Just to keep them settled?"

Karen got up with a nod and climbed the grand staircase. A moment after, awkward footsteps pattered down it. The nine-year-old boy Jo and Arnett had seen on the security tape, with the same dark hair as Nicole and Gia, crossed haltingly into the room. He sank against the arm of the couch, next to his mother.

"Aunty Karen said you wanted me," he said to her.

She put her arm around him. "I want you to meet our visitors. This is Detective Fournier and Detective Arnett."

"They're police detectives?" His eyes widened slightly.

"That's right. You remember what I told you about police, right?"

"Yes." His wide eyes stayed on them.

Gia nodded to Jo.

"Hi, Nicholas, my name is Jo. Is it okay if I ask you a few questions about recess today at school?"

He nodded.

"Do you remember what you did during recess?"

"I played tetherball with Michael and Braydon."

"I used to play tetherball when I was in fourth grade, but I wasn't any good."

He eyed her skeptically. "Boys are better at tetherball, that's why."

"Could be. Sounds like you're pretty good at it, huh?"

He shifted slightly away from his mother. "I'm pretty good. But Braydon's the best. Especially today 'cause I can't hit very hard—" He stopped short and looked back at his mother.

"Oh no! Why's that?" Jo asked.

Gia reached over and gently extended his hands to show her. "He skinned his palms this weekend. We went bike riding, and he took a spill. Luckily, he wasn't hurt much, but he's upset because his rims were bent and he couldn't ride anymore. We had to carry the bike back and take it to a repair shop."

Jo screwed up her face as she glanced at the road rash on his palms. "That always hurts so much, like a thousand little cuts, and then the scabs are so itchy."

Nicholas' eyes widened. "I know. I hate it."

"So did you play tetherball for the whole recess?"

"Yeah, except when Gavin tried to cut the line. He's always messing around like that, but Braydon got upset and shoved him, and then I shoved him, and then Mr. Karnegi came over and yelled at all of us because that's not acceptable behavior. So he made us apologize and then made Gavin go to the end of the line." He frowned.

"That sounds fair. It's not nice to fight."

"No, it's not, but then Mr. Karnegi stayed nearby for a long time watching us."

"Oh, I get it. It's never as fun when the teachers watch you."

Nicholas moved farther from his mother. "No, it's not, because you have to watch everything you say, and—"

"Nicholas!" his mother cried, but with a laugh. "You'll make the detectives think you like to say naughty things!"

Nicholas looked back at her, then returned to her side.

"Did you do anything else before you played tetherball?"

"Nah, because the trick is you have to get in line super fast. Otherwise you might not get a turn if a lot of people want to play. So we all run straight there so at least we know we'll get one turn."

"And you didn't have to go to the bathroom or anything in the middle?"

He gave her a *boy-are-you-stupid* look. "I'm not a baby. I can hold it."

Jo laughed. "Did anything weird happen at all?"

He thought for a minute. "Just Gavin being a jerk, like I said."

"Nicholas." His mother's tone held a warning.

"Sorry. Just Gavin being mean."

"So nobody over the fence, or any fights, or anything like that?"

He thought for another minute. "No. Why?"

"No reason. Thanks so much for talking to us." Jo looked up and nodded at Gia.

She reached over and kissed Nicholas' head. "Can you tell everybody to come down here now?"

He nodded, and started out of the room. When he reached the doorway, he stopped and turned back toward Jo, his chin quivering. "I'm not stupid. I know something happened to Nicole. She didn't come home and now police are here. Is she okay?"

The pain in his eyes broke Jo's heart, and she was relieved when Gia responded before she had to.

"Everything's going to be okay, honey. We'll talk more when your father gets home."

CHAPTER EIGHT

Molly Hayes walked the detectives to the door for Gia, then watched through the peephole as they returned to their car and drove away.

Her heart was broken for Gia, absolutely broken. To have your daughter taken from you was the worst thing in the world she could imagine, and she'd been sick to nearly the point of vomiting since she'd heard about it all. Fear and anger and helplessness all roiled inside her, trying desperately to find some way out. Gia had always been there for her when she needed anything, and here she was, helpless to do anything in the face of Gia's pain except make her cups of tea.

The children had been sedate when talking to the police, muted by the unexplained tension in the room. People didn't give children nearly enough credit—they were intuitive, they were smart, and they knew when things weren't right. They'd wanted to help, and had been visibly disappointed when they had to admit they hadn't seen or heard anything unusual on the playground. The detectives, especially Detective Fournier, had been good at putting the children at ease and trying to keep their expectations neutral, but even little Willie was smart enough to know that police didn't come asking questions unless something bad had happened. Shauna had made her proud—she stood tall, looked the detectives in the eye, and answered all their questions thoughtfully.

Molly crossed back into the living room, where Gia was attempting to clear the tea mugs onto a tray.

Karen reached for the mug closest to her. "Let me do it, Gia, please. Sit and rest."

Gia waved her off. "Stop fussing, Karen. I'll do it. I need to keep busy."

"Okay, I get that." Karen straightened up and tugged at her blonde ponytail, then followed when Gia picked up the tray and headed toward the kitchen. She flashed Molly a deer-in-headlights look. "I'll get something started for dinner then. I took the first slot of the meal circle like you asked. I figured something simple, like spaghetti and meatballs."

"There's really no need, I just didn't want anyone else over here." Gia set the tray down. "Nobody's going to be hungry, anyway. You know how Nicholas is."

Molly knew. The last time Nicholas had been upset, it was *her* lap he'd thrown up all over. And then he'd been upset about that, and she'd had to tell him over and over again that everything was okay. Poor little guy—he was so anxious and sensitive, and she completely felt for him because she'd been the same way as a child. Always trying to please her parents, always worried she was failing them.

Karen pulled open the refrigerator. "But you have to eat something. You have to keep your strength up."

"We'll order something in." Gia rinsed the mugs in the sink, then put them in the dishwasher.

Karen turned toward Molly, eyes wide, and mouthed, "What do I do?"

Molly glanced around, trying to figure out the answer to that, but she had absolutely no idea what to do. She'd been at a complete loss ever since Karen had called with the news, and now on top of it, Gia's reaction made her feel like she was in a speeding vehicle whose brakes had failed. Four months ago, when little Nicole had broken her arm ice skating, Gia had spent a week crying so hard she had to hide behind sunglasses, and when Nicole had to go to the hospital for a severe case of pneumonia a month later, Gia had been nearly inconsolable. But now, in the midst of something so much more horrible, Gia was calm and collected, focused on logistics and details.

She must be in denial. That was the only explanation Molly could come up with, either that or something in her mind had broken. Either way, reality would set in eventually, and Molly didn't want her to be alone when that happened. And Anthony—at the best of times he was oblivious, and never home, and even when he was home, completely hands-off. If Molly didn't know better, she'd think the kids weren't his, that's how little he seemed to care about being together as a family. But that's how some men were—they saw their roles as breadwinners, not caretakers.

She said a quick prayer of thanks for her Don. She'd won the lottery when she found him—he loved her deeply and dramatically, and frankly she'd never understood why. She wasn't ugly but she wasn't the sort of woman who captured men's attention, either. Some women lit up a room when they entered it—she was lucky to be noticed. Some women could wear clothes and do their makeup and hair like natural-born starlets—but clothes wore her, the slightest misstep with makeup made her look like she'd been in a street fight, and her hair frizzed or fell flat rather than curled and bounced. She was so lucky to have found him and she knew it, because even though he didn't know his ear from his elbow when it came to raising Shauna, he cared and he tried, and that was more than so many men did.

Not that it was their fault. Men might be physically stronger, but women had the emotional strength. It would be up to her and Karen to see Gia through this, and she was damned well going to do whatever she could to ease this pain for her friend.

It was the very least she could do. Gia had always, without fail, been there for her. Harristown wasn't a welcoming sort of place, and when Molly's family moved to town three years before, the Briar Ridge mothers were frosty and supercilious. Don was a skilled attorney and made a good living, but they were on the lower rungs of Harristown's ladder, and besides that, wealth was only one of the items that had to be checked off Harristown's criteria list. Truth be told, after three years she still wasn't quite sure what all of the items on that list were. The phrase you heard bandied about was the *right kind of people*, and it took a while for the people that mattered to decide you were one of them. Don't even think about not vaccinating your children—the Montessori School in the next town over was the right place for you if that's what your deal was. And if you weren't willing to donate significant time and money to the 'right' causes, just show yourself out—good Harristowners believed in a sense of community, and expected you to do your part. And, ironically, if you were *too* eager to be on the committees and give your money, well, doors would slam shut then too. Desperation was *not* a good look in Harristown.

The lack of acceptance had been disconcerting for Molly. She'd never been what you'd call popular, but she'd never been shunned either; the upside of being the sort of woman men didn't notice was other women didn't feel threatened by her, and she'd never had difficulty finding a friend or two. So when the Harristown mothers met her with frowns and stares, she wasn't quite sure how to react. But she kept trying, and had the good fortune to be assigned to the playground-supervisor volunteer committee with Gia and Karen. They were beyond excited to learn that her hobby was glassblowing, and declared her a fellow *artisan*, a term that still made Molly smile. They'd already been thinking about opening a shop in the ever-so-quaint Main Street area, but didn't have enough time between them to run the shop amid the demands of stay-at-home motherhood. But with Molly, they'd have three different types of goods to sell, and each of them would only have to tend the store for a couple of days a week.

And just like that, Gia decided Molly was *in*. And if Gia Marchand decided that, the deal was sealed. Her husband's family had lived in Harristown since before the revolution, and had patriots through every thread of the family. As the closest thing to royalty that Harristown had, a slight against one of her two best-friend-business-partners was a slight against her. Within weeks, the invitations had started trickling in, then streaming in, and the Hayes' place in the community was sealed.

Gia had done so much for her, and all she could do was watch, impotent, with absolutely no idea how to even interpret Gia's strange mental state.

Gia turned to them. "I know you both just want to help, and I promise, as soon as there's anything you can do, I'll call you. I'm so grateful for the moral support when the detectives were here. But now I really need to talk to my son."

Karen answered. "Are you sure you don't want us to hang out down here while you do it? It may be harder than you think, they've always been so close—"

"That's exactly it." Gia reached for Karen's hand. "I know how hard it's going to be, and I need Nicholas to have the space to react any way he needs to react. He can't do that with you and the other kids here."

Molly shot a glance at Karen. It didn't make sense to them, but what did they know? Gia's child had been murdered, and Molly couldn't even imagine what that felt like. She only knew that just the thought of Shauna being in danger was enough to send her over the edge of sanity.

"How about this," Molly said. "I know neither Karen or I is going to feel okay leaving you without something to eat. So why don't I go get some takeout from that Thai place you like and bring it back for you? I can get something for Don and Shauna while I'm there, too. It'll take at least an hour, and if you aren't done by the time I get back, I'll just leave it on the porch. You can text us if you need anything else, okay?"

Gia smiled and nodded. "Sure. That sounds perfect. Thank you."

Karen started to object—she must also have felt like Gia was just placating them. But Molly gave a quick little headshake, and she backed off.

They bundled up the kids, and Gia watched in silence from the porch as Karen and Molly packed them into the cars. She waved as they climbed in, then turned around and closed the door behind her.

As soon as the two cars rounded the corner, a text beeped through on her phone from Karen:

What the hell was that?

CHAPTER NINE

Fifteen minutes later, Jo and Arnett grabbed a table at Sal's and plopped their notes in front of them. The smell of tomatoes and meat and cheese normally made Jo salivate the moment she entered, but despite not having eaten since breakfast, today her stomach flipped.

"Split a pizza?" Arnett asked.

She really should try to put something in her stomach other than coffee. "Get a small, I don't think I'll have more than a piece."

Arnett ordered as Jo sipped her water, willing the waitress to bring her coffee as quickly as possible. "You want to start things off?" she asked.

Arnett nodded. "Arlo's out, although Lopez might come up with other options, and something may come up from the neighborhood canvas. But as things stand right now, I think we agree we're not looking at a stranger. Which leaves us with the school staff."

The waitress dropped off coffee for both of them, and Jo curled her hands around the warm cup. "And even there, a random element feels less likely after meeting Gia. What did you think of Gia's reaction?"

Arnett blew out a long puff of air. "Definitely not what I expected after what Karen Phelps said about her."

Jo fingered the diamond at the base of her neck. "Possibly she was just projecting her own response onto Gia. But she made reference to previous incidents when Gia had been emotional, so I don't think it's just that."

"Maybe the news about her pregnancy took it all over?" Arnett gulped his coffee.

"If anything, that would have made her more emotional, not less. I promise you, pregnancy hormones are not a joke."

"I'll take your word on that. And in that case, my vote's on denial. Hasn't hit her yet. What's your take?"

"Her response reminds me of something, but I can't figure out what. My gut says something isn't right. Her answers seemed… I'm not sure what the right word is. Not guarded, exactly, but definitely *careful*, which isn't something I've ever seen from a parent who's lost their child. Taken together with the nature of Nicole's death, that makes me wonder what Gia isn't saying, and if Nicole's death has something to do with the family, or someone with a grudge against the family."

"I still can't believe Anthony Marchand's office wouldn't break through to him," Arnett said. "Not the mark of a happy family setup."

Jo tapped her nails on her mug. "And Gia seemed very protective of her son, which I guess is normal, so maybe she was just channeling her emotions into protecting him. But it felt like more than that, and for a minute I even wondered if she was worried he was the one who hurt Nicole."

"He wouldn't be the first kid to hate their little sibling. And he's big enough he could have accidentally killed her if he got angry."

Their waitress appeared with their pizza, and asked if they needed anything else. They said no, and she left.

"Thank goodness the waitstaff here know us." Arnett cast a glance at the waitress as she walked off.

"I'm pretty sure they all learned to tune out our conversation years ago, you know, so they can sleep at night." Jo pulled a slice onto her plate, working up the motivation to take a bite. "As far as Nicholas, I've been going back and forth. He's old enough to lie well, and you could almost see an invisible rope pulling him in to his mother. But at the end, that little speech he gave—either he was really worried about his little sister or he could give Sir Kenneth Branagh a run for his acting money."

"It would explain a lot." Arnett slid a slice onto his plate. "And in terms of the father, anyone who's that intense about their business has likely put noses out of joint."

"We need to look at who might be angry with the family."

"People close to them, extended family members." Arnett shoved most of the slice into his mouth.

A vision of Nicole being throttled by someone she loved flashed through Jo's mind, and the bite of pizza she'd just taken stuck in her throat. She washed it down with her water and pushed away her plate. "When was the last time I couldn't choke down pizza?"

Arnett swallowed, then leaned forward. "I don't think it's bad for you to be sensitive to things like this. For God's sake, a murdered child is horrific, and a heightened reaction after you lost your own child is normal. So many cops shove everything so far down to do the work they turn into emotional zombies. Cut yourself a break."

"Yeah, well." She tossed her crumpled napkin onto the table. "Next steps. While we're waiting for Lopez's and Marzillo's results, maybe we should focus in more on the family and people close to them. Right off the bat, I'd like to verify that Nicholas was actually playing tetherball at recess, so we can eliminate him if possible."

Arnett nodded through a mouthful of pizza. Jo pulled out her phone and put a call through to Briar Ridge's front office, and got Jim Karnegi's cell phone. She dialed the number and waited as the phone rang.

"Hello?" he answered.

"Hello, Mr. Karnegi, this is Detective Fournier. We spoke with you earlier about Nicole Marchand's death?"

"Of course I remember," he said, voice apprehensive. "How can I help you?"

"We have a few more questions we'd like to ask you. Could we come talk to you?" Jo glanced at the clock—it was just past six. "Are you still at the school this late?"

He paused before answering. "I'm not. I just got home, and I was about to go for a run before dinner. If you can come by in the next few minutes, I can talk with you before my wife puts dinner on the table."

"We'd really appreciate that." Jo took down his address, ended the call, and programmed the GPS.

"Let's do it." Arnett shoved the rest of his pizza slice into his mouth and waved for the waitress. She brought a box before he'd managed to swallow, and each of them dropped several bills on top of the check.

Jo's phone buzzed as they left the restaurant—a text from her sister.

Forget about the phone call. I need to talk to you in person.

CHAPTER TEN

Jim Karnegi lived in Wiltshire, a larger, less affluent town next to Harristown. In five minutes, they pulled up to his house, a modest yellow-clapboard saltbox with slightly overgrown landscaping.

As they walked up the driveway, Karnegi opened the door wearing a black tracksuit, a Red Sox cap pulled over his short brown hair, and a worried expression on his face. Without a word, Karnegi gestured them inside. The door opened directly into the home's living room, which had a comfortable, lived-in vibe with mismatched furniture and a scattering of ceramic Hummel-like knick-knacks. Jo and Arnett settled onto the blue couch while Karnegi took a brown armchair.

"Mr. Karnegi, we're sorry to bother you again so soon. We'll be fast, we realize we're already intruding on your evening."

"You can call me Jim. And it's not a problem, I understand investigations like this move quickly. Have you found a suspect?"

"We have several leads, and a few details we'd like to pin down to help us clear our path. First, do you remember seeing Nicholas Marchand at recess today?"

The tension in his face relaxed. "I do, actually. He and the boys he hangs out with always play tetherball."

"So you just know generally, or you remember today specifically?" Arnett asked.

"Specifically today, because one of the fifth graders came in and tried to cut the line, and got into a scuffle with the other boys, including Nicholas. That was near the beginning of the recess, and I kept an eye on them from that point on. That's why I was in the back-west corner for most of the time."

That mapped on to what Nicholas had told them. "So he was playing tetherball the entire time?"

"Yes."

"Gia Marchand mentioned you had Nicholas in your class last year?" Jo asked.

He paused. "I did."

"How did that go?"

His voice was cautious. "How do you mean?"

Arnett shifted in Jo's peripheral vision. "Was he a good student? Well behaved?"

Jim raised his eyebrows and scratched the space between them for a long moment. "Look, it's clear Gia already talked to you about this, so I may as well be up front. I don't like to speculate when I'm not on solid ground, but you'll find out soon enough, anyway. Last year I had a talk with Eileen, Principal Pham, about Nicholas. He'd always been a bright child, eager to please, and quiet. But midway through the year his grades started to slip, and he became withdrawn at times. At other times he was more disruptive than usual. These are signs we're trained to watch out for, so I reported them."

"More disruptive than *usual*," Jo said. "How so?"

"Most kids have bad days for whatever reason. So maybe I'll have to warn them about whispering to their friends in class when they're really excited about something. Issues like that. But this was different. He was more reactive than usual, faster to get upset."

"Violent?" Arnett asked.

Jim shook his head vigorously. "Not at all. I've never seen him even threaten violence."

"You said these are signs you watch out for," Jo said. "What do they signal?"

"There are a variety of possible reasons, some as simple as hormonal changes in some boys who start puberty earlier than others.

And that age is a time of big change in kids. They're getting more responsibility, that sort of thing. But the signs can also signal issues like dyslexia." Jim shifted uncomfortably in his seat. "Or stressors at home. We see it a lot when parents go through a divorce."

"What did Principal Pham say?" Jo asked.

"Not much. Like I said, Nicholas is a quiet child to start with, so it was possible I was being oversensitive to the change. But I feel it's better to be safe than sorry."

"That seems responsible of you," Jo said.

"Yeah, well, Mr. and Mrs. Marchand didn't think so. They pitched a fit, and demanded to put a letter into Nicholas' file rebutting what they called 'my accusations.' Eileen told me to tread carefully, but to let her know if there was any further change. There wasn't, either for the worse or the better, so that was that."

Jo watched Jim carefully. "Speaking of Mrs. Marchand, did you ever have any exchanges with her that were, well, perhaps a bit flirtatious?"

Jim's expression turned indignant, and he glanced over his shoulder briefly before leaning in to answer. "No way in hell. I'm married. Why would you think that?"

Jo kept her face blank. "I apologize, I may have misunderstood."

Jim sat back in the chair, unmollified. "That's a dangerous mistake to make."

Jo raised both hands, palms out in a conciliatory gesture. "I understand that, but we do have to follow up on everything we hear. Please don't worry, our policy is to always be discreet. And if you don't mind, I'd like to backtrack a little. The behavioral changes you mentioned in Nicholas. You must have had an opinion about what caused them?"

Jim raised his brows pointedly. "I don't like to speculate when I don't have facts. Reputations are easy to damage and very hard to recover."

Jo pushed down a flare of temper—she never liked this type of overcoat integrity, but in the current situation it just plain pissed her off—and considered her best approach. "Mr. Karnegi. I appreciate your circumspection, I do. Idle gossip is surely something that should never be condoned. However, Nicholas' sister was murdered today, and we need to find out who killed her. And your opinions on Nicholas and the Marchand family aren't idle, they're informed and buttressed by experience."

Jim grimaced. "I can't see how. Surely she was killed by some sick opportunist."

"We have to explore all possibilities, and that includes the Marchand family dynamics. So whatever your opinions are, we need to hear them. I promise we'll take them with a disclaimer."

Jim's heel bounced up and down. "I don't have facts, and I won't speculate. But I will say that if I were to guess, I don't think Nicholas has a learning disorder and I don't think this is some sort of hormonal issue. His friend group has remained robust. So, that leaves his home life."

"And do you know of anyone who has any reason to be unhappy with the Marchand family? A grudge of any sort?" Jo asked. *Other than you.*

"I don't have any specific knowledge of anything like that, no."

Jo weighed his response and decided that, whether he was hedging or not, he wasn't likely to be any more precise. She stood up, and Arnett did the same.

Arnett held out a card. "Thank you very much for your help. If you think of anything else we should know, please call at any hour."

*

"Well, that was a blazing case of CYA," Arnett said as he pulled away from the house.

"And quite an interesting little he-said-she-said about the flirting," Jo replied.

"First rule of detecting—everybody lies."

"The question is why," Jo said. "In this case, I can see a clear motive for Karnegi to lie—I can't imagine Briar Ridge looks highly on teachers having relationships with parents. I can't see why Gia would lie about it, but then, my read on her is still cloudy."

"But he seems fairly clear—Nicholas Marchand was playing tetherball during recess."

"And he doesn't have motivation to cover for Nicholas, in fact, quite the opposite." Jo tapped her coffee cup.

"Should we drop back by the Marchand house?" Arnett asked. "It hasn't been that long, but the husband might be home by now."

"It's worth a shot—it's on the way back to Oakhurst anyway," Jo said.

They drove by the house. The same Lexus Jo had seen earlier was still in the driveway, parked parallel to the garage. The Volvo and the Audi that had been parked on the curb were now gone.

"Looks like Karen and Molly are gone, but hubby isn't home yet," Jo said.

Arnett grimaced. "Dammit. But I have to admit, I'm already beat and I promised Laura I'd take her to the movies tonight."

"I'm supposed to have dinner with Matt, anyway. And I still have to go see my sister."

"Ugh. May God have mercy on your soul." Arnett laughed.

Arnett dropped Jo off in front of her house, and she stared longingly up at it, pulled to it as if by a siren's call. She wanted to take a nap, or dive into background checks on predators, or regrout her shower—pretty much anything other than go deal with her sister. But there was no point in putting it off.

She climbed in her Chevy Volt and drove as slowly as she could justify. She'd spent a cluster of intensive therapy sessions over the past two weeks examining every trauma in her life, back to her childhood, and Sophie figured prominently among the things that caused her grief. She and her sister had had a rocky relationship since their parents' divorce when Jo was thirteen and Sophie was eight. Sophie had pointedly taken their mother's side, but with a few more years' maturity and a lot more awareness of their parents' fights, Jo hadn't been able to reduce things down to black and white so easily. And while her mother and father managed to get along just fine after they weren't married anymore, the upheaval had a lasting effect on Jo and Sophie's relationship. As did Sophie's tendency to make life choices their mother approved of, like marrying and having children, rather than joining the police academy and spending time that should have been reserved for 'family' doing 'unsavory' things like catching killers.

Still, one of the things she and Nina, her therapist, had focused on was the cumulative effect of trauma. One aspect was how PTSD caused you to be overreactive, and to interpret situations that might be perfectly harmless as potential hazards—was she doing that with Sophie? Was she so used to every encounter with Sophie being unpleasant that she braced automatically for it and overreacted to her sister, thus creating a self-fulfilling prophecy? Possibly—possibly not. But even if she wasn't, it wouldn't do any harm to go into the situation assuming something different, in the hope that it would lead to something different.

And in fact, she might be able to go one step better than that, and actively restructure their dynamic. She was becoming more and more convinced that Nicole's death was caused by someone inside the school, and if that was the case, Sophie's insight could be valuable. She knew most of the teachers, all of the administrators, and probably the majority of the parents. She knew the school procedures and traditions and all the peccadilloes that didn't make it into the guideline manuals. If Jo approached it right, maybe she could turn this interaction from an accusatory inquisition into an ally-recruitment session. And at the very least, maybe all of this would give Sophie a little more appreciation for what Jo did, and why she couldn't drop everything every time someone in the family called.

She checked her e-mail again when she arrived, and found a message from Principal Pham waiting for her with the key-card access records. She'd take a look at it later at home; in the meantime she forwarded it on to Lopez. Then, when she could delay no longer, she forced herself up the drive to her sister's slate-blue two-story colonial, reminding herself to stay positive.

She pressed the doorbell, then tapped her finger on her thigh in time to the chimes playing the first notes of Beethoven's 'Ode to Joy'.

Sophie pulled open the door and stepped back, then gave Jo a quick, stiff side-hug once the door was closed again. "Coffee?" she said by way of greeting.

"Yes, thank you."

Jo followed behind Sophie as her yellow, kitten-heeled sandals tapped their way along the parquet floors. Sophie had changed clothes from when Jo had seen her at the school, and was now in jeans and a light yellow sweater. She might have been wearing the sweater under her trench, and only changed her pants and shoes, but somehow Jo doubted it. Her sister moved through life in outfits, not clothes.

When they reached the kitchen, all stainless steel and white cabinets, Sophie pulled out a mug and a Keurig pod and stuck them both into the machine. With a swift tug she closed the lid, impaling the pod within, then pressed the start button. Only then did she turn and address Jo, who'd slipped into one of Sophie's spindle Windsor kitchen chairs.

"One of the few benefits of having a sister who's a police officer is, I'd like to believe, that she'd alert me when something is happening that might affect my children."

Police detective, Jo thought, and bit the correction on her tongue. She held up a hand. "Here I am, Soph, doing just that."

"Yes. *After* I've had to endure hours of frightening speculation flying at me through e-mails and text chains and phone calls, especially since everyone knows my sister is a policewoman. The most credible rumor I've heard is a little girl went missing from the kindergarten class."

"I have to find out what's going on before I can tell you, and I have to do my job effectively. So do you want to argue about how long it took me to check in with you, or do you want to know what's going on?"

Sophie crossed her arms across her chest. "You're right. I apologize. But this has been a terrifying afternoon."

Jo gave her a quick recap of the basic facts of the case. "We can't rule anything out yet, but in my opinion the possibility that an outsider climbed the fence, snatched Nicole, and managed to kill her without being seen in such a short window of time is nearly nonexistent." This next part was risky—any implication that Emily and Isabelle were in danger could freak Sophie out and render her useless. "I think it's more likely someone associated with the school or the family is involved, or was careless somehow. So I need your help. You know that school and the families that attend inside and out. Where should I be looking?"

Sophie stood slightly taller. "That's a complicated question, and it depends on what you mean, exactly. I wouldn't have the girls there if I knew of anything obvious, or if I didn't think the teachers and admin were top-notch. But there are always little things, like the time I smelled alcohol on one of the cafeteria workers, and there are always whispers and gossip. I guess I'd start with the yard supervisors. Who was on playground duty today?"

Jo was pleasantly surprised by Sophie's calm and focus. But then, her father did always claim Fourniers were made of stern stuff; maybe she was just as guilty as Sophie of misjudging one another. "Jim Karnegi and Karen Phelps."

Sophie's brows popped up, and she leaned against the counter. "Karen Phelps? Well, well, well. That's almost certain to cause a fracture within the Witches of Briar Ridge."

"The what?"

"The Witches of Briar Ridge. That's a little nickname a number of the mothers call Karen Phelps, Gia Marchand, and Molly Hayes."

"Sounds like there's quite a story behind *that*."

Sophie pulled the now-full mug of coffee from the machine and slid it in front of Jo as she sat. "Not really, it's not as negative as it sounds, it mostly has to do with the fact that they're a tight little trio of friends. Nobody likes to be excluded, and some people get their feathers ruffled easily."

Jo straightened. "How so?"

"The perception by some is that Gia Marchand thinks she runs Harristown, and Karen and Molly are her two henchmen."

"And does she run it?" Jo asked.

Sophie shrugged. "Pretty much. Her husband's family is rich, and she's not afraid to use that money and the power that goes with it to get what she wants. Molly's also fairly well off, although not nearly as much as Gia, and while Karen used to be rolling in it, things have changed since she got divorced. But she'd still be more than fine if she'd stop trying to keep up her old lifestyle."

Jo grabbed the mug with both hands and sipped. After seeing the Marchands' house, news of their wealth wasn't a shock. But to hear her sister refer to it in those terms was jarring—Sophie's husband, David, came from a family with one foot dipped deeply into the upper-middle-class pool, and Sophie wasn't easily impressed. "So people are jealous."

Sophie waved her hand. "Of course they're jealous, but like I say, it's not that simple. It's more that nobody likes to feel they aren't in the in-crowd."

"So you're saying they're mean girls." Jo sighed internally—high school never ended.

Sophie scrunched up her face. "No, not exactly that either, at least not in my experience. I've never seen them be nasty or spiteful. They're just… exclusive. I know I'm being vague, but it's hard to explain. It's like, have you ever seen a couple who're in that beginning phase where they only have eyes for each other? They'll be perfectly lovely if they have to interact with you for some reason, but for the most part, they just pay attention to each other and aren't going to think to invite you in. Does that make sense?"

"I think I get what you mean," Jo said.

"And Gia's an interesting character. She's warm and friendly, and very fun to be around, but if you try to get to know her, it's like pounding on a cement wall. So it feels a bit like she pulls you in only to keep you firmly at arm's length. It happened to me when I first met her. She was very kind to me, and invited me to a charity luncheon she threw, and then we chatted at a baby shower for a mutual friend. It felt like we were becoming fast friends, but then when I started getting to that place where you talk about your kids and your husbands, all that, it was like the barriers at a railroad crossing dropped down into place. It made me feel like I'd said or done something wrong, but then I saw the same thing happen to several other women and realized it was just Gia. And along with her general *to the manor born* situation, a lot of people find it insulting. Others find it annoying, and some people would just do anything to turn the trio into a quartet."

Jo wondered briefly where Sophie landed on that scale. "So it sounds like there's no shortage of people who'd like to take her down a peg."

"Take her down a peg, certainly. But killing her daughter? That's a whole different level of evil."

Jo wagged her head. "You'd be surprised at what can trigger people sometimes. I had a call once where a man shot another man in the leg because the second man asked him to be quiet in a theater."

Sophie's brows shot up. "Was alcohol involved?"

"You'd think so, wouldn't you? But no. Which makes it even more bizarre."

Sophie took in a breath and stared at the ceiling. "I mean, I know of little things, everyday you-stepped-on-my-toes issues. The biggest thing is they snap up the volunteer assignments they want so they can either work them together, or make sure they're able to cover shifts at their boutique. Our school is small enough that probably everyone's had their nose put out of joint by that stuff over the years. But seriously, if someone's going to kill an innocent little girl over something like that…" She shook her head at the implication.

"They're probably not all that stable," Jo finished for her. "So if you know of anyone who has shown any questionable behavior in the past, that would help."

"I can't think of anything offhand, but let me ask around and see what I can come up with."

"That'd be great. Back to the playground—what do you know about Jim Karnegi? He claims nothing unusual happened on the playground. Should I trust him?"

"I'd say so. He's Isabelle's teacher, and he seems fine. I don't have any issues with him, but then, you know Isabelle, she's well behaved and does well in school. Our parent-teacher conferences are always perfunctory."

"Is he the flirty type?"

"He's never flirted with me." Sophie looked her up and down. "Did he hit on you?"

The sip of coffee Jo just took went down the wrong way, and she coughed. "No, nothing like that. But Gia Marchand says he hit on *her*. Last year. And she rejected him. Some men don't take kindly to that."

Sophie *tsk-tsked*. "Well, well, well. Gia's beautiful, so I suppose that's not too surprising. He's married, although I guess *that* doesn't mean much."

Sophie's tone caused David's face to flash through Jo's mind. She'd sensed tension between them over the last few months, and it worried her. But Sophie continued before she could ask about it.

"But to kill Nicole because Gia rejected him? I just can't see that. He's a dedicated teacher who seems to really care about his students. I've seen him go out of his way to help them inside and outside of the classroom."

But Nicole wasn't his student. "Is Gia the sort of woman who thinks all men are in love with her?"

Sophie considered the question. "I'd say she's the sort of woman who's oblivious to the effect she has on men. She's deeply in love with her husband. The kind of love that led her to drop out of college after her junior year because he graduated and got accepted to grad school and they couldn't bear to be apart."

"Beauty, brains, money, love—seems like she has everything." Jo tapped her fingernail on her mug. "In my experience, the more perfect someone's life appears from the outside, the more of a shambles it is in reality."

Sophie nodded, but remained quiet.

"What about the other yard monitor, Karen? Is she careless? Do you trust her supervisory skills?"

"She's a little bit of a wannabe—she actually named her kids Catherine and William, so take from that what you will." She flashed Jo an eye roll. "But she's well-meaning and good with kids. I'd trust her to watch over the girls. I would not, however, trust her alone with David for half a second. If you want to talk about the flirty type, there you go. If it's male and it has a pulse, she'll make cow-eyes at it. I'm not even sure she realizes she's doing it. I think she's one of those women whose self-esteem requires constant feeding and watering, and since her husband left her she's been in famine and drought."

"What about the kindergarten teacher?"

Sophie's face lit up. "Stephanie Roden? She's a delight. I was genuinely sad when Emily moved on from her class. She's so good with the kids, and they just love her." Her expression fell. "I should call her. Finding Nicole must have completely destroyed her."

"I'm sure she'd like that." Jo tapped and swiped on her phone, and pushed it toward Sophie. "Do you recognize this?"

Sophie looked down, then up again quickly as though the question were a trick. "It's Gunter. From *Sing*."

"Gunter. From *Sing*."

Sophie gave an of-course-you-don't-know headshake. "He's a character from a kids' movie called *Sing*. He's a pig. With a German accent. He sings 'Shake It Off' with another pig called Rosita. Stop me when you know enough."

Jo threw up her hand. "Got it. Do you know who it belongs to?"

"Not specifically. Isabelle used to have one, but she outgrew it and we donated it with a bunch of old toys to that domestic abuse shelter in Springfield. Why?"

Jo sighed. "We found it in the dumpster near Nicole's body, and Gia says it's not Nicole's."

"That's strange." Sophie grabbed Jo's mug and took a sip.

Jo waved her hand at the mug, fighting flashbacks of Sophie stealing sweaters from her closet. "Sure, help yourself. It is your house, after all."

"Sorry, my brain needs caffeine." Sophie slid the mug back. "Could it have fallen out of the dumpster? It is an older toy, maybe somebody didn't want it anymore."

Jo cradled the mug. "The area was clean otherwise, so it's not like some bag burst, and the toy didn't have any detritus on it. It's possible someone threw it over the side thinking it would go into the dumpster. I can't imagine most kids bring their toys to school to throw away, but maybe one kid grabbed it from another and threw it over in a moment of blossoming junior assholery."

"But you think it's more likely someone used it to lure Nicole." Sophie rose and crossed to the Keurig.

Jo was impressed again. "You wouldn't make a half-bad detective."

Sophie pushed another mug into the machine. "I don't know about that. I've just spent hundreds of hours obsessing about all the horrible things that could happen to my kids."

"Yes, well. The ability to generate possibilities is the first step."

"I'll tell you one thing, though." Sophie pushed the start button. "That should cut down on your suspects, at least if you're considering parents as a possibility. That's a fast-food toy, it came in one of those kid's meals. Half the parents at Briar Ridge wouldn't be caught dead anywhere near food that's not fully organic and gluten-free, et cetera et cetera."

"Lots of people say that, but when push comes to shove…" Jo said.

"True. But they sure as hell wouldn't allow their child to have a toy around that proved their transgression," Sophie said.

"Probably true." Jo drained the rest of her coffee and stood up. "Anyway. If you can keep your ear to the ground, I'd appreciate it. I'll go so you can fix dinner."

"I will." Sophie walked over to Jo, gave her a hug, then pulled back and looked at her. "I need you to be straight with me. Are my girls in danger?"

Jo considered her answer. Normally she'd assure any parent at a school where something like this happened that this was likely an isolated case, and that the school would be taking steps to ensure child safety. But Sophie wasn't stupid and she wouldn't appreciate being finessed. "I hope not, Soph. But if they were my girls, I'd walk them all the way to their classroom in the morning and pick them up there at night. I'd also tell them to stay in the center of the playground during recess, where both supervisors can see them, and not to go anywhere alone with any adults. Even their teachers."

CHAPTER ELEVEN

Jo sat in her car for a long moment outside Sophie's house, trying to get the vision of Nicole's tiny broken body out of her head.

Already, within the space of a few hours, it had become inextricably linked with her own lost baby, as though the tragic image had slipped into the blank slot of the picture she'd never been able to form. On an intellectual level, she understood what was happening; it was another aspect of cumulative traumas—they stitched and molded together, like layers of a cake turning into one cohesive dessert. First Marc, the boyfriend she saw gunned down when she was a teenager, then Jack, the fiancé she'd failed to save during a drug-addled mugging. Now the only child she was ever likely to have. Three souls she should have protected, three souls now merged into one blinding pit of fear in her chest, sucking in everything she saw and experienced, filtering it all through a lens of tragedy, morphing the safe into the terrifying.

Add in the horrors of the job, particularly a sweet, innocent child, and you had a recipe for disaster.

Jo's therapist, Nina, had been right—two weeks hadn't been enough time to process it all before she returned to work. Jo had thought she had the cognitive-behavioral tools she needed to cope, but she was wrong and it was too late now, the damage was done, and the layers of her cake now contained Nicole's indelible image. Her hand clasped the diamond at her throat, taken from the engagement ring Jack had given her, and she squeezed her eyes shut. The first step in working through her trauma had to be figuring out who killed Nicole.

She checked the time. She was desperate to head to HQ and jump into background checks, start digging into everything about everyone inside and out of that school until she had a solid lead. But she'd promised Matt she'd come over for dinner to celebrate her last night off work, and she was due there in twenty minutes. And she was self-aware enough to know that an evening in his bed would go a long way to soothe her frazzled mental state and allow her to focus more effectively tomorrow.

After a quick stop-off at home to change and run a comb through her hair, Jo arrived at Matt's house. He opened the door and pulled her into his arms, kicking the door closed behind her as he kissed her slowly. Her body relaxed as she sank into his embrace, proof of how stressed the day had made her.

She gazed up into his handsome face. Matt Soltero was tall, with black hair and eyes the color of dark chocolate, and the musculature of someone a decade younger than his forty-five years. They'd met the month before, when he, as a neurologist, attended to a woman who'd wandered out of the woods with no memory of who she was. He'd given them advice on how to help the woman remember who was after her, and in the process had asked Jo out. She'd enjoyed his company far more than she'd expected to, and when she pulled away after realizing she was pregnant from her previous relationship, he hadn't become petulant or demanding. That had been a refreshing change from her recent experiences with men, and had, ironically, increased her attachment to him.

He reached up and rubbed her shoulders, then gave an exaggerated wince. "Very tense." He dropped his hand, picking up one of hers as he did so, and led her into his kitchen. "Don't worry, I already have a bottle of wine open. And I'd be happy to give you a little massage, if that would help."

She smiled. "One glass. I need to be up early tomorrow."

His laugh was deep and sexy. "And I feel much safer out on the streets of Oakhurst County because of it."

The scent of onions and bell peppers reached her, and she glanced at the gray granite island in the middle of his sleek, gray-and-black kitchen. "What's for dinner?"

"I thought I'd try my hand at some jambalaya." He kissed her hand and pointed at the shrimp waiting to be deveined.

She took an exaggerated deep breath. "I don't know—that's a dangerous proposition."

"I know, I know—your father makes the best jambalaya in the world and I'll never come close. So if I can't get it right, you can teach me what I'm doing wrong."

"Actually, my aunt Claudette makes the best jambalaya in the world, but don't tell my father I said that." She reached up and kissed him. "Because if you ever do, I'll tell him you're a protestant and he'll order you out of his house."

He shot her a skeptical look. "Like when he hears the name Soltero and looks at my obviously Latino face he'll believe anything other than one hundred percent Catholic."

"You make a good point." She peered into the pot hissing on the stove, relieved he hadn't latched on to the implied suggestion he'd meet her father. "You've got your holy trinity sweating, so you've started out on the right foot. But I see two problems."

He crossed to the far counter and grabbed the already-open bottle of wine, and a glass. "Do tell."

"Always brown the andouille first. Then use the drippings to sweat your trinity. And"—she pointed to a can on the island—"Cajun jambalaya doesn't have tomatoes."

He poured the wine into two glasses. "Well, I guess I should just be very glad you got here in time for the tomatoes, at least." He handed her a glass. "Cheers."

She sipped, then added the sausage into the vegetables. "Thank goodness."

They laughed and chatted as they cooked, and by the time they'd finished dinner, her wine was gone and the knot inside her had loosened, until only the underlying numbness remained.

"Now, then," he said as he pushed away his empty bowl. "Tell me why you're so het up. This seems like more than just being stressed about returning to work tomorrow."

"Turns out, I went back today." She caught him up on the events of the day.

He leaned back in his chair and rubbed the side of his face. "A little girl. I don't know how you do what you do."

She stared down into her bowl. "At the moment I'm not really sure how I do it, either."

He reached for her hand, and threaded his fingers through hers. "It takes a lot of strength to face the dark side of human nature. And nobody can be strong all the time." He was silent for a moment, then seemed to think of something. "Why did you go back early?"

Her automatic reactions kicked in—whenever conversations with men got too emotionally intimate, she deflected by turning the moment to physical intimacy. She looked up at him, ready to give him a sexy look and lean forward for a long kiss, but stopped short when she saw the expression on his face. Concern, but mixed with something else she couldn't identify, and whatever that something else was, it tugged at her soul.

"I haven't told you the full truth," she said before she realized she was saying it. "I told you I took the time off because of my injury, and that's technically true, but it's incomplete. I was pregnant when he shot me, and I miscarried. I didn't know I was when we first met," she hurried to add. "I found out shortly after our first date. And I didn't know you well enough to feel comfortable telling you about it."

"You don't owe me any explanations." He squeezed her hand. "But now I understand why you made me promise not to read your medical records."

She smiled, thankful for his attempt at humor. "So, when this came up, Bob tried to pass it to another team, because he didn't want to put me through it. But nobody at HQ knows about the miscarriage, so he couldn't really explain. And he knew that if we were going to be on the investigation, I'd want to be a part of it from the start, because my nieces go to the school where it happened."

He tensed, and leaned forward slightly. "That's terrifying."

She nodded, silent.

He stroked the back of her hand with his thumb. "There's more."

She paused a long moment. "It's all running together in my mind. Nicole and my nieces and the baby I lost. My brain does that. It makes connections, too many. People remind me of other people I've known, and situations bring up emotions and reactions I've seen before. It helps me solve my cases, because I see things other people don't. But it also sabotages me, because I can't seem to let go of pain, I just transfer it on to new situations and live it over again and again."

"Sounds like a version of PTSD."

"My therapist agrees with you. One that transforms my strengths into my own personal demons."

He squeezed her hand, and she squeezed it back. She watched his eyes trace a path across the table, bracing herself for whatever wrong thing he was about to say. Would he tell her not to feel what she was feeling, that none of it was her fault and she shouldn't take it on? Would he try to find a solution for her, suggest she take more time off or that she see her therapist more often or find a new one, or—the worst possibility—suggest she quit her job? Or maybe he'd ask a series of invasive questions that would feel like she was being prodded by some sort of emotional speculum.

He took a big breath, then sighed. "Why does life have to be so complicated?"

Something deep inside Jo, in a part of her soul that hadn't moved for over twenty years, shifted. "You know what I'd really love right now?"

He met her eyes. "What?"

"A long, hot bubble bath and another glass of wine. Would you mind very much?"

His smile was gentle, and teasing. "You saw the whirlpool jets in my tub, didn't you?"

She smiled back. "I must admit I did."

He kissed her forehead, disappeared into the bathroom to draw her a bath, then came back and refilled her wine glass. "I put towels on the stand next to the tub. Give a shout if you need anything else."

She kissed him, and padded off to the bathroom. By the time she stripped down, the bath had filled; she tested the water with her hand, then slipped in. She turned on the jets, leaned against the built-in ridge that doubled as a headrest, and sipped her wine until the water turned cold.

When she emerged from the bathroom wrapped in his blue terrycloth robe, he was on the couch, reading.

"Good book?" she asked.

"It is. It's about Steve Jobs."

"I didn't realize you were a tech buff."

"I am, but I admit it's more that I'm addicted to biographies. I love learning about people's lives, especially people who did extraordinary things." He patted the cushion next to him. "Come sit with me. Do you want to watch a movie?"

"Sure."

She sat next to him, and he pulled her into his chest. The movie started—some black-and-white classic he found On Demand—but she fell asleep before the opening credits had finished. She woke briefly as he carried her into his bed, allowed herself to be settled under his sheets, then fell asleep again to the feel of his strong arms around her.

CHAPTER TWELVE

Molly woke in a panic, gasping for breath, sweat drenching her nightgown.

She checked the time on her phone and tried to calm her breathing. Three in the morning, and the house was quiet.

Her nightmare had been about Shauna—not surprising giving the day's events. Shauna had been running, trying to escape a mysterious black shadow chasing her, and hadn't noticed a looming cliff. Molly ran toward her as fast as she could, but she was too far away to make it in time, and she had to watch her baby plunge over the side and fall to her death. Shauna's screams still echoed in her ears.

She pulled back the covers and shifted out of bed gently, careful not to wake Don. He needed his sleep for work the next day, but had taken far longer than normal to fall asleep, and had tossed and turned all night long, waking Molly several times. The hardwood floor sent a chill up her legs, and the cold night air pricked her exposed skin. She grabbed the robe she'd tossed over her armchair, wrapped herself in it, and crept as silently as she could down the hall to Shauna's room.

The blanket on Shauna's bed was tossed and rumpled and tugged up over her head. Molly pulled it back and watched the little ruby lips blow slightly in and out with Shauna's breath. She couldn't bear to even think about losing Shauna—Shauna was her heart, her soul, her world. Just thinking about the possibility raised her blood pressure and shortened her breath. She forced herself to inhale deeply and waited for the relief to kick in, picking up the book Shauna had knocked off her nightstand in her sleep.

Of course the dream was just a dream, but it had been so terrifyingly real, especially in light of the day's events. Poor little Nicole—she was such a lovely child, well behaved and kind, the sort who'd share her last bite of popsicle with the other children without having to be asked. It was normal, she told herself, for anxiety to rear up after something like this. Tears sprung into Molly's eyes and she hurried out of the room before they turned into sobs that would wake Shauna.

But a different sort of anxiety hovered in the back of her mind—Gia's reaction *wasn't* normal. She wasn't handling it all well, or rather, she was handling it *too* well. Most likely that was just a front, and if that was the case, when that sort of facade crumbled, the results weren't likely to be pretty.

Still, what if it were more than that? Because it wasn't like Gia to put those walls up with her and Karen. Other women, yes, but you couldn't blame her for that. Everybody wanted something from her or was jealous of her, and that made it hard to trust other women. But their friendship was different, as Gia herself had said a hundred times: *Thank God for the two of you. I don't have to explain myself to you, I can just be me.*

So why had she shut them out today?

She'd held them at arm's length, then practically kicked them out of the house, unable to get rid of them fast enough. Molly had talked Karen down after the fact, because Karen always overreacted to everything; that was just her normal insecurities at work. But Molly had to agree it felt wrong. Like they were on the outs, and Gia no longer trusted them. And it took Molly right back to those early days in Harristown when everyone looked at her like she was a hopeless, outsider loser.

She slid back into bed and slipped her leg next to Don's, taking solace in the warmth of his skin.

Don rolled to face her, his eyes sleepy. "Can't sleep?"

She tried to put on a smile. "I had a nightmare that someone was chasing Shauna."

He reached out from under the covers and grabbed her hand. "It's freezing, come under here."

She snuggled in and tucked her head into his shoulder, inhaling his musky scent.

"Shauna's safe. You're safe. We're all safe."

"I'm also worried about Gia's reaction. It's not like her. I feel like something's going on."

"People have all sorts of reactions when something like this happens." He reached across with his other hand and stroked her hair. "You've done everything that can be done. And we'll both continue to do whatever we can. Obsessing about it all night isn't going to undo it or fix it or help anyone move forward."

She nodded, rubbing her cheek against his chest. "Do you think it's safe to keep Shauna at Briar Ridge?"

"Stop. Something like this can happen at any school, at any time. We can't just uproot our lives over it, that isn't the solution. Don't overreact." He lifted her chin so he could look into her eyes. "I really need you to make that appointment with the therapist. It's past time, and you promised me."

She pulled him close. "You're probably right. I just—well, I'll look into it tomorrow."

He reached over to the nightstand, and felt for his bottle of Excedrin PM. "In the meantime, you need your sleep. And this has been a huge shock."

"No, I'm fine. I'm already feeling drowsy."

He kissed her forehead. "Good. But if you have another nightmare, wake me up. Promise?"

She smiled. "Promise."

She lay listening to the thub-dub of his heart, and in less than a minute, his breath slowed. She was so lucky to have him. Funny how these things worked—Gia was so beautiful, so elegant, so everything, but she had a husband who treated her like she was invisible. Anthony worked such long hours and left her alone so much, in most ways she was a single mother. She was strong and she was competent, but that didn't mean it was pleasant to have to do it alone, and then when you added in something like this—that's when partners were the most important, when life's unexpected twists turned into tragedy. Not that she was judging, because to each their own—she'd long ago learned to never judge what happened inside someone else's marriage.

She rolled onto her back and lay staring at the ceiling.

*

Gia lay awake in bed, staring up at the ghostly outlines of the crown moldings highlighted by the moon, when a desperate cry carried through the still house.

She jumped out of bed and hurried down the hall to Nicholas' room. He was sitting up in bed, his face red and sweaty.

"Mommy," he said.

Mommy. He only called her that when he was upset, it was supposedly too babyish for a boy in the fourth grade. She was *Mom* usually, and when he was annoyed, she was *Mother.*

She sat beside him on the bed. "Are you okay, baby? Did you have a nightmare?"

He nodded. "Can I come sleep with you?"

"Of course, darling."

He climbed out of the bed and grabbed her hand, and she led him through the hall.

They both jumped as the door to Anthony's office flew open. The lamp on his desk backlit him so she was unable to see his expression, and they stood for a moment, staring at each other in the darkness. He stepped back inside and closed the door, sending an eddy of air toward them. A whiskey-scented eddy.

Once in the bedroom, she flipped back the eiderdown cover for Nicholas. She climbed in next to him and pulled him close, wrapped around him as though he were still in her womb.

She sang to him as she lay staring now at the shadows on the wall—'O-o-h Child' by The Five Stairsteps always put him to sleep—and chased her thoughts around her mind.

In the silence, the sounds of sobbing crept in from Anthony's office.

*

Karen forced her tears back as she stood in Willie's room, watching him sleep. She'd crossed back and forth from Katie's room to Willie's, over and over, unable to stay in her own bed for more than a few minutes. For once, she wished they lived in a smaller house and the two shared a room—then she'd be able to curl up into a chair and keep watch over them both at the same time, and maybe she'd even be able to drift off herself.

Although, the way things were going, it might not be long before that happened. If something didn't change, she wouldn't be able to make the house payment. Not that money was the important thing—both her babies were alive, and that's what really mattered. But money was a reality she couldn't ignore, either. Maybe this was all a sign she should just give up and put the kids in public school.

That would certainly be the final nail in the coffin of her flagging social life. As it was, her friendship with Gia was the only thing that kept any of the invitations coming since the divorce. But so what? Who cared about friendships with people that were based on status and money and not who you really were? Vacuous conversations and pointless events, all of it.

But pain stabbed her heart at the thought of leaving it all behind. It made her feel important and glamorous, like she was *somebody*. Not in a superficial way, not because of the money. But she mattered. People knew her name, they smiled when they saw her, she belonged. She was a part of something, and she was real. Without her social circle she'd shrink back into nothingness, and would be nobody.

Then again, maybe she *was* nobody, and the life she led just hid that.

She shook herself—she shouldn't be so ungrateful. She had two lovely children, and a new man who was crazy about her, who thought she was pretty and sexy and fun. That's what mattered. After struggling through this year alone, she'd give up all the trappings of her Harristown existence if she could just find a husband to love her again.

She wiped the tears away as she crossed back to check on Katie again.

CHAPTER THIRTEEN

Frost covered the ground when Jo left Matt's house the next morning. She peered down at the ice crystals on his blades of grass as she trudged to the car, marveling at the intricacies of physics and the natural world. And how temporary they were—the cold snap would have to end soon, and she'd be sad to see it go. Especially right now, when hiding inside against the cold felt cozy and comforting, and the temperature made the world seem calmer and a little less threatening.

After a stop at Starbucks along the way, she pulled around the charming redbrick facade of the HQ building to its far less charming industrial back side. She grabbed the two drinks and strode inside, briefly responding to the *welcome backs* and the *look what the cat dragged ins* with laughter and rejoinders. She set Arnett's coffee on his desk and settled into her chair, then checked in with a group text to Lopez, Marzillo, and Arnett. Lopez had, as usual, made considerable progress before leaving the night before, and Jo had barely begun checking into it all before Lopez returned her text. She grabbed her latte and headed into the lab.

Lopez had made a permanent home next to Marzillo's workstation in the front of the lab area, and between the two of them they'd taken over a medium conference-sized room for their set-ups. Jo found Lopez sitting cross-legged in her chair, inspecting a screen, her long black ponytail wound around the fingers of her left hand.

"You're up early today," Jo said. "That's usually my specialty."

Lopez turned, and bounced her eyebrows up and down. "I had a very fun night last night, and woke up energized and ready to kick some ass."

"Anybody I know?" Jo teased, trying to remember the last time Lopez had taken enough of a liking to someone to go home with him. She'd seen far too much both as a cop and as a cyber-specialist to trust most dating sites or apps, and her romantic sensibilities were slow to warm up.

"No. Someone I met at a video game conference a few months ago. We've been talking since, and finally went out about a week ago." Her eyes widened. "He's thirty-one."

It took Jo a moment to realize the implication of this—Lopez was thirty-nine. Jo pulled over a chair. "Congratulations?"

"Jury's still out. He seems to have his act together more than you'd expect from a dude his age. He owns his own computer-repair-geek-squad-Apple-bar type store, and he knows his stuff. But he spends a little too high a percentage of his time watching shows that are animated or that involve people getting hit in the genitals. He's got a lot of energy, though, I'll give him that," she finished with a smile.

Arnett rounded the corner into the office. "Who has a lot of energy?"

Lopez turned a naughty grin to Jo, and they both burst out into laughter.

He closed his eyes and jutted a hand out. "Yeah, never mind, I don't want to know."

"You really don't," Jo said, and pulled over a chair for him. "Christine was just about to walk me through what she found out yesterday."

Arnett's eyes swept Lopez's desk. "I'm not sure I trust anything she says until she's had her morning Rockstar."

Lopez met Arnett's eyes and held his gaze as she extracted a Rockstar from the mini-fridge next to her desk, cracked it open, and took a long sip.

Arnett laughed as he dropped into his chair. "Now we're talking."

Lopez tried not to smile. "Okay, so. Early yesterday I identified four more registered sex offenders who live close enough to be viable suspects in Nicole's death. But, I asked local PD to follow up on alibis, and they can all account for their whereabouts during the time Nicole was murdered. And, there was a report from the responding officer waiting for me when I got in—his canvassing didn't turn anything up. Nobody saw or heard anything unusual."

Jo was disappointed, but not surprised. Every cell in her body was screaming that no stranger had done this—Nicole had known her killer, or at the very least, had reason to trust them.

"While they were checking on that, I sorted through the key-card access records. I didn't see any suspicious timing anywhere, including the cafeteria. Pham explained to you that it's impossible to tell who exited the door out of the cafeteria to the dumpster area, you only need the key-card to get *in*. But the last recorded key-card entry into the door was a full hour before morning recess had started, so nobody came in after killing Nicole."

"Nothing during or after recess?" Arnett confirmed.

"Nope. So someone might have ducked out and hid somewhere waiting for a child they could snatch, but they didn't go back in that way after the fact."

"Got it," Jo said.

"Then I started in on the background checks. At your suggestion I've been working backward from the newest hires. Nobody hired on so far this year, but last year they hired two cafeteria workers and a janitor." Lopez paused to take another draw on her Rockstar. "Now, before I say anything else, I want to give kudos to Principal Pham. Not only did she do all the state and federal mandated background checks on everybody she hired, fingerprint scans, criminal records histories, the whole nine, she went above and beyond. I'm double-checking as I go to make sure nothing has changed, but I gotta say, if I had a kid I'd have no problem putting them there based on her caution."

"I'll be sure to pass that on to my sister." Jo tapped her cup on her knee.

Lopez's head snapped back to Jo. "Your nieces go to Briar Ridge? Your sister must be losing her shit."

Jo wagged her head. "Not as much as I expected, truth be told."

Lopez inhaled skeptically and turned back to her displays. "Anyway. Of course I'm going deeper. Residential histories, employment histories, financial records."

Jo and Arnett nodded. All of those searches would check for far more subtle flags than criminal histories. Individuals from out of the area, or who were jumping from job to job, might signal someone running from their past. Financial records uncovered all sorts of difficult or questionable circumstances.

Lopez pointed to her screen. "All three are from western Mass, and all three had legitimate reasons for leaving their previous employers. In fact, when I checked up, the employers had only good things to say. And nothing strange in their financial histories that I could find. So I moved on to the following year, when two teachers and two staff members were hired. Three of these had also turned up clean."

Jo waited—Lopez loved nothing more than a dramatic reveal.

"The fourth was Jim Karnegi."

Jo leaned forward. "He didn't come back clean?"

"If his life was a Facebook status, it'd be *it's complicated.* He moved to Wiltshire three years ago from Lippitt, Rhode Island, after leaving an elementary school there. He also divorced his wife that same year. He married his new wife the following year; she's from western Mass, so I assume he met her here. Other than the period directly after his dismissal, he's been stable financially. I dug into the local newspapers from the period right around his departure, hoping for some salacious scandal, but no such luck.

But even if it didn't make the papers, I'm guessing there's quite a story there."

"Why did he leave his previous school?"

"They wouldn't say. I got the whole 'all we can say is he worked here, and when' deal, and we all know that means they have nothing good to say about him. But I had a contact check the unemployment rolls, and he filed a successful claim. Which means he was fired."

"A kid is dead and the school wouldn't tell you anything?" Arnett asked.

Lopez scrunched up her face. "Well, the principal wasn't in when I called, and the person I talked to was new enough to not want to make a decision about disseminating information without permission. I figured you might want to talk to him yourself, and if not, I'd call him back today. I have his info in the notes."

"Perfect," Jo said. "I'll call today."

"In the meantime, I'll keep moving on down the employee list."

"Great. But before you do, we're thinking we need to take a close look at the Marchand family," Jo said.

A disappointed, jaded expression took over Lopez's face. "I was really hoping since this happened on school grounds, that the family didn't have anything to do with it."

"I was hoping that, too, but it turns out we can't rule them out. They both entered the premises yesterday morning, but we don't have evidence either of them ever left. But more than that was the mother's reaction. I've seen a lot of different forms of mourning, but this one was an outlier, and I finally remembered what it reminded me of. Camilla Wharton, when her husband was murdered." Michael Wharton was the first of a series of murders that had occurred at Oakhurst U the previous fall. "She was cold and resigned, almost like she expected it. Which, in Camilla's case I get—everyone hated her husband, including her, and it probably was only a matter of time before someone killed him. But I don't see how that logic can possibly apply to a five-year-old child."

"Unless killing the child was a way to get at one or both of the parents," Arnett said.

"Exactly. Which would mean something ugly is going on somewhere around or inside the family, and if so, we need to find out what it is. My sister gave me the general lay of the land yesterday." She caught them up on what Sophie had told her. "I asked her to keep her ear to the ground for us, since she knows the ins and outs of the school, but I think we need to jump on it more aggressively."

"I'll get started on the cyber stakeouts." Lopez tilted her Rockstar in a *cheers* motion.

Movement outside the room drew their attention seconds before Marzillo trudged in. They stared open-mouthed at her—gone were the platform heels and flattering cloud of curls she normally wore, now replaced by sneakers under her jeans and red sweater, and black hair pulled back into a severe bun.

She caught their expressions and looked down at herself. "Yeah, well. All I can tell you is, if you're ever in a situation where you have to go through two dumpsters' worth of garbage from an elementary school, at all costs, delegate. You don't want to know what we found in there. In fact, I'm gonna have *nightmares* about what we found in there. It took me two showers to get the smell off, and I didn't have time to condition my hair."

Arnett's eyes were billiard balls. "You used to work in the ME's office. What can smell worse than decaying bodies?"

Marzillo set the stack of papers she was carrying down on her main desk. "It wasn't so much that it was worse. It was different, and unexpected. When you work with dead bodies, you expect certain things, and those things happen in fairly controlled ways. When you think of innocent little kids…"

Lopez burst into laughter. "Innocent little kids. They may be innocent and they may be little, but speaking as someone who helped raise my younger brothers and sisters, first and foremost they're *nasty*. Vomit, urine, feces, snot. All the bodily fluids, all the places, all the time."

Marzillo tapped her nose with her index finger. "Bingo. Any fluttering I had left in my ovaries, yesterday killed it."

Arnett pointedly avoided looking at Jo—neither Marzillo nor Lopez knew about her miscarriage. She had planned on telling them at dinner that night, until Marzillo announced to her and Lopez that she was hoping to bring a date. She could tell them another time.

Jo cleared her throat. "I assumed we didn't get a text from you because you didn't have an update for us, but maybe it was because you were in it up to your neck?"

"Literally," Marzillo said. "But no, no update. You know as much as I do. The ME's office won't have a chance to do an autopsy until this morning because there was a multiple-fatality car accident on the pike about the same time Nicole was dying. He said he should have the information to you by this afternoon. He did mention that Anthony Marchand came and ID'd the body last night, and apparently wanted to be sure you were aware of it, so there's that. Otherwise, it'll take time to sort through all the fingerprints we had to take, but Hakeem is a whiz at that. And I took swabs off Nicole's jacket and the toy we found near her, but it'll be a while before we hear back."

"Good to know Anthony Marchand actually exists; now we just have to get him to return our calls," Arnett said, and turned to Jo. "So as it stands, we don't have much to go on. Sounds like our best chance for a lead is those background checks, priority on the Marchand family, and following up with Karnegi's last principal."

"Also, I'm thinking we should disseminate the photo of the Gunter toy to the parents at the school," Jo said. "It's the sort of detail I'd normally like to hold back, but with so little to go on, I'm not sure we have that luxury."

"I agree. In this case I don't think having to rule out a false confession is our big worry right now," Arnett said.

Jo stood up. "Sounds like we at least have a plan, then."

CHAPTER FOURTEEN

"Mrs. Marchand, please, wait a moment."

Gia turned to find Eileen Pham hurrying toward them, down Briar Ridge's main hall. She stopped still between Karen and Molly, and waited for her.

"We didn't expect to see you here today, given the circumstances," Eileen said when she caught up to them.

"Life doesn't stop just because my daughter has been ripped away from me," Gia said, face blank.

"But surely you deserve to spend a few days—" She stopped as Molly and Karen each took a protective step toward Gia, then started again. "Is there anything I can do to help you through this difficult time?"

Gia weighed Eileen's change of approach, trying to measure her agenda. "What my son needs most right now is normalcy. For his life to continue on as much as possible as it did before."

"That makes sense." Eileen glanced back behind her, toward the east wing. "Ms. Madani just mentioned you were still planning on chaperoning the field trip on Thursday?"

Gia's shoulders tensed, recalling the awkward conversation she'd had with Ms. Madani minutes ago. She must have called the principal literally as soon as Gia left the classroom. "Absolutely. I see no reason to break my commitment, and I see no reason to reschedule my volunteer hours."

She watched the conflict on Eileen's face. Gia and Anthony were the school's most generous donors, and normally she went out of her way to appease them.

Eileen planted her feet and pushed her shoulders back ever so slightly. "I understand that different people mourn in different ways, and business as usual is what works for you. However, the problem is we need our chaperones to be fully focused on the children. And there's some concern among the other parents that you'd be—understandably—distracted."

"You've had complaints?" Gia bristled.

"We've had concerns." Eileen stood her ground.

"Gia." Karen placed a gentle hand on her arm. "Not everybody knows you well. It might be best to just keep everyone comfortable. I'd be happy to take it over for you, and we can swap days at the boutique?"

Eileen shot Karen a pathetically grateful look, and Gia was tempted to continue stonewalling on principle—the idea that she was too distracted to watch over a group of children was ridiculous.

When she hesitated, Molly jumped in. "People don't understand how it's possible that you're holding together as well as you are. They're expecting you to lose it at any moment, and they don't want it to happen around their children."

Gia glanced from face to face. At the end of the day, was this really a fight worth having? She had bigger things to worry about, and this would give her a few extra hours to help sort things out. Maybe it was just as well.

"Thanks, Karen. I appreciate that," she finally said. "I'll make it up to you."

Karen beamed, ecstatic to have something to do. "No need. I'm happy to help. And I'm excited to get to see the museum."

Eileen clapped her hands together in a *namaste*-esque thank-you gesture. "Excellent, that's settled then. And I very much appreciate your understanding."

The capitulation still niggled at Gia, but she couldn't let pride derail her. "I always want to do what's best for the children."

"I have no doubt. Thank you again." Eileen turned and hurried back down the wide hall.

*

The scene with Eileen left Gia unsettled as she went through her tasks that morning. Eileen's face and her words kept flying through her mind on endless repeat, and she wasn't quite sure why. She needed to refocus.

Kintsugi was the answer. It was the only thing that would calm her down, the only thing that ever really managed to center her when she faced hard situations and hard decisions. She'd almost run out of Kintsugi pieces for the boutique, anyway, and they were always her best seller.

When she arrived back home, she crossed straight through the house and garden, into her studio. Just entering calmed her mind—something about the combination of the familiar smell, earthy clay tinged with the tang of chemicals, and the warm light flooding the open space, illuminating her tools and tables and pottery wheel. The only place that was truly hers, and always as she left it. Always reliable.

After slipping into her green smock, she surveyed the finished bowls she'd created the week before. A large pasta-sized bowl she'd glazed with several shades of blue called to her, and she carried it, along with a linen napkin and hammer, to the round table she dedicated to her Kintsugi. There was a transcendence to it, almost a spirituality to the art, that she protected carefully.

As she wrapped the bowl in the linen, she probed why the exchange with Eileen had mattered so much to her. Being at the field trip wasn't vital, she could manage without it. So why couldn't she let it go?

She turned the linen-wrapped bowl over, bottom facing her. With her eyes closed, she ran her hands over it, following the curves and ridges of the bowl through the material, gauging its shape and strength, allowing the piece to speak to her. Finally it did, and she paused for a moment, cherishing the intact piece for the final time. Then she anchored the bowl with one hand and brought the hammer down in a single, precise strike. The satisfying crack rippled through her fingers and echoed in her ears, followed by the gritty rasp of the newly broken edges rubbing together under her fingers.

The problem wasn't Eileen's request itself, she realized. What bothered her was the *reason* for the request, or rather, the likelihood that there was more behind it than Eileen had admitted.

She turned the bowl over and gently peeled back the linen, inspecting the break. Six large pieces, but importantly, several smaller chips from a web of fissures that radiated sideways. That gave her plenty to work with.

Careful not to jostle the table or the pieces, she crossed to her workbench to make the adhesive. She lifted an approximate tablespoon of flour with a palette knife, then sprinkled in a few drops of water. With the edge of the knife, she mixed and scraped, mixed and scraped, producing a thin paste, then added in a small dab of urushi lacquer. She carried the resulting adhesive, and her jar of toothpicks, back to the table. She lifted the first piece, the largest, and used a toothpick to coat the broken edge with the glue. So many people used a brush for this step, and it annoyed her. Why choose to engage in an ancient art form and refuse to do it the right way? People made no sense.

Gia's status in the community would only function as a shield for so long, she'd always known that, but the cracks had appeared far sooner than she'd hoped. Maybe she was being paranoid, maybe not. But she couldn't take that risk. The time had come to make a decision. Except that wasn't really right. There was no decision to make, no choice. The time had come to gather her courage, and act.

She lifted the second piece and fit it into place, then wiggled the two pieces together until the coarse grind ceased, signaling the paste had formed a perfect join between the sections. After a minute she carefully removed one hand to test the bond—the pieces held. She continued on to the next piece.

She just had to work out the details. And she was being watched, so she'd have to be stealthy. But also fast, because the clock was now ticking. Every day was a monumental risk.

She worked her way through the shards, painting and joining, painting and joining. And planning.

CHAPTER FIFTEEN

After leaving another message for Anthony Marchand to contact them, Jo spent part of her morning at a physical therapy appointment for her recovering arm, then the rest of it sorting through as much legwork surrounding the case as possible, starting with Jim Karnegi. She pulled up the information Lopez had gathered about him and created a timeline for herself. He'd lost his job at Mary Dyer Elementary at the end of 2016. His wife filed for divorce shortly after that, at the beginning of 2017, citing irreconcilable differences as grounds—which told her exactly nothing. He applied for the position at Briar Ridge in spring of 2017, was hired, and moved during the summer so he could start officially during the 2017-2018 academic year.

When she called Mary Dyer Elementary, the principal was still gone—the school functioned on a year-round model, and was currently on a three-week break, during which the principal had gone on a two-week vacation to Hawaii. She left a message for the assistant principal asking him to return her call as soon as he was able.

After that, she and Arnett spent the rest of the day filling out paperwork for warrants and digging into backgrounds, their primary focus on direct connections with the Marchand family. Sophie's description of the family's background had been on target; they were so established in Massachusetts they had a family history book published about their genealogy, a general overview of which was proudly displayed on a Marchand history website. The lineage extended back to the late 1600s and featured war heroes, abolitionists and suffragettes, daughters who'd married all manner of high-powered people across North America and Europe, and politicians at every level. A Marchand had even made a bid for Governor. Families like that didn't get, or stay, where they were without making enemies.

In terms of recent history, however, she couldn't find anything overt. No police reports filed by the family in the last few years, so nobody had blatantly victimized them in any robbery, assault, or trespassing sort of way, and nothing that could have started a feud. She switched databases and searched for civil cases filed against any of them; there were several, but all on a corporation to corporation level, and nothing with outcomes that seemed particularly crushing to anyone involved. She spent most of the afternoon and early evening working backwards through press coverage—charity events, business mergers, ribbon cuttings, birth and engagement announcements. Several spats here and there—protests when a Marchand company knocked down a marginally historic building and the like—but nothing with the deep, emotional connection that would engender the rancor required to murder a child.

Just as she decided to switch to social media, her phone rang with a call from a law firm she didn't recognize. She tapped to take the call. "Detective Fournier."

"Hello, Detective. I'm Tom Barclay, calling on behalf of Anthony Marchand. He mentioned you'd like to talk with him about his daughter's murder."

She shot her rolling chair over to Arnett and rapped on it to get his attention, then put the call on speaker. "We'd very much like to talk to Mr. Marchand, and as soon as possible. Are you his attorney?"

"I am. He asked me to set up an appointment with you, so I can be present. The first opening I have is a week from today, at three in the afternoon. Will that work for you?"

She shot Arnett a you-have-to-be-kidding-me look. "Mr. Barclay, I don't think I have to explain to you that every day we delay makes it harder to find his daughter's killer."

"I'm afraid I don't understand how, given the circumstances of her death, he can contribute anything useful. And I'm sure you understand that both his and my schedules are booked out weeks in advance."

Jo was momentarily speechless—why was this man giving them the run-around? "Nicole may well have been hurt by someone who holds a grudge against Mr. Marchand, and we need as much information as we can get from him to point us in the right direction."

"I'm happy to ask him to send me any information he has in that regard, so I can forward it on to you as soon as possible."

Arnett threw up both hands in a 'huh' gesture.

Jo tried again. "We'd also like an explanation for why Mr. Marchand was on campus during the time of Nicole's murder."

"Ah. Your question sounds very much like Mr. Marchand is a suspect in your investigation. In that case, it's all the more vital that I'm present when he talks to you."

"I have to tell you, Mr. Barclay, I'm at a complete loss to figure out why a father would be so obstructive about helping us find his daughter's killer. Why does he feel the need to hide behind an attorney?" Jo prodded.

"If Tuesday at three doesn't work, I can also make Thursday next week at ten."

Jo gritted her teeth. "Tuesday at three works. We'll see you and Mr. Marchand here."

"Tuesday at three. Thank you, Detectives." He hung up.

Jo stared at Arnett. "What am I missing? Why on earth would an innocent man put us off like that? Or even run to an attorney in the first place?"

Arnett rubbed his mouth and chin. "If this had happened to one of my girls, I'd be camped out on the detectives' desks, demanding action and information. Something's not right with this guy."

The alarm on Jo's phone went off. "Dammit. I'm supposed to go out to dinner with Lopez and Marzillo. I have to head out." She pushed her chair back to her desk.

"No problem. I need to head out soon, too, if I want to stay married."

Jo half-smiled as she pulled her blazer on, and waved at him as she hurried out. As she crossed town as quickly as speed limits allowed, a call came through from her mother. Wincing, she let it go to voicemail. When she pulled into the parking lot of Fernando's, she tapped on the message to play it.

"Josette, your sister called and told me about what happened at the girls' school, and that you're the one in charge of the investigation. I know I pressured you to take more time off work, but I have to admit I'm glad you didn't. I'm worried about the girls, and I'm worried Sophie isn't telling me everything. Please call me as soon as you can and let me know what's going on."

Jo sighed, and saved the message. Now both her mother and her sister were waiting by the phone, and somehow she doubted keeping both their minds at ease was going to be simple.

*

Jo headed into Fernando's. Lopez had arrived just moments before she did, and was settling herself into the table when Jo spotted her. Lopez stood again for a quick hug, and the two of them sat down as a waiter brought chips and salsa and took their drink orders—a margarita for Lopez and a Diet Coke for Jo.

"Any luck today?" Lopez asked.

"Not really." Jo gave her the few details she'd picked up. "I'll start checking out Facebook profiles tonight when I get home."

"You'll have mixed results. You'll be fine with the older parents, but the younger ones are less likely to be on Facebook. A lot of younger millennials consider it a 'boomer app.'" She marked the phrase with air quotes, then cracked apart a group of four chips that had fused together during frying. "They'll be on WhatsApp instead, maybe Snapchat, and you won't get anything worthwhile from those without hacking the accounts. Of course, you can see users' content on TikTok if you have a high appetite for silliness."

"Whatever it takes. But for now I'm going to hope we get clearance to go hard into their financials." Not in the mood for her usual chile relleno, Jo eyed the menu. "What about you, any luck?"

"Yes, actually. Your sister said she smelled alcohol on one of the cafeteria worker's breath a while back? I found her. She went to rehab nine months ago, with the school's help. She's been back at work for six months, and has had an exemplary record. No problems inside or outside work since, and because the school knows about what happened, it's not like someone can be holding it over her head."

"I don't suppose Gia turned her in to the principal, something like that?"

"No, I followed up on the notation with Principal Pham directly. She said the woman came to her asking for help, because one of her co-workers had noticed too many problems and figured out what was going on."

"Scratch that off the list, then."

"In fact, you can scratch off the whole list. I ran through the entire list without coming up with anything significant," Lopez said.

"Anything insignificant?"

Lopez shrugged. "Everybody has their secrets, but nothing relevant to this. Like, one of the teachers is an active member of the communist party, something I suspect wouldn't go over well in this conservative bunch. Little things like that, but no flags I can see. And, more than half of the parents who we didn't see leave the campus that morning turn out to have iron-clad alibis, regardless. So unless your sister comes back with something to point the way, I'm at a dead end."

Jo fingered the diamond at her throat. "I think the most efficient path to finding out who might be upset with Gia is the little phalanx she has guarding her. I think I need to have a more pointed chat with Karen Phelps and Molly Hayes."

"Should I start with background checks on the two of them?"

"Might as well. And hopefully I'll hear back from Mary Dyer Elementary tomorrow, and we can see exactly how much more attention we need to pay to Jim Karnegi."

"Hello, ladies!" Marzillo called as she made her way to their table, her date by her side. "This is Ellie. Ellie, this is Jo and Christine, the two co-workers I was telling you about."

Jo exchanged a quick look at Lopez. Ellie was five-foot-eight and model thin, with flowing honey-blonde hair, hazel eyes, and a heart-shaped face. In other words: a dead ringer for Zelda, Marzillo's very recent ex.

"Lovely to meet you," Jo said, resigning herself to an evening getting to know a person she'd clearly never see again.

CHAPTER SIXTEEN

The following morning broke crisp and sunny. Jo stared up at the sky as she drove to work, hoping some of the sun's cheer would penetrate her mood, or at least help to keep her thinking clear.

While she waited for Arnett to arrive, she returned a call to Eileen Pham, who was also, apparently, an early riser. None of the teachers or staff had recognized the Gunter toy; she'd talked to everyone, she assured Jo, but nobody remembered ever seeing it. Jo asked if she could e-mail the picture out to the parents, and Pham agreed.

"Morning." Arnett plopped a mocha in front of Jo.

She savored a large gulp and stood up. "Ready to go pay Earthly Delights a visit?"'

He shot her a befuddled look. "Earthly Delights?"

"That's the name of the boutique Gia Marchand owns with Karen and Molly." She pulled her black blazer off her chair and threw it on.

Arnett's expression made clear his position on cute shop names. "Let's do it."

The shop was set in a large, contiguous Greek Revival building with white columns and yellow clapboard that housed several small shops. A gentle chime sounded when they pushed open the door, and a subtle waft of lavender and rosemary greeted them. The store was small, but gave the illusion of being larger due to effective use of negative and positive space, along with luxe natural wood decor. Three distinct displays, staged to feel like art gallery exhibits, guided them through the store. The first showcased ceramics: vases, plates, bowls, cups and a variety of art pieces. Some were sculpted, some were thrown, and many had intriguing gold lines threading throughout. The second contained a similar array of blown glass pieces, and the final section showcased hand-designed jewelry.

Karen Phelps stood up from her chair behind the sales counter at the back and made her way toward them, a smile failing to mask the concern on her face. "Detectives. I didn't expect to see you here. How can I help you?"

Jo took the lead. "Your store is very impressive, like walking into a gallery. These items are all made by the three of you?"

Her smile morphed to genuine. "Completely, only artisan goods produced by us. The pottery is Gia's, the blown glass is Molly's, and I'm the jewelry maker."

Jo bent to inspect a red platter with the intricate gold threading. "This is beautiful, like golden cracks—so delicate, and so random."

Karen also bent close to the piece. "That's exactly what it is. Isn't that gorgeous? It's a technique called Kintsugi, which takes broken items and repairs them in a way that, rather than hide the break, incorporates it as part of the beauty of the piece. Nowadays artists break their pieces on purpose, but the principle is the same. And look at this vase." She stepped over to the blown-glass display, warming to her topic. "Doesn't it look like it's made of some sort of lace? It's called Merletto canework, and although I have no idea what it means, it's my absolute favorite."

"Just beautiful." Jo stepped past to the jewelry. "And your pieces are stunning. Art deco?"

Karen blushed and beamed at the same time. "I don't have the sort of artistic skills Gia and Molly have, most of my work is just about assembling elements in a way that appeals to me. But they've been encouraging me to branch out, so these over here are my very first few pieces of handcrafted metalwork. I love art deco, so I tried to let that help me get past my fear of metalworking.

They're not quite what I envisioned, but I'm hoping I'll get better with time." She looked up at Jo, and her smile turned back to its plastered-on form. "But here I am going on and on when I'm sure you didn't come here looking for a gift."

Jo straightened up from the jewelry display. "No, we didn't. We have a few more questions we'd like to ask you about Gia and Nicole."

Karen crossed her arms over her chest. "I'm not sure what more I can tell you."

"When we spoke Monday, you were worried about how Gia was going to handle the news about Nicole. But when we arrived at the house later, Gia seemed very calm, almost like nothing had happened. What did you think of her reaction?"

Karen's eyes bounced between them. "I guess you can't ever tell how someone's going to respond to something as horrible as this."

"That's true." Jo shifted slightly toward her. "But I got the sense you had reason to believe she'd react differently. You and she, and Molly, seem to be close, so we'd like to understand better what's going on with her."

Karen shrugged, but the jerky movement didn't convey the nonchalance Jo suspected she was trying for. "Gia tends to be emotional. When something upsets her, she doesn't hold back. But it never lasts long, it's like a flare that burns itself out quickly. She always jokes it's because her mother is Italian. So, yes, I guess I expected wailing and gnashing of teeth, but I underestimated how much shock she'd be in. This wasn't a broken arm or a baseball to the chest."

Jo weighed the response, and decided to prod. "We've heard she can be frosty to outsiders, to people she doesn't trust. I know you were worried she might blame you, do you think that's a part of her reaction, maybe she's shutting you out?"

The desperate expression that flashed over Karen's face was all the answer Jo needed.

"Not at all." One of Karen's hands shifted to her hip. "I told her everything, and she told me I was being ridiculous. Gia's not the sort to hold grudges."

Jo gave an *ah-that-explains-it* nod. "That brings me to another question. Gia may not hold grudges, but other people do. Who might have a grudge against Gia?"

The hand dropped, and Karen's spine stiffened. "Plenty of people are jealous of Gia, and get an attitude because she doesn't want to be BFFs with them. But Gia would never, ever do anything to hurt anyone."

"Her husband, then. Powerful men make powerful enemies, and we're having a difficult time getting him to call us back," Jo said.

"I don't know anything about his business affairs, other than he's extremely busy."

"Nothing?" Arnett asked.

She shifted her weight. "She doesn't talk about his work much, except for the charity events she's involved in. She doesn't really talk about him much at all."

Jo dug in. "As close as you are, she doesn't talk about him? About that whole side of her life?"

Both hands sprang to her hips and red slashes crawled up her neck to her cheeks. "We *are* close. She talks about him, just not in that way. I know he's not home much because he's trying to build a business and she supports that by taking care of the kids and running the house so he doesn't have to worry about any of that. When they see each other it's mostly for events and parties, and of course she tells us about *that*. And I'm divorced. What is she going to do, rub in how rich and important her husband is? We talk about our kids, and the school, and our art." Her arm slashed out an angry circle.

Arnett threw up his hands. "Right. I get it. But the details of Nicole's murder don't fit with a stranger. This was swift and targeted, like someone had an agenda. And since very few agendas are pointed at five-year-old girls, that suggests someone's pissed off at Gia or Anthony and we need to know why. You must have an idea, and if you want us to catch the killer, we need your help."

Karen turned to meet Jo's eyes. Jo nodded in agreement with what Arnett had said. Karen's hand flew to her throat like she was strangling herself, and she took a deep breath. "Maybe Anthony's ex? I don't know the whole story, but he broke off an engagement before he met Gia. That's all I can think of, and even that's iffy. And please, please don't tell her I told you."

Jo's radar perked up. "Gia doesn't want you talking to us?"

Karen waved a hand as if to erase a board in front of her. "No, nothing like that. She's just very private about her life in general. And loyalty is big to her—a lot of people she's been friends with are no longer her friends because they talked too much to other people about her life."

"But this involves her daughter's killer."

She hurried to backpedal. "I'm sure she'd probably be fine with it, but I just don't want her to think I'm spreading gossip about her family. That's her only real blind spot."

"I get it. Some people get very sensitive about those things. We'll be as discreet as possible." Jo looked around the ceiling of the shop, and spotted two security cameras, one pointed at the door, and one pointed at the counter with the register. "How long do you keep your security footage?"

"For a week. We have six memory cards, one for each weekday and one for over the weekend, and we rotate them out." She looked confused. "But why would you care about our footage?"

"Because if someone is upset with Gia or obsessed with her or Nicole, they might have come here. Who knows, maybe Gia even insulted someone accidentally recently, and we might see that on the footage. Would you be okay with us looking it over?"

She shrugged. "I don't see why not. I'll get it for you."

Jo followed her into the back; Arnett raised two fingers to signal that he'd wait behind. The room was larger than Jo expected, with a large desk on the right-hand side, and the rest of the room lined with deep shelving units filled with office supplies and cardboard boxes.

She motioned to several of the shelves. "I admire your organization."

Karen followed her gesture. "We have to be organized, since we're each dealing with one another's stock. And, we have to keep it packed safely away in bubble wrap, that way if one of us has a clumsy moment we don't smash hours and hours of someone's work."

Karen continued over to the desk, and pulled open the top drawer. "Do you want the one from this morning too?"

"If you can manage that—do you have extra cards?"

"We have one extra, and I can pick up some more when I leave later, no problem."

"Then yes, we'd appreciate that."

Karen handed the cards to her. "Hopefully something on here will be helpful. And if I think of anything else, I'll let you know."

She crossed her arms back over her chest. Jo wouldn't get anything else out of her, at least not today.

*

"She folded like a cheap suit at the end there," Arnett said once they were back in the car.

"Why, do you think?" Jo asked.

"Don't suppose it's as simple as she finally got the reality of the situation?"

"Possibly. But even though she started talking when you told her flat-out that a stranger didn't do this, I didn't get the sense it was exactly a revelation to her."

"No. Which means she'd been thinking it, but hoped we hadn't." Arnett turned onto the pike. "Nice call with the security footage, by the way."

Jo's phone rang, and she answered. "Detective Josette Fournier."

"Detective Fournier. This is Lee Capillo, I'm the Assistant Principal at Mary Dyer Elementary School. I'm returning your call."

Jo put him on speakerphone. "Thanks so much for contacting us. We're calling about Jim Karnegi."

"Right. I got the messages, and I've been trying to dig out the information for you. That's why it took me some time to return your call. Unfortunately, there isn't much I can tell you."

"Did the message you received make clear this is about a homicide investigation? That a little girl has been murdered?"

"Yes, I absolutely understand. The problem is I managed to locate his file, but it doesn't say much of anything. Only that he was dismissed because of 'inappropriate conduct,' but it doesn't say what that conduct was. And since I wasn't here during that time, I have no first-hand knowledge of the situation."

"How is that possible? Most employers document any disciplinary steps they take with employees."

"And so do we. Normally there's at least a warning letter, and then something that documents the termination. I don't know if the documents are just missing, or if they were never there to start with."

"And you have no idea what 'inappropriate conduct' could mean?"

"My best guess, given the wording, is that it's something that refers to our code of conduct. All our educators have a morality clause in their contract. It covers a range of activities from stealing to inappropriate language, to, well, anything to do with sex."

"I'm guessing that would include things like child molestation?"

"Well—I—yes, of course it *would*," Capillo sputtered. "But in that case, we'd also have brought charges with the police."

Jo shot a glance at Arnett. "Ah, right. Because if you didn't, you'd be in serious trouble yourselves."

"Exactly."

"Your principal was at the school when Karnegi was fired? Can he tell us what happened?"

"He can, yes. I can have him call you when he returns from his vacation."

"This really can't wait. Is there a way we can contact him?"

"He didn't leave us contact information. He trusts me to take care of any situations that arise in his absence."

Jo rubbed the bridge of her nose and bit her tongue. "Great, thank you. If you can have him call us as soon as he's back, we'd greatly appreciate that."

"I will. And I hope you find out who killed that little girl."

Jo thanked him again and hung up, then turned to Arnett. "So, yeah. Inappropriate conduct, and the routine paperwork is missing. That *reeks* of covering your ass. My guess is they didn't report whatever he did because it would have been bad press for the school, but now that they're getting a call from the cops, they can't have us getting a warrant for the records."

"So he probably wasn't fired for swearing in class."

"No." Jo's nails tapped against her phone. "His wife left him right after he was fired, so I'm thinking whatever it was, she wasn't happy about it. And when someone cuts bait and runs like that, there usually aren't good feelings involved."

"You want to go talk to the ex-wife?"

"I have a feeling she has an interesting story to tell." She looked at her watch. "Three hours' round trip, but it's not like we have any better leads to follow, anyway."

Arnett nodded agreement.

"I'll call Molly on the way, see if she can give us any more insight into the Marchands' enemies."

CHAPTER SEVENTEEN

Karen stared at the door after the detectives left, struggling to decide: should she tell Gia what just happened? Surely Gia would understand that she just wanted to give the detectives something to focus on? And wouldn't it be better than hearing it from someone else?

But the detectives were right, she didn't seem to be able to predict Gia's reactions right now. Usually Gia only shut out people she didn't feel safe with—and that meant Gia knew something, or suspected something, and she didn't feel safe telling Karen about it.

Had she told Molly about whatever it was? Twice now she'd reached out to Molly to figure out what to do, and Molly had told her she was overreacting. But maybe that was Molly's way of sidelining her? Would Molly do something like that? She didn't feel sure of anything anymore.

Karen picked up her phone and called Gia. The call went to voicemail.

A cold ripple ran through her. Was Gia dodging her call?

A few seconds later, a text came through: *Am running errands. Can't answer right now. What's up?*

Karen let out a relieved breath. Not dodging, then. At least not completely.

She sent a response: *Detectives were just here. Call when you can.*

Gia's reply came almost immediately: *Will call in five.*

Too anxious to stay still, Karen crossed to her display and rearranged her items. No matter how much she tried, her jewelry looked like an afterthought next to Gia's pottery and Molly's glass. Like the cheap souvenirs at the end of the museum next to the prints and postcards of all the beautiful artworks inside.

Stop being so insecure, darling. You're so beautiful and so popular with the boys, her mother's voice ran through her head.

Why do you even try? her father's came right after, and also echoed.

She tried to shake the thoughts as she sorted a set of bracelets strung with millefiori beads Molly had made for her. She layered them one over the other, then separated them again. She pulled out a glass hand from under the counter and strung the bracelets over the fingers, hoping to create the effect of a handful of jewels pouring out of the palm. It looked cheap and bohemian in the exact wrong way, so she stripped them off and replaced them as they originally were.

The answer was in the metalworking. She'd keep at it, keep improving, until she could replace the trashy pieces with art that deserved to be in the same room with the other beauties.

But it was so slow going. She didn't have any natural talent for it, and working with molten metal scared her. One wrong move, and she'd be scarred for life, maybe even lose a finger, so she spent her metalworking time tense and unhappy, not like the zen that took her over when she made her other jewelry. Selecting the right pieces, combining them together and stringing them, creating links—all of it was meditative, almost hypnotic, and she missed it.

Her phone rang, startling her, and she almost dropped the glass display hand—but she caught it as it slipped from her fingers, clasping it into her thigh. She shook her head, set it on the counter, and answered the call.

"What did they want?" Gia asked without preamble.

"They wanted to know why you weren't more upset, and they're really ticked that Anthony won't call them back. And they wanted to know who might have a grudge against you or Anthony. They don't think it was random."

Gia gave a frustrated grunt. "What did you tell them?"

"I told them I couldn't imagine anyone having that sort of grudge against you, and that if I had to stretch, the only person I could think of was Anthony's ex."

Gia was quiet for a long moment. "Well. It's ridiculous, isn't it? Obviously anybody who'd harm a child like that is mentally ill, and that just can't be anyone in our circle."

"I know, right? I hope it's okay I said what I did, I just didn't—"

"No, no, that's fine. You did the right thing. I'm sure they're going to be digging into all of our lives now. But they'll check and they won't find anything, and then they'll realize it had to be some disturbed individual."

Relief rushed through Karen. "I just—shouldn't they be looking at vagrants, or people with arrest histories, or—"

"You'd think." Gia's voice was clipped. "Look, I have to go. Let me know if they come back, okay?"

"Oh. Okay," Karen said.

"I'm sorry, I don't mean to snap, I just—thank you for being a good friend. I'm just in line and I have to go." Gia hung up.

Karen stared down at the phone.

*

Molly drove up to the boutique's back entrance and parked in the alley. She'd just had to assure Gia three times that the detectives hadn't contacted her again—they were digging into Gia and Anthony's personal relationships, apparently, and Gia was agitated.

But *of course* they were going to dig into those relationships, how could Gia expect anything different? And not just people who had it out for them, but Gia and Anthony themselves. Gia had said it herself when the detectives were there, when they'd asked about her alibi—loved ones always had to be considered and eliminated. Even if the police had bloody footprints leading up and over the chain-link fence and into one of the neighboring houses, the detectives would still need to consider it could be an inside job. Everyone knew that—everyone, at least, except Gia.

The point was, it was only a matter of time before the detectives asked her, so it was probably good to be on the same page about it all. Molly hadn't been in Harristown before Gia and Anthony were married, but she'd heard all about his ex, Lauren McKay, many times and from many sources. When Anthony had dumped her for Gia, she'd released a howl that was still echoing in space. No way was Molly *not* going to mention it if she were asked.

Carefully balancing the box of wrapped vases against the wall, she unlocked the back door and let herself in. She set the box down and headed toward the front—but froze as she reached the door.

Karen was talking to someone, and she sounded distressed. There was no second voice, so she must be on the phone. Was she talking to Gia again?

Molly cracked the door open slightly to hear better, but still could only make out a few words here and there.

Only a matter of time

I know it isn't safe, but

Molly held her breath, trying to eliminate all noise. But the conversation was over—Karen spat out "fine," something clattered onto the counter, and angry footsteps clacked across the room.

Molly carefully closed the shop door, then backtracked out the door. She opened it again and closed it loudly this time, then set about unpacking her vases.

Karen peeked her head in. "Oh, Molly, you scared me! I expected you earlier."

"I'm running late today." Molly smiled apologetically, then put on a concerned face. "Is everything okay? You seem flustered."

Karen waved a hand like she was chasing away a gnat. "I'm fine. The detectives stopped by earlier is all. This whole thing is really freaking me out."

"Ah." Molly dug into the Styrofoam peanuts cushioning the vases. "This whole thing is like a nightmare that won't end."

The front door chimed.

"Be right back," Karen said, and left to tend the customer.

Molly lifted the vases out of the box, inspected them for damage, then tagged them and brought them out to the floor. She sent a cheery smile and wave to the customer, who was looking at one of Gia's museum-worthy platters, then threw a kiss to Karen as a goodbye.

Once in her car, she sat for a moment, squinting back toward the shop.

If there was one thing Molly hated, it was being lied to.

Her phone's ring pulled her out of her thoughts.

Detective Fournier.

CHAPTER EIGHTEEN

Jo's conversation with Molly was short, and only yielded confirmation that Anthony Marchand's ex-girlfriend might be relevant. Unfortunately, that lead fizzled out quickly. Lauren McKay, who was now happily married to a man in France, had been living in Paris for the last six months, and a few phone calls established she hadn't left Europe since the beginning of the year. Jo asked Lopez to add her to the research list, but didn't have any confidence they'd find anything. In fact, the whole thing left her with a nagging sense she'd been sent on a wild goose chase.

She shifted her attention back to the footwork she was doing on Jim Karnegi's ex-wife as they headed into Rhode Island. Kaitlyn Karnegi had legally changed her name back to Kramer the day she filed for divorce. She also moved out of the house they shared that day, but still lived in Lippitt. She currently worked as a claims adjuster for Pilgrim Insurance, and an hour later Arnett pulled up to the large white federal-style building in the downtown area that housed the company. The receptionist called Kaitlyn out without asking what business they had with her, and she appeared almost instantly. Five-six with her heels, around thirty-five years old, she was a pretty, petite, curvy blonde with large blue eyes wearing a black pencil skirt and pink twin set.

She greeted them with a friendly smile and extended her hand toward Jo. "I'm Kaitlyn. I apologize, I didn't recognize your names. Am I working on a claim for you?"

Jo shook her hand. "Not at all. I'm Detective Josette Fournier and this is Detective Bob Arnett. We're with the Oakhurst County SPDU in Massachusetts. Is there somewhere we can speak to you in private?"

"Certainly. What's this about?"

"We'd like to ask you a few questions about Jim Karnegi."

Kaitlyn's smile didn't just fall, it crashed.

"Come with me." She twirled on her heel and marched them toward a glass-fronted conference room in the back of the building, and pointed to the large black lacquer table. "Sit wherever you like. There's water in the pitcher, unless you'd like some tea or coffee?"

"We're fine, thanks." Jo selected a chair near the door, and Arnett sat across the corner of the table from her.

Kaitlyn dropped into a chair that faced both of them. "What has Jim done?"

"We were hoping you could tell us. We're trying to find out why Jim was let go from Mary Dyer Elementary," Jo asked.

Kaitlyn's eyes narrowed slightly and her face, previously sunny and pretty, became pinched and calculating in a way that pricked up Jo's instincts. "Ask them," she said.

"We're asking you," Arnett rejoined.

She stared at him for a moment. "Why are you asking at all?"

Jo explained about Nicole's death.

"And you think he may have hurt this little girl?" she asked, looking back and forward between them.

"We don't know. Do you think he's capable of that?"

"I have no idea. Jim turned out to be capable of lots of things I never thought he'd do."

An image of a cat watching a mouse hole flashed through Jo's mind, and she forced her face to keep a pleasant, neutral expression as she readjusted the dynamic. "You seem angry."

Kaitlyn reached over and poured herself a glass of water without responding.

So much for that. Jo kept the expression in place. "Angry or not, there's a little girl who needs justice, and a school full of children who may be in danger. So I'll ask you again. Why was Jim fired from Mary Dyer?"

Kaitlyn snorted a small puff of air over a half-smile. "They didn't tell *me*. The information was confidential."

"What did *he* tell you?" Jo asked.

Kaitlyn took a sip of water before she answered. "That he was accused of inappropriate conduct."

Jo kept a close watch on Kaitlyn's face—she was trying to maintain a poker face, but with limited success, and her calculations leaked through. "And you didn't ask Jim to explain what that conduct was?"

"He said a lot of things to me, most of them untrue. But no, he never gave me the full details."

"I'm sure there was talk?"

Kaitlyn narrowed her eyes at Jo. "Oh, there was plenty of talk. I suspect what you're looking for is the part of that *talk* where the mothers felt he was far too friendly with their children. Too *attached*."

Jo didn't like the way she'd phrased that. "Were they right?"

She shrugged, and swirled the water in her cup. "Maybe. I don't know."

"You divorced him right after he lost his job. Why?"

Kaitlyn gave a sarcastic laugh. "Let's just say he cheated on me."

"Did he, or didn't he?" Arnett asked.

She tilted her head at him. "Oh, he definitely did."

Jo drew a deep breath. There was clearly no love lost between Kaitlyn and her ex-husband, but there was a rancor here that didn't sit well with Jo. She'd reached her limit; sometimes when you were pulling teeth that wouldn't come, you had to tie them to a door and slam it. "Where were you on Monday morning between ten and eleven?"

Kaitlyn's expression snapped like she'd been slapped. "Are you serious?"

Jo held her eyes, and didn't respond.

Kaitlyn shifted in her chair, posture taut. "I was here, at work, all morning. You can check with my boss."

"Going out to inspect damage is a part of your job. You're sure you were physically in the office that morning?"

"Luckily for me, the only cases I've worked this week were auto cases that brought their vehicles here. I had one such appointment on Monday, and was out of the building for less than thirty minutes. We log everything and have cameras out in the inspection lot, so you can check it all for yourself." She stood up. "And since this has taken a turn where I appear to be a suspect, I think it's best if I end this interrogation now. If you have any further questions, I'll direct you to my attorney."

*

"Well, that was fun." Arnett pulled the passenger-side car door closed with a little more force than required. "So glad we drove all the way here. That was quite a nasty little implication she left hanging out in the wind, about the cheating paired up with his affection for his students. Well done by the way, calling her out on her bullshit."

"I don't like being played." Jo turned over the engine. "And given her little game, I have no idea how much of what she said we can believe."

"I'm surprised you believe any of it." Arnett pulled over his seat belt.

"She was too careful for it to be flat-out lies. She implied, but didn't veer into territory that could have gotten her in legal trouble. But she had an agenda, and for the life of me I can't figure out what it is. Scorned woman out to destroy her ex-husband? Or wronged wife who either doesn't fully know the truth, or is worried about being slapped with a lawsuit?" She pulled away from the curb and headed for the highway.

"The upshot is, something shady's going on. I say we go lean on him," Arnett said.

Jo didn't respond.

"You don't agree?"

She signaled a merge. "No, I do. I'm just not sure that leaning on him is going to work. And, what I keep coming back to is, I don't see how he could have hurt Nicole without Karen spotting it. According to both of them, he was on the other end of the playground. She was distracted, yes, but he'd have had to cross the playground and pass Karen without her noticing, then be gone long enough to kill Nicole without her realizing."

"Interesting point."

Jo could see Arnett's brain spinning. "Can you call Lopez and see if she has anything new for us?"

Arnett pulled out his phone and put the call through the car's speakerphone.

"Bob. Jo. How'd your little road trip go?" Lopez asked.

"It provided a lovely glimpse into the dark side of the human psyche that left me feeling like I need a shower," Jo said. "We were hoping maybe you had something to help guide our focus."

"I've been pushing forward on the background checks, but I'm not sure how useful the information will be. I started with Karen Phelps. She's a local girl, grew up in Wiltshire as Karen Hirshner. She's an only child, and her family was middle class. I found her yearbook online—she was a cheerleader, the kind of cute preppy girl that made me vomit back then and kinda still does. Prom queen, the whole shadoodle."

Which fit perfectly with the well-groomed, fake-lashes-even-in-the-morning, yoga-mom persona Jo had tagged Karen with.

"She married Rob Phelps ten years ago, and divorced him three years ago; he remarried the following year, so I'm gonna pin that donkey tail on an affair. She got alimony and child support in the divorce decree, but from what I can tell, it's not enough to pay the bills. Her credit card balance seems to be gently but steadily climbing, so even with whatever money she brings in from the boutique, she doesn't seem to be flush."

"No job other than the boutique?" Arnett asked.

"Nope. Same with Molly Hayes, both stay-at-home mothers who split time at their store, and she, like Karen and Gia, has no siblings. Molly, however, is the relative ragamuffin of the group. She grew up Molly Raynes in East Pinkers, Connecticut, another middle-class town, but her parents divorced and then her father died in a car accident when she was a teenager, both of which dropped their tax bracket. She managed to earn herself a scholarship to Harvard, where she met her husband. He's a family-law attorney who used to work at the Boston office of his family's firm; they lived in Quincy, and he commuted. Her husband was transferred to the Harristown branch of the firm three years ago. And from what I can see, family-law attorneys make pretty decent money, so Molly's come up in the world."

"Did you manage to get the warrants, so we can get into everyone's accounts?"

"Should have them by tomorrow. In the meantime I've been plugging away at the other parents who go to Briar Ridge, but it's slow going. I finished up with all those who didn't sign in and out the morning Nicole died, and I found nothing. So I'm going through the rest of the parents in Nicole's class, and I'll check Nicholas' class roster after that. I will say I'm finding some cool little secrets, though, even if they're not relevant. I found a father who does drag shows on the weekend in Springfield, which I didn't know was a thing, so I've found my newest hangout."

Jo laughed. "And just to check, you haven't found anything else in Jim Karnegi's background?"

"Nope. I checked out his current wife and his ex-wife, but didn't find anything suspicious. I'll give you a buzz if I do."

They said brief goodbyes and ended the call.

"Well," Arnett said. "After all this driving, by the time we get back I think we definitely earned a meatball sub from Sal's."

Jo nodded, but stayed silent.

*

After quick update phone calls to Sophie and her mother, Jo spent the rest of Wednesday evening putting a second set of eyes onto Lopez's background checks. She retired well past midnight, knowing she had a little time to sleep-in the next day; she'd taken a few hours off for an appointment with Nina and a physical therapy appointment after.

Despite a show of professional equanimity, Nina's body language the following morning leaked her consternation with Jo's choice to remain on the Marchand case. Jo tried to reassure her that she saw the case as a chance for healing, and that if her pain had transferred so easily to the vision of Nicole's face, hopefully solving that case would help bring closure to her own loss.

"Has that approach worked for you in terms of resolving your emotions about Marc's and Jack's deaths?" Nina asked, in what struck Jo as an impressive display of passive-aggressive behavior for a therapist.

And yet, she had to admit Nina had a point—so far, no number of apprehended criminals had made up for the feelings of inadequacy that haunted her about their murders. "My job is my job, so my hope is that together we can find a way to break through that pattern this time."

Nina's brows had bounced up. "That sort of positive intention is a very strong first step."

Jo clung to that positivity as she worked through her exercises during her physical therapy appointment, particularly the dreaded arm ergometer. Like a bicycle for the arms, the machine always gave her the same feeling of futility her grandmother's rotary eggbeater had when she was a child. So much effort, with so little apparent result.

As she left physical therapy, a notification chimed on her phone—she'd missed a call from Arnett. She called him back.

"Jo. When do you expect to be back?" Arnett asked.

"I just finished. I'm on my way now," she answered. "Why?"

"Briar Ridge's fourth grade teacher, Layla Madani, is dead."

CHAPTER NINETEEN

Jo picked Arnett up from HQ and drove into Wiltshire, where the third- and fourth-grade Briar Ridge classes had spent the morning on a field trip.

"How did I not know there's an Ancient Egyptian Museum smack in the middle of downtown Wiltshire?" Jo asked half an hour later, as she turned onto the right street.

"They just finished it two years ago. It's the sister museum of one out in California," Arnett said.

Jo craned her neck, trying to match the location of the GPS dot with the block in front of her. "And apparently it's hidden."

"You just drove past it." Arnett tried to hide his smile.

"What the— Oh, I see it now." She did a quick U-turn and pulled up to the building. "No wonder I didn't know it was here."

The museum complex was surrounded by several multi-story buildings and was set several hundred feet back from the sidewalk. A large courtyard lined with inward-pointing sphinxes led to a small, partially enclosed hall outside the entrance of the museum, whose opening was decorated by a row of columns painted with a blue Egyptian-lotus pattern. In the distance, the tip of what looked like a pyramid seemed to spring up off the roof of the museum. Two uniformed officers stood securing the perimeter, while two more took statements from Karen Phelps and Jim Karnegi, both looking shaken and frightened, the second standing next to Principal Pham. Jo and Arnett approached the officers at the tape and identified themselves.

One, a tall woman whose nametag read 'Norton', pointed back and up. "One of the teachers fell off the pyramid. Straight back through this courtyard, then through the building. The main crime scene is in the back courtyard."

Jo followed her gesture to the pyramid tip that she'd mistakenly thought was a part of the building's roof. "Holy—is that an actual, literal pyramid?"

"Yup. It's a reconstruction with burial chambers inside. Kids love it."

She looked left and right. "Speaking of, where are the kids now?"

Norton jutted her chin toward Eileen Pham. "The principal sent the assistant principal back in the bus with the kids."

Jo and Arnett thanked her. As they turned to approach the main building, a man pushed out of the door and hurried to greet them. He thrust his hand out toward Arnett.

"I'm Dr. Neil Gamal, I'm the curator of the AEM. The CSI team said the detectives were on the way, I'm assuming that's you?"

Arnett shook his hand as he kept walking. "Yes. The crime scene's this way?"

"Yes." Dr. Gamal pushed open the door again, and led them quickly through a series of chilly rooms with a vaguely chalky, dry scent. Jo's eyes ran over clear-glass display cases filled with coffins, mummies, faience bottles, and other assorted artifacts. She noted the positions of the cameras.

Dr. Gamal kept glancing back at them. "She fell off the pyramid, but she must have done something wrong. We're very clear with everybody, we talk to every group that comes through. The proper pathway is very clearly marked."

Arnett shot Jo a look, and Jo returned it. Prioritizing liability issues over human life never made sense to her—but that was this man's reality. Probably just as well she had no desire to oversee a museum or any other sort of public institution.

"The school signs liability waivers, don't they?"

"Yes, right, of course. They do, yes." He flicked a glance back at her as he pushed open the door to the inner courtyard. "But I want to make it clear, we are extremely careful to take all necessary precautions."

Jo stepped out of the yard and stared up at the pyramid looming in front of her. It dominated the courtyard, far taller than she'd anticipated—that's why the tip had given the illusion of sprouting out of the roof, it was actually much farther away. She now understood Dr. Gamal's hurry to assert the museum's safety protocols. At least five stories high, the pyramid was modeled after those in Giza, made to look like exposed, rough-hewn beige stone that ascended up in what would be, if someone were brave enough to try to climb it, an extremely treacherous staircase. Protective ropes ran the length of the huge base to prevent anyone from attempting just that. A deep channel ran up the front of the pyramid, containing a normal staircase that switched back on itself twice. Not quite midway up, an entryway led into the pyramid; the staircase continued on above that, switching back several times as it climbed to a viewing platform at the top. Sturdy, waist-high handrails lined the staircase throughout.

Dr. Gamal pointed. "It's completely safe, you see. The rails are sturdy, and even if you fall against them, you wouldn't tip over. Unless you do something you shouldn't."

Jo scanned the pyramid. "I noticed several cameras in your galleries. Where else do you have them?"

"Just in the galleries, both in the main museum, and in the pyramid."

"But nothing out here, or at the entrances?"

He looked at her like she wasn't very bright. "There's no need. Our main concern is to protect the exhibits against theft or vandalism. And we have guards. Not many people try to sneak into the museum."

Jo peered into the space surrounding the pyramid. Landscaped into lush gardens, it was separated from the surrounding buildings and alleys by a ten-foot stone wall decorated with frescoes. At the far-left corner, Jo spotted a door cut into the wall. She pointed towards it. "And that entrance? Is it monitored in any way?"

Dr. Gamal shifted from foot to foot. "It's exit only."

"Unless someone going out gives someone the opportunity to sneak in."

"As I say, not many people look to sneak into museums, and if they do, we'd catch them on the gallery cameras." This time he looked at her like she was full-on insane. "And why would you come around the back alleys rather than the front?"

Jo didn't push the issue. "We'll need to see all the footage from your cameras for today up until the time of the accident. Can you arrange that for us?"

"Immediately, yes." He turned and darted away.

Jo and Arnett crossed the remaining distance to the police tape, where Marzillo was waiting with Hakeem Peterson, the tech who'd worked Nicole's crime scene with her. Before they were close enough to see Layla Madani, they were greeted by the smell of vomit.

"You just missed Dr. Speedy—in and out of the scene in twenty minutes, which might be a new record. To be fair, cause of death is pretty clear on this one," she said. Dr. Don Caputo, one of the county medical examiners, was known for making quick work of his initial examinations at crime scenes, and generally managed to avoid coming to them at all when possible. "She fell, nearly all the way from the top, and broke her neck. Among many, many other things."

"Could the fall have been an accident?" Jo asked.

"From what I've seen so far, it's impossible to tell. And nobody was around when it happened. One of the other teachers came looking for her and found her like this. But since we didn't find any broken railings or anything like that, I'm not quite clear on how it could have been an accident."

Arnett grabbed a stack of PPE and outfitted himself. Jo did the same, then lifted the tape and stepped over to Layla Madani's body, skirting the pool of vomit several feet from where she lay.

"Who vomited, one of the responding officers?" Arnett asked.

"Nope, nobody for you to haze, Mr. Sensitivity. It was the teacher that found her, or so I'm told," Marzillo answered.

Jo bent over Layla. Her limbs extended out at impossible angles—not just because they were askew, but because they'd each been fractured in at least one place. Her head jutted back from her neck, and her eyes stared out blankly behind her, as if trying to see the long black hair splayed out over the cement. A slash of skin had split across her jaw, revealing the white bone beneath. Refusing to look away, Jo fought the clench that roiled through her stomach, and squatted down next to Layla's face. She looked into the eyes, and for an instant, would have sworn that Layla Madani was staring back at her, trying to communicate silently.

She looked up at Marzillo. "This is horrific."

"If it makes you feel better, I'm fairly certain she died almost instantly, so she didn't feel most of it."

"Why do you think that?" Arnett asked, circling the body.

"See how little blood there is, despite all the damage? Her heart stopped either before those injuries or simultaneously with them. My guess, given she'd have hit several spots on her way down rather than a single impact at the bottom, is that the first or second impact broke her neck." Marzillo pointed to the bend in the spine.

Jo stood back up, and did a quick measurement. "She's what, fifteen feet from the base? I'm guessing that's the inertia of the fall?"

"Correct. Bodies bounce, as horrible as that is to think about. And in this case, because of the sloped surface of the pyramid, she was likely bouncing out more than she would have had she fallen straight down."

Jo peered up at the pyramid. "Has the team had a chance to examine the structure for signs of impact? Do we have any idea how high up she'd have to be to have this level of injury?"

"Hakeem examined the staircase, but couldn't identify any areas of impact. I have a small drone in the van we can use to examine it, but I'm not going to send anyone out there looking. It's far too dangerous, and the swabs wouldn't tell us anything we can't get directly from her, regardless. But I think it's safe to assume she was high up, nearly to the top."

"A fall from farther down wouldn't have killed her?" Jo asked.

"A fall from a few feet can kill you if you land wrong," she said, and rubbed her nose with the back of her forearm. "But the chances of that happening are small. So could it have happened, according to the laws of physics, et cetera? Yes. But you don't just accidentally slip and fall over those rails. You can't even just accidentally push into someone and have them go over. So if someone intended murder, which is what I think you're really asking me, the higher the better."

"Great. You said Hakeem examined the staircase. I don't suppose he found a convenient cigarette butt that may have our killer's DNA on it up near the top?" Jo asked.

"No, nothing. Sadly, with the ever-increasing restrictions on smoking, DNA-laden cigarette butts around public buildings are few and far between."

"Damn the anti-smoking legislation," Arnett deadpanned.

"But, the more eyes, the better," Marzillo said.

"Right." Jo turned and headed toward the evidence tent. She grabbed a portable kit and started up the staircase, which turned out to be even more secure than it had looked from a distance. The steps were wide and deep, and each had two strips of anti-slip tread. At the bottom of the staircase, railings blocked easy access to the ridges of the pyramid. As the stairs went up, their angle cut farther into the pyramid, which made it impossible to reach the outside edge until the staircase switched back on itself. Where it neared the edge again, sturdy rails resumed their effective barrier.

Arnett stopped at one of the landings, and grasped the guardrail, attempting to shove it. "Doesn't move an inch. The gaps between the balusters aren't big enough for a child to slip through, and it's too high for even an adult to accidentally fall over, just like Marzillo said."

Jo tried to bend over the top of the rail, and had to lift herself off her feet to do so. "Unless you're seven feet tall, at least. Dr. Gamal's right. Someone did something they shouldn't have been doing."

"If it were one of the kids, I'd say someone got stupid and tried to climb out on the edge. But a teacher, that's a whole different story."

Jo continued up the stairs to the observation deck. She turned and glanced out. The building was about the same height as several of the surrounding structures, and looking out through them gave the strange illusion that she was staring out from the past, into a future that had built itself up around her.

Arnett caught up, breathing hard. She turned and shook her head at him.

"Don't. I quit smoking and I work out three times a week. That's as good as it's gonna get," he said.

She turned forward again and peered down, hoping for something to clue her in to the spot where Layla Madani had gone over the railing. What she found was a scatter of coins amid a healthy sprinkling of bird droppings. "I guess the kids treat this like a wishing well."

"Sweet, but not helpful for us."

Something larger caught Jo's attention. She pointed to it. "Do you see that there?"

Arnett peered over. "Looks like some kind of watch."

"Come on." Jo turned back down the stairs, taking them two at a time, until she reached the level nearest the watch. She pulled out her phone and took several shots.

"You think it's relevant?" Arnett asked, catching up faster on the descent.

"I'm not sure." She stood back and surveyed the area again. "But I don't see anything else other than pennies and feces, so either things don't get dropped over often, or the staff cleans it up. And, it's on the same side that Madani fell from. Maybe she was trying to grab it, and fell? Maybe the clasp broke, and it fell off her wrist?"

"Could be. Looks valuable from here." Arnett sidled up to the railing closest to it, careful not to brush up against it. "It's just a bit out of arm's length. If you lifted yourself and pivoted over the top of the railing, you could reach it."

Jo tilted her head. "Safely?"

Arnett stepped to one side and the other, judging the angles. "I guess it depends on how tall you are, and how long your arms are. We'd need to test it out—you're close to her height."

"Right. Let's get the team up here to swab the railing just in case some touch DNA can identify someone who shouldn't have been here."

As Hakeem processed the area around the railing, Jo hurried out to the unmarked Malibu and retrieved several bungee cords and a length of rope from the kits in the trunk. By the time she returned he was finished, and gave his go-ahead for them to continue.

He glanced at the rope in her hand, then at the railing. "Should I stay and help? I feel like the more arms you have to secure you, the better."

Jo surveyed the area. It was a tight fit on the landing with the three of them, but she'd feel far safer with Hakeem's six-foot-two, workout-five-days-a-week strength to help. "That'd be great. I'm going to tie the rope to my waist and the railing, and if each of you can grab one of my ankles, that should keep me as safe as I'm probably going to get."

Once she secured the rope, they knelt behind her and she pushed herself up onto the rail.

She stretched an arm out. "I can't quite reach it. I'm going to have to lean farther forward."

Arnett and Hakeem each grabbed one of her ankles, and she shifted her weight forward over the rail, one hand grasping the railing while she kept the other gloved hand clean for evidence retrieval. She then reached her clean hand out toward the watch.

"Oh, yeah, this is scary. The rail is now acting as a fulcrum, and most of my weight is forward. I feel close to falling on my own, never mind if one of you shoved me. And if you did, and I tried to keep hold of the rail with my hand at that angle, I'd almost certainly break my wrist." She made a final stretch, then pushed herself back down onto her feet. "But, I did manage to grab the watch."

Hakeem pulled on a clean set of gloves and opened an evidence bag so Jo could drop the watch in.

Arnett peered at it. "That didn't come out of a Cracker Jack box."

"No." Jo snapped several pictures, then studied it. The watch face was an elegant art deco rectangle, with four small diamonds and sapphires amid the decorations at each corner and the word 'Solrex' printed on the dial. "Gold, and those gems are real. And, it's vintage."

Hakeem manipulated it through the bag. "Clasp seems to work just fine."

"What are the odds that an expensive watch, unmarred by the surrounding bird scat, happens to be hanging just out of reach on the day someone falls to their death over the side of the pyramid?" Jo took off down the stairs.

Arnett's footsteps kept close pace behind her, and a few minutes later they reached the bottom.

"Back so soon?" Marzillo said as Jo strode over to Layla Madani's body, still waiting to be transported to the ME's office. Not wanting to change out her protective gear again, Jo leaned around from the edge of the tape.

"Is one of her wrists broken, by chance?"

Marzillo turned back to the body. "I didn't specifically check her wrists yet, but—" She examined the one, then the other. "Yep. Her left wrist is broken. How did you know?"

Jo held up the evidence bag. "And we need to know if she's wearing a watch."

Marzillo held up the wrist, which flopped over like a rotten fish, so Jo and Arnett could see.

The sun glinted off a silver watch.

CHAPTER TWENTY

While Marzillo's team finished processing the scene, Jo and Arnett returned to the outside courtyard. The uniformed officers had continued to keep Jim Karnegi and Karen Phelps separate, sitting each at the base of one of the sphinx statues. Eileen Pham stood several yards away, talking on her phone.

"Karnegi looks like he was just visited by aliens," Arnett said. "I'm gonna go out on a limb and say he found her body."

They confirmed with Norton, then strode over to him and signaled the officer next to him away. "Mr. Karnegi, we understand you're the one that found Ms. Madani?"

"I did." He sat slightly hunched, his black slacks and jacket now covered with slashes of dust from sitting on the stone. He shifted uncomfortably, like he wasn't sure what to do with his hands, and his glance flicked around the courtyard. "Awful. Just horrible. *What* is happening?"

"We need you to walk us through it all," Arnett said.

He stared up at Arnett like he didn't understand. "I—but—I told everything to the officer already." He cast around looking for the officer he'd spoken to. "I need to go. When can I go?"

Jo exchanged looks with Arnett. The last time they'd seen Karnegi, he'd been cool, calm, and in control—why was he falling apart? She stepped forward slightly. "We understand you've been through a lot today. But we need you to go through it with us one more time, because we'll have additional questions for you. Can you do that for me?"

He met her eyes, and nodded. "Sorry. Yes. What can I tell you?"

Jo took him back to the beginning of the day, to orient him in non-traumatic ground. "The third and fourth grades came here together on a field trip?"

"Yes, that's right. It's the kids' favorite field trip of the year. They've been looking forward to it for months."

"So you arrived, and went through the museum?"

"Yes. No. We split them in half by grade because the spaces are small, especially inside the burial chambers. So Layla's class went through the tomb this morning while mine were inside the museum. We were going to reverse after lunch." His gaze flicked back in the direction of the pyramid. "The kids are going to be so disappointed they didn't get to go in the tomb."

Jo exchanged another look with Arnett. Somehow, she imagined they'd be far more concerned that a teacher was dead—but then, logical thinking wasn't exactly a hallmark of shock. "Were the kids inside the pyramid when it happened?"

He shook his head. "No, they finished, and we all met back out here for lunch. We bring them out here so they can eat their boxed lunches in an open space after being inside for so long. That way they can move around, play, all where they have restrooms easily at hand."

"Then what happened?"

"Layla stepped away to do her check-in. Whenever we have a field trip, we have set points where we report in to Eileen, let her know how everything has gone and if there are any problems. I actually did mine first, then came back to help Karen watch the kids while Layla did hers."

"She stepped away?" Jo asked.

"Yes. Not far, just there, around the corner, to get away from the noise of the kids." He pointed to the enclosed hall that surrounded the entrance to the museum. "There are restrooms back on the left side, and we take the opportunity to use them, then make the call.

Normally she'd only be gone a few minutes, but she didn't come back. The kids finished their lunches and it was time to go back inside, but she still hadn't returned. So I went to look for her."

"In the hall?"

"Yes, at first in the hall. Then I had Karen check the restroom for her. When she wasn't there, I went inside the museum, wondering if the curator had pulled her aside or some such. But she wasn't there, so I went out to the pyramid, and—" His voice froze, and his face paled further, something Jo hadn't thought was possible.

"I know it's unpleasant, but what happened then?"

"I saw a figure on the ground. I ran over and it was so—impossible. Just impossible." He gazed up at her, his eyes searching her face for answers. "You know what I mean? It looked fake, and at first I thought it was a joke. Like some horrible set dressing they'd brought out for some reason. And I almost went back inside to give the curator a piece of my mind, because, you know, that's not appropriate for when you have children present. But then it hit me. If it were a prop, why did it look like Layla? And that's when I threw up."

"Did you touch her at all? Try to resuscitate her?" Arnett asked.

Karnegi looked at Arnett like he was insane. "Did you see her? How could she possibly be alive? Her bones were—" His throat seized again.

Jo hurried to reassure him. "You did the right thing. We just have to ask, because we need to know who touched her or moved her, and how. What did you do then?"

"Like I told Officer Reyes, it's a little fuzzy. I know I called nine-one-one, and I know I went searching for the curator. I think I was already on the phone by the time I found him. Then I must have led him out to her."

"What then?"

"I came back out here to let Karen know what was happening. I told her there'd been an accident, and we needed to get the kids onto the bus. They were upset, but I think they could sense something was wrong, so they didn't give us too much flack."

"And then?" Arnett asked.

"That's it. We waited with the kids, playing games on the bus to keep them occupied. We drove them around the corner so they wouldn't see the police arrive, but once they did, the officers asked that Karen and I come back here and stay in sight. Luckily Eileen and Sally had arrived by then, and Sally rode back with them."

"Okay, let's backtrack just a bit. What time did you bring the children out for lunch?"

"Eleven thirty."

"And when did you find Layla?"

"Twelve twenty."

Arnett's eyebrows rose. "That's extremely precise."

Karnegi bristled. "We'd planned forty-five minutes for lunch, and I went to look for her when we hit that mark. And when Officer Reyes asked me the same question, I checked my phone to see when I'd placed the nine-one-one call."

"When Ms. Madani went to check in with the principal, you and Karen were here with the children the whole time?" Jo asked.

"Yes, we try to always have at least one chaperone per fifteen-ish children."

"And neither of you left the whole time she was gone?" Arnett asked.

"Karen had to go to the restroom at one point," he said.

"When? Early in the lunch period, or later?"

"If I had to guess, I'd say about fifteen minutes in? She waited a few minutes for Layla to return, but then asked if I'd mind if she went."

"And how long was she gone?" Jo asked.

"A few minutes. Maybe five?"

Jo examined his face—he still looked dazed, and Jo wasn't sure how accurate his judgment could be. "Thank you so much, Mr.

Karnegi. One of the officers should have a statement ready for your signature shortly. Do you have a way back to the school? If not, we can arrange a ride for you."

"I can ride back with Eileen. Thank you."

Jo and Arnett strode to the other side of the courtyard where Karen Phelps, whose black leggings were today paired with a red workout jacket, sat with her arms wrapped around her abdomen.

She watched them approach, then spoke just before they reached her. "This has to be a coincidence. It *has* to be."

Arnett remained standing while Jo sat next to her. "It may be. We haven't made any determinations yet."

Karen nodded at her, blonde ponytail bobbing.

"What happened?" Jo asked.

Karen took her through a version of events that paralleled Karnegi's. She'd spent the morning with the children in the museum proper, spread out among the galleries. The children had been excited, but well behaved, and the morning had been pleasant. "I just don't understand. You'd have to climb purposefully over the railing. I can see a child doing something like that, but not Layla."

"But you just said you thought it must be an accident?" Jo watched her closely.

Her eyes raked across the paved stone on the ground in front of her. "I guess I don't know what to think. I can't see how it could have been an accident, but I can't see how it could have been anything other than an accident."

Jo pulled out her phone and brought up one of the pictures of the watch they'd found. "Do you recognize this?"

She studied the picture for a moment. "It's a watch, but I don't think I've ever seen it before. Was that hers?"

Jo stood up. "Thanks for your patience. Once you've signed your statement, you're free to go."

As Jo and Arnett turned to cross back to the car, Jo's phone rang. Her brow creased at the name on her screen. "Ms. Roden?" she answered.

"Detective Fournier?" Stephanie Roden's voice was thick with fear. "What's happening? I'm hearing that Layla had an accident?"

Jo paused, confused. "There's been an incident, yes, but—"

She sobbed. "Oh, God. She's dead, isn't she? Sally wouldn't look me in the eye."

Jo glanced at Arnett, who nodded—there wasn't much point trying to deny it. "Yes, I'm sorry, she is. Were you two friends?"

Little halting gasps came over the line as Stephanie tried to keep control. "More than friends, Detective. She was my girlfriend. We were supposed to move in together once my lease was up next month."

The news sank into Jo like a punch in the abdomen. "I'm so, so sorry."

Stephanie choked, then cleared her throat and resumed with an undercurrent of steel. "There's something you should know. The day before yesterday, I didn't get a chance to talk much to Layla. She was busy making preparations for the field trip, and then she had dinner with her mother and sister. Her mother is very… traditional, so I wasn't invited. Layla and I only had a short phone conversation, but while we were talking, she mentioned she might have remembered seeing that toy pig you found near Nicole."

Jo's chest tingled. "Whose was it?"

"She didn't remember exactly. She just remembered seeing it during a birthday celebration, and believed it belonged to one of a particular group of children. She said she was checking into it. At that point her sister yelled for her to come help in the kitchen, so she said she had to go."

"So she didn't say which children?"

"No."

"Did she say whose birthday celebration it was?"

"No, and I'm not sure she remembered for certain herself, because she has a group birthday celebration once a month for all the children who have birthdays. She only remembered a group of three children playing a particular game during the celebration, and saw something that might have been the pig among their belongings set off to the side."

"And you didn't ask her about it the next day?"

Stephanie gave a shuddering sigh. "No, it didn't occur to me. She wasn't even sure she remembered the right toy, so I didn't take it too seriously at the time. And maybe I'm making something out of nothing now, but…"

But, two days later, she'd mysteriously plummeted to her death down a five-floor pyramid. "You did the right thing telling us. We'll check into her phone records and see if we can figure out who she might have talked to about it," Jo said. "I'm going to text you a different picture. Can you tell me if you recognize the item?"

"Of course," Stephanie said, voice wavering.

Jo selected a snapshot from her gallery and texted it to Stephanie's number. "Let me know when it comes through."

"Got it," Stephanie said. "It's a watch."

"Do you know whose?"

She paused a moment. "No. I can't remember ever seeing it before."

"So definitely not Layla's?"

"Not that I'm aware of." Stephanie's voice contracted.

"Okay, thank you. If you remember it, please let us know." Jo paused a moment, listening to Stephanie's muffled sniffles. "And I promise you, we'll find out who did this as soon as possible."

CHAPTER TWENTY-ONE

"First things first." Jo dialed Lopez as they continued to the car.

"Jo." Lopez's voice was tight and heavy over the speakerphone. "What's the news?"

Jo gave her a quick recap. "So we need to hunt down the watch, and we need to get hold of Layla's phone records. You got Gia's and Anthony's records from right before Nicole was killed, right?"

"Correct. I'm guessing you want me to take another dip in that pool?"

"Yep. And I'm thinking we broaden the search," Arnett said. "Karnegi, for sure. I don't like that he's been on both scenes, and he's the one who found Madani."

"On it."

Jo hung up and turned to Arnett. "Talk it through?"

Arnett nodded. "In terms of suspects, both Karnegi and Phelps were alone for long enough that they could have gone up the pyramid, pushed Layla off, and come back down."

"But it could have been someone else, too. You can walk all the way through to the pyramid without registering on any of the gallery cameras if you beeline it. Or, sneak in that back entry as someone's going out."

"But you'd risk being seen by one of the chaperones or kids."

"A parent could just claim their child had forgotten something."

"Still risky that you'd get Madani alone."

Jo shook her head. "A parent would very likely know the field trip protocol."

Jo's phone rang, and she swore under her breath when she saw her sister's name. Harristown was small, but how in the hell had her sister heard about this already? *The school*, she realized—they must be contacting all the parents who had children on the field trip, and Isabelle would have been with the third graders.

Wincing, she tapped the phone. "Sophie. I guess you heard."

Sophie paused. "Heard what?"

Jo dropped her head into her hand, and gritted her teeth against the torrent of profanity bounding through her head. She hadn't made a mistake that stupid since she was a rookie.

She took a deep breath and kept her tone steady. "I need you to stay calm, Soph."

"Are the girls okay?" Sophie's voice rose.

"Yes, they're fine. But Ms. Madani isn't. She fell off the side of the museum's pyramid. The fall killed her."

There was another pause as Sophie processed the news. "Something's happening, Jo. I don't know what it is, but something's happening." The panic edging Sophie's voice had hardened into steel.

"I agree. We're processing the scene now." Jo found herself again impressed at Sophie's reaction. "But hang on. If you didn't know about it, why did you call?"

"I found out something I think you'll want to know. I sent out a few tendrils and two different sources told me they're certain Karen Phelps is having an affair with a married man. Anthony Marchand."

"Two sources. Impressive. Have you ever thought of being a journalist?"

"Don't be ridiculous, Josette," she said, but with a trace of pride in her voice.

"Okay, let's back up. First, why do they think she's having an affair?"

"She's made a few mysterious comments about dates, but won't say who they're with, and that isn't like her. Normally people can't get her to stop talking about whoever she's dating, in excruciating detail. But then someone heard her sitting in her car talking on her phone, and her tone was extremely sexy and flirty. She didn't see them until they were right up on top of her, and she ended the call quickly and tried to say it was a friend from college."

"Could it have been a friend from college?" Jo asked.

"I asked the same question. The answer I got was 'If it was really a friend from college, why did her face turn fire-engine red?'"

"Yeah, that's a fair point." Stephanie and Layla flashed through Jo's mind. "But, is there another sort of relationship she could be hiding? People in Harristown can be pretty conservative, maybe she's bisexual but is worried about people knowing that."

"Jo. You know better than that. They're fiscally conservative, yes. But socially conservative? Absolutely not. One of the main goals of their charity work is to show how *woke* they are. If that news leaked, her social calendar would fill up by the end of the day."

Jo laughed. "Sophie, promise me you'll never use the word 'woke' again."

Sophie was quiet for a quick second, then matched her laugh. "I guess it's not really me, is it?"

The sound jabbed Jo. How long had it been since she and Sophie had shared a laugh? She couldn't remember, and that was answer enough. "Any other alternative explanations you can think of?"

"I haven't been able to come up with anything. There's nothing wrong with flirting with your boyfriend as you sit in the car, so short of some sort of paid gigolo, I'm not sure what else she'd have to be embarrassed about."

"Can we add the word 'gigolo' to your no-speak list?" Jo laughed.

"That one I refuse to give up," Sophie said, and Jo could hear her smile.

"So the next question is why Anthony Marchand?"

"The main reason is there's been a strange shift in the Witches of Briar Ridge's dynamic, which means there's definitely tension, and this would explain it. There's no way she's sleeping with Molly's husband, because Don's so in love with Molly it's nauseating, but everyone knows Anthony Marchand is never home. Which just goes to show, really."

"Goes to show what?"

"That there's a lid for every pot. Gia Marchand literally used to be a model. Molly looks like Goodwill vomited on her and her husband worships her. It gives you faith in humankind, really."

Jo winced—every so often Jo got a glimpse of the mean girl her sister had been in high school, overlapping into her adult years. It was one of the many root reasons why their relationship was so complicated, even if Sophie had mostly matured out of the tendency. But, she told herself, this was her sister rejecting that superficiality—or so she would choose to believe.

"Let's back up again. What's the shift in dynamic you mentioned among the three ladies?"

"This part I've seen and felt myself. They've each been spotted alone much more often in the last few days, for one."

"That may just be because of Nicole. When someone loses a child, everything changes."

"Except I'd still expect Molly and Karen to be together, and besides, Gia's acting like nothing has happened. She even tried to go on that field trip today as chaperone, until Principal Pham pulled her off because some of us weren't happy about that."

Jo's brows knit. "Wait. Karen wasn't supposed to be here today?"

"No. She volunteered to take over for Gia when Eileen pushed the issue."

Jo's fist bounced on the side of her leg. "So the three friends have been less friendly."

"You could put it that way. When they're together they seem fine—somber, but fine. But it's things like missing their morning trips to Starbucks together after they drop off the kids, that sort of thing."

Jo turned that over in her head. Would she want to go meet with one of her friends if the other habitual klatch member was suffering? Possibly not. "Maybe Gia's the glue that holds the group together."

"She certainly is. But like I say, she's still around, but the vibe is different."

Jo had learned over the years to trust her instinct when it came to vibes—did her sister have that same skill? "Got it. And the more I think about it, I suppose it might help account for how Gia has reacted to all of this, if she suspects her husband is cheating on her. Thanks for letting me know."

"I'm glad it's helpful. Call me later and let me know what's happening—I'm beginning to think it might be a good time for David and me to take the girls on an impromptu vacation."

They said brief goodbyes and hung up.

"So what's the theory there, that Karen wants Anthony March-and to leave Gia, and when he doesn't, she kills his daughter?" Arnett said.

Jo half-shrugged as she pulled open the passenger side door. "It's the first hint of an actual motive we've had. So far, the best we've managed are hints and rumors about Jim Karnegi behaving *inappropriately* around children, and the possibility that Nicholas killed his little sister in a fit of anger or some such."

Arnett slid into the driver's seat and pulled the door closed behind him. "If we hadn't already eliminated Nicholas, this would put the kibosh on that, at least. Some sort of accident or fit of anger with his sister is one thing, but this"—he gestured toward the building—"this is something else entirely."

"Agreed. Layla's death narrows things down considerably, actually. If we're working on the assumption her death wasn't just a coincidence, and I think that's a safe assumption, can we agree the motive to murder her was to cover up the killer's tracks, especially in light of what Stephanie Roden told us?"

"Sounds solid to me."

Jo pulled on her seat belt. "So if we follow that through, it means we're not talking about somebody who's pissed off because of some lawsuit involving the Marchands, or some ex from their past. Whoever did this is a part of Briar Ridge's inner circle. Most likely Layla Madani contacted them about the toy pig, and they knew about the field trip today. Down to the details about field trip procedure, including that she'd step away from the others to do her check-in."

"So not janitors or cafeteria workers." Arnett switched on the ignition, and pulled away from the curb.

"Exactly. Our killer is a teacher, administrator, or a parent," Jo said.

"And we should be able to rule out the vast majority of the teachers and administrators easily—no way they left campus for long enough to get here and back without someone noticing."

"Right, especially since, if I'm remembering correctly, the students here ate their lunch half an hour earlier than the scheduled lunchtime for Briar Ridge. So even if one of the teachers or admins tried to sneak out during their lunch break, they couldn't have arrived in time to kill Layla. So for the teachers it's a simple case of who showed up to work today and who didn't. The admin may be more complex, but still fairly easy."

"So apart from any strange discoveries we make there, we're looking at Karnegi and Phelps, since they were both on site, and the parents."

"And again this should help us winnow that field. Lopez said she already confirmed half of the possible parents have alibis for the time of Nicole's death—I'm sure we'll be able to knock out more who have an alibi for today," Jo said.

"But in the meantime, your gut is telling you this situation with Karen Phelps and Anthony Marchand is our best bet?"

Jo's hand flew to her necklace. "I'm not sure. When I look through that lens, a lot of things start falling into place. Anthony

Marchand's strange priorities. Gia's strange reaction. And Karen was on site for both deaths—she could have taken advantage of the few minutes when Jim was breaking up that fight with the tetherball players, and maybe when she supposedly went to the restroom today, she really somehow tricked Layla into going up the pyramid, and pushed her off."

"But?"

She pressed her lips together and shook her head for a moment before answering. "But, I just don't see her planning out the cold-blooded murder of her friend's daughter like that."

"Some sort of accident? Maybe she took out some frustrations she had with Anthony on Nicole and before she knew it…" He gave the steering wheel a sharp squeeze for emphasis.

"It's possible," Jo said, deep in thought.

"And Karnegi's still a viable possibility. He could have killed Madani easily—he's big enough he could have shoved her over the side of that railing no problem."

"Especially if he used the watch to divert her attention somehow. Maybe that's how he got her back up on the pyramid, said he noticed something that might belong to one of the kids?"

"And he could have killed Nicole when Karen was dealing with the little girl that got hurt. If he was molesting her, maybe she reached some sort of breaking point, and he realized he was in danger of being found out, so he seized the moment when Karen was helping that little girl." Arnett eased the car to a stop at a red light.

A thought occurred to Jo, and she sat up straighter. "Or—hold on—Anthony was on campus right before Nicole was murdered, right? Maybe he ran into Karen—"

Arnett's head snapped around toward her. "And Nicole saw them playing a little grab-ass and threatened to tell Mommy? Holy shit."

"That sure would explain why he doesn't seem to be very eager to return our calls," Jo said. "And possibly Layla remembered something that implicated him, and mentioned it to Karen or Gia—"

"And it got right back to him." The light turned green, and Arnett stepped on the gas. "So our little chat with Anthony and his lawyer just became a much bigger priority."

CHAPTER TWENTY-TWO

"Gia. I need to talk to you. Please call me back as soon as you can."

Karen threw the phone onto the passenger seat as she pulled into her driveway. She'd left three messages, in addition to a text she'd sent both Gia and Molly. Molly had also been slow to answer, but at least she *had* answered eventually, unlike Gia. The store had been busy all day, Molly had told her when she finally called. She said that if Karen had been upfront in her text about what was going on, she'd have ushered the customers out and called immediately. But what was Karen supposed to do, send a text that said, *Hey guys, guess what? Layla Madani just nose-dived off the side of a pyramid, and for the second time this week someone died on my watch—but how's your day going?*

After two failed attempts to click off her seat belt, she finally found the right button and jumped out of the car. She unhooked Katie first, then Willie, and corralled them toward the porch. They glanced up at her briefly, aware something was wrong, but not concerned enough to keep from pushing each other out of the way for the privilege of opening the screen door. Normally she'd remind them to be nice to each other, but right now she didn't have an ounce of extra energy, so she just unlocked the door, then watched, annoyed, as they dumped their backpacks in the hall before bolting up to their rooms. Then she marched directly into the kitchen and poured herself a very large glass of wine.

All she wanted to do was give her friends a heads-up about what happened. Warn them as soon as possible—

No, that wasn't true, it wasn't only that. She needed someone to talk to. She needed her *friends*. Twice in a week she'd been on the scene when something *awful* had happened. Was it so strange to expect her friends to be concerned about her? Okay, yes in the first case, because Gia's needs were obviously primary—her daughter had been murdered, after all, and Karen's potential state of mind had no priority in anyone's thinking. But today had been traumatic, and unlike them, she didn't have a husband to hold her and tell her everything was going to be okay. Since she couldn't have *that*, she at least deserved a friend's shoulder to collapse on for a few minutes.

She gulped down half the wine and closed her eyes as the warmth of it spread through her abdomen and her chest.

Whatever. Just, seriously—whatever. None of this mattered. What really mattered was she now had to go upstairs and explain to Katie why her field trip had been cut short, and explain to both kids that Ms. Madani had a bad accident. It was the absolute last thing she wanted to do, but it'd be all over school the next day and she needed to prepare them for it.

And she had to deal with it alone.

But she only had to be alone for a little longer. Soon he'd leave his wife and be free to be with her. Then she'd have that shoulder to cry on, and someone to help her with the kids, and someone to sit with at the end of the day and sip wine rather than down it alone in rushed glugs while she struggled to keep hold of her sanity.

She sighed, tossed back the rest of the wine, and braced herself as she headed upstairs to talk to the kids.

*

Molly shoved her phone away across the counter and forced on a smile for the woman who'd just entered the boutique.

No, the store hadn't been busy all day, she just hadn't wanted to call Karen back until she figured out what to say to her. Because what she *wanted* to say was "I know you're hiding something from me," but that would have gone over like a leprous roach on a dinner plate. And if there was one thing she'd learned from dealing with her father, it was that if people didn't want to be upfront, they wouldn't be. Trying to force the truth out of someone was like wrestling a greased pig. And now with Layla Madani's death, she just wanted to scream, *This isn't about you, Karen!*

Because of the aborted field trip, Molly had to close the shop to pick up Shauna, and now she had to paste on fake expressions and answer silly customer questions as her daughter huddled in a chair in the corner of the shop, when all she wanted to do was run to her and pull her into her arms. Of course this was horrible for Karen to deal with, but it was horrible for everyone involved—first and foremost, Gia and Anthony, and Layla's family. Didn't Karen understand that? Didn't she get that *every* parent at Briar Ridge would have to have another nightmarish discussion with their children? Didn't she see that so many children who loved their teacher would be traumatized and heartbroken? Everyone would be sleepless tonight, trying desperately to figure out if their children were safe and what to do about it all. Karen wasn't special just because she was there when it happened.

She stared over at Shauna, bent over the book she was reading, her long auburn hair tucked behind her ear and one hand rubbing at her nose, a gesture that indicated Shauna was stressed. Thank God Shauna had always been able to find comfort in books. Molly envied that—she'd give anything for a way to escape all of this, to not have to think about it, to not be filled with fear and uncertainty. *Be grateful*, she reminded herself as she watched Shauna turn a page. Her daughter was here with her, safe and sound.

What worried Molly far more than Karen's state of mind was that Gia hadn't called or texted either of them. Molly couldn't remember a time when Gia took more than an hour to respond to them with at least a text, unless she was on vacation or something like that. And even then, she was in near constant contact.

Molly reached for her phone, but stopped. The same principle applied here—if Gia was pushing them away, forcing the issue would just make things worse. Gia knew where she was. And if she called, Molly would be there to pick up.

And if she didn't, well, that sent a strong, clear message, too.

*

Gia ended her return call to Karen without leaving a message, then tucked her phone back into her purse, shaking her head in frustration. Three missed calls from Karen, but when she's finally able to return them, Karen doesn't bother to pick up?

Which was fine, anyway, because she really didn't have time to deal with any of it. The day had been beyond hectic and stressful—she'd never realized exactly how small Harristown and the surrounding area was until it was desperately important she wasn't recognized—and now she had to get all the way to Springfield and back before Anthony got home. Her head was splitting with all the details she needed to navigate, and she couldn't shake the nagging feeling she'd forgotten something important. She'd gone over her mental list a hundred times and she was almost certain she had everything covered, but it only took one slip.

The hard part was going to be waiting until Monday. The documents wouldn't be ready until then, and she couldn't do anything without them. So she'd spend the weekend obsessing about every tiny thing that could go wrong, all while maintaining layer upon layer of pretense.

As she merged onto the pike, she took a long, deep breath. She was losing it, and she didn't have that luxury. She had to keep it together, just for three more days, and everything would be fine.

She glanced at Nicholas in the backseat, fidgeting while he played *Box Island* on the iPad, and placed one hand on her abdomen.

Three days. She could manage that. She had to.

CHAPTER TWENTY-THREE

On the way back to HQ, Lopez sent a text asking Jo and Arnett to call or come by as soon as they were able. When they arrived, they headed straight in to see her.

"What do you have for us?" Jo asked.

"The warrant came through and I've been digging into Molly and Donald Hayes' finances."

"Anything interesting?"

"Not as interesting as I'd like, unfortunately, but a bit strange. Each week there are several small cash withdrawals on their debit card. Since a lot of them happen during the day around other purchases, I'm fairly certain it's Molly who's responsible for it. And the minute I saw it I channeled your superpower, Jo—because it reminded me instantly of my abuela. She used to play this little game with my grandfather where he'd always tell her she needed to stop buying clothes, and she'd agree—and then funnel money out of the household budget and buy the clothes anyway. Then she'd wear them, and my grandfather would say, 'Hey, isn't that new?' and she'd get offended and say, 'No, it's not new and that just goes to show how little attention you pay me, you don't love me anymore, what's happening to our marriage,' and he'd feel so guilty he'd go out and buy her a new pair of shoes or something."

Arnett's chin jutted back into his neck. "That's horrible."

Jo waved him off. "Oh, come on. Do you really think he didn't realize what was going on?"

"Wouldn't he have put a stop to it if he had?" Arnett said.

Lopez gave him a *come-on-now* head tilt. "If he kept falling for it, that sorta makes her point about him not paying attention, right?"

He narrowed his eyes at her.

Jo tried to hide her smile. "So what you're saying is, Molly's a secret shopaholic?"

"That's my theory: pull out the cash here and there and justify it however you can so there's no credit card records ratting out your clandestine purchases."

"Interesting. Anything else to report?"

"Not yet. Still waiting on the phone records, so there's not much more we can do tonight. And for now I have to clock out anyway, because I'm taking my mother out to play Thursday night bingo over at St. Bede's." She pointed at Arnett. "And before you say anything, I'll have you know I deeply enjoy bingo. It's so hypnotic searching for the numbers, it's like a form of meditation."

Arnett raised both hands. "Hey, far be it from me. I'm looking forward to the days when I can retire and Laura and I can play bingo all day long on cruises around the Caribbean."

Lopez raised her fist and Arnett bumped it.

As Jo packed up and headed out for dinner and a movie with Matt, she pushed down visions of Layla's broken body and Nicole's swollen face, and contemplated the potential healing powers of bingo.

CHAPTER TWENTY-FOUR

Molly woke Saturday morning feeling like a small boat being tossed on very rough seas, with danger all around, unable to find safe port anywhere. She hadn't felt that way, at least not with the same intensity, since the day her parents took her for ice cream and then, while she happily lapped up her bubblegum cone, had announced they were getting divorced. Her father moved out the next day, leaving her mother alone and scared and barely able to support herself even with the alimony and child support. He moved to Maine with the woman he'd fallen in love with and Molly barely saw him until he died in a car accident three years later. To this day, the artificially sweet taste of gumballs nauseated her, and rose up from her memory whenever she felt overwhelmed.

Last night's fight with Don brought the smell right back for her, like she was standing in that very same ice cream parlor.

She needed to think clearly, and she did that best when blowing glass. So when Don took Shauna off on a trip to the bookstore, she drove to the studio.

She pushed through the doors with one straight-armed shove. She waved to a man heading out for the day, then laid her tools out onto the worktable. After tugging on her safety glasses she added sand into the furnace to melt, then stood back and considered.

She'd make something easy, because she needed to think, but pretty, because she needed stock for the boutique. Paperweights would be perfect. They always sold well, and they were nearly impossible to mess up in her distracted state.

The problem was she'd just had too much to deal with. Nicole's death, and now Layla Madani's, the whole situation more and more terrifying, and on top of it Karen was lying about something and Gia was pushing her away. And when she told Don about it all, he'd lost his temper. It happened so rarely—only once before in their entire marriage and not nearly as bad as this time—that she had no idea how to process it. She tried to tell herself it was only a fight, that every couple had them, but she knew that wasn't true. She and Don didn't have them. They weren't that type of couple. Her heart tossed around her chest and the memories of her father's departure flooded back, and she knew without a doubt her marriage was in trouble, and she had to figure out what to do.

Molly surveyed the line of blowpipes and selected one—it didn't really matter which, but there was always one that called to her. She located it, hefted its weight before inserting it into the furnace, then twirled it, picking up a bulb of molten glass. Or, as she liked to think of it, a seed of molten glass. Both because its shape resembled the pip of an apple or a pear, but also because it was the beginning that would grow into her finished piece after she molded and pulled and shaped it into something beautiful. She rolled the molten glass in a dish of granules, picking up the red-orange glass she'd be swirling through it.

Gia was at the core of it all. At first, she tried to convince herself that Gia was just struggling to deal with Nicole's death. But her behavior had escalated, communication had all but shut down, and she was barely going through the motions with them anymore—Molly hadn't heard from Gia at all on Friday. Then there was Karen. What was she lying about, and why? So much for her two closest friends in the world, her only friends, really, the only people outside immediate family that she trusted. Both acting sketchy.

She was obsessing, Don had said. She was driving herself insane, and it wasn't healthy. She needed to focus on her family—on him and on Shauna, and on what was best for them, and if she did that, none of the rest would matter.

But it did matter, couldn't he see that? Two people were dead and her daughter was in danger—that meant any secrets popping up *mattered*. They just did, no matter how much Don wanted to pretend otherwise. And she'd told him just that—sticking your head in the sand didn't make the situation any less real, and calling her obsessive didn't change that.

She inserted the blowpipe into the glory hole—she hated that term—and twirled again, allowing all the granules to melt and fuse into the bulb of glass. The process always mesmerized her—the two becoming one, distinct, with clear visual delineation, but also now inseparable.

Karen was the complicating factor, or rather, whatever she was hiding. Did Gia know what it was? Is that why Gia's behavior had shifted? Maybe Gia wasn't upset with Molly at all, just with Karen, but since they were a trio, she was pulling away from both of them?

Molly rolled the glass over the marver's cool, flat steel surface, shaping the orb into a capsule, red-orange spots now popping like a leopard's rosettes waiting to be molded.

A sudden thought chilled her. Maybe the exact opposite was true—maybe Gia and Karen were distancing themselves from *her*, and Karen's protestations were just a big show so Molly wouldn't figure it out.

She squeezed her eyes shut and shook her head. Maybe she *was* being ridiculous and paranoid, maybe Don was right, maybe she *was* letting her fears and insecurities sabotage her. Gia would come directly to her if she was upset about something, she wouldn't plot and plan with Karen.

Setting the pipe on its stand, she spun it and blew into the end, watching the glass expand outward. When it reached the right size, she stuck it back into the furnace and watched it collapse on itself like a deflating pool toy.

But no, she needed to admit to herself that Gia and Karen weren't actually at the root of the fight, as much as she wanted to deflect it to that. The real problem was she'd been delaying. Saying she'd make an appointment with a therapist, but finding excuses not to. That's why Don lost his temper last night and put his foot down. He'd been clear: her resistance was destroying their family, and he couldn't allow it any longer.

Which was a truly low blow because everything she said and did, every moment of her life, was all about their family. Nothing even came a close second to how important he and Shauna were to her, and just because she didn't agree with him didn't make that any less true. So she'd screamed back at him that he *just didn't trust her*.

He'd stormed out of the house, drove off, and didn't come back for over an hour. And when he finally did, he didn't say a word to her, just slammed the door to the spare bedroom and went to sleep.

She grabbed and twisted the molten glass with her huge tweezers, trying to find comfort in the pliant, taffy-like texture as she swirled the dots into streaks, pulling and pushing until the piece looked like ruffled lace on a girl's collar. Because he'd never—not once—slept in a different bed over the entire course of their marriage.

He'd left his phone next to his keys on the counter. Of course she knew his password, just like he knew hers. She'd only meant to check the location tracking, so she'd know where he'd been. He often went on long drives when he was worried about something, work or Shauna or money, and she always checked afterward because if he was cheating on her, she wanted to know—she wasn't going to be blindsided like her mother had been. His drives were always consistent and the only stops appeared to be for gas.

But last night when she checked, the browser tab was open, and his search was still up. He'd taken the matter into his own hands, and googled therapists in the area. He'd reached his limit. He wasn't going to let it go, and that put her in an impossible situation.

When she finished the lacy design, she dipped the piece in more clear glass to preserve the pattern, then spun it inside a block, shaping it into a ball. As it took shape, the panicked fear of losing Don bubbled back up. Why was he so adamant? Why did he have to push her to do something she was so dead set against? Therapy wasn't the solution, she'd watched her mother go through decades of it, until she'd finally given up and killed herself. Love and patience were the solutions. That's all she was asking for, love and patience, two things he'd always been good at. Surely that wasn't too much to ask.

So much for thinking it all through and coming up with a solution—she was right back where she started.

She sighed and used her jacks to score into the base of the glass, then with a careful, pointed tap, broke the bulb off the pipe. She smoothed the edge with a blowtorch and stuck it into the kiln so the piece could slowly cool off rather than crack or explode.

Head tilted, she considered the kiln.

A cooling-off period—that was the answer. She'd ask him for a few days—with a definite endpoint—to prove to him she could deal with it on her own. And she'd agree that if he was still worried at that point, he could make as many appointments as he liked. She smiled to herself, relieved that she'd come up with a potential solution.

But as she turned to pick up another seed of molten glass, the smell of bubble gum hovered over her.

CHAPTER TWENTY-FIVE

By Sunday morning, all of the teams' leads had run dry. They had finished checking out the last of the parent alibis—the requested phone records had arrived on Friday afternoon, and Jo and Arnett spent the rest of Friday, then into Saturday, going through them. Jo had hoped Layla Madani's phone records would point clearly toward whoever she'd suspected of owning the *Sing* Gunter toy, however, the list of calls she made the day before she died was extensive. The vast majority of them had to do with preparations for the field trip, including clarifications for which children needed special box lunches or other accommodations. Narrowing the field down to one, or even a handful of suspects, was impossible.

They moved on to the previous week's phone and text records for Jim Karnegi, Molly and Don Hayes, Karen Phelps, and Gia and Anthony Marchand. The vast majority of Anthony's calls and texts were business related—in fact, he'd barely communicated even with his wife, and that contact was short and perfunctory. Jim's were nearly non-existent; apart from a few organizational texts to Layla Madani the day before the field trip, he had no work-related communications, and his only others were to his wife. Molly and Don texted each other regularly, and it warmed Jo's heart to see the affection between them. Molly, Karen and Gia were in near constant contact at the beginning of the week, although that had tapered off in recent days. Out of sheer desperation, she asked Lopez to start work on warrants for everyone's

WhatsApp histories, hoping that someone had tried to hide their communications via the app.

After tossing and turning all night, alternating between nightmares and trying to come up with some lead they'd overlooked, Jo struggled through a disastrous attempt to make herself breakfast, cutting a finger and burning her eggs. She dumped the ruined food into the garbage and sagged over the sink, eyes squeezed shut. A scene from one of her nightmares flashed back through her head: a doctor telling her she'd miscarried, then handing her Nicole's broken body.

Her body's signals were clear—trembling, nausea, the light around her too bright, every muscle in her body taut like a cat about to jump. Fight-or-flight mode, as if someone were chasing her with a chainsaw, telling her *you're under attack, there's danger all around you, you aren't safe.*

She dropped into a chair and tried to turn her attention inward, the way Nina had taught her. *You're safe. Everything's fine. You're at home, nobody's trying to harm you.* She took a series of deep breaths, but the anxiety wouldn't subside. She tried again, telling herself there was no need for panic, they'd find the killer, some solution would come to her, everything would make sense. It had to, because if it didn't, she wasn't sure she'd be able to keep her walls up and keep moving forward.

Nothing worked.

She desperately needed to get out of the house. She was overdue for a practice session at the shooting range anyway, and that would allow her to let all the information running around in circles in her brain bubble away on the back burner while she kept her marksmanship on point. The sooner she stopped obsessing about it, the sooner something would come to her. She grabbed her keys and headed out.

Half an hour later, Jo slipped on her safety glasses and earmuffs, then pushed through to the indoor range and selected the lane farthest from the other two shooters.

She pulled her Beretta out of her hip holster and unloaded the boxes of ammo onto the table, then clipped a target to the motor and sent it ten yards down the lane. She ran the bullets over her fingers one by one as she positioned them into the magazine—as ridiculous as it was, the process always reminded her of a PEZ dispenser, and the regularity of it soothed her. Once both magazines were full, she slid the first into the gun until it clicked into place, then cycled a round into the chamber.

As she stared at the silhouette deciding what to target, an image of the mugger who killed Jack flashed into her head.

What would Nina say about that? That it would be cathartic to picture him there, to envision herself unloading her weapon into his chest? Or was that too slippery a slope, one that would lead to something far less benign?

Better to be safe than sorry, so she pushed the image out of her head and refocused. The heart first, she decided as she squared herself to the target, feet slightly apart for a solid stance. She closed her eyes for a moment and settled into the position, rooting herself firmly to the earth. She lifted the gun and released the safety, then gazed down its length, aligning the front and rear sights into position on the target, and braced herself.

She fired, allowing the jolt of the recoil to power through her. She aimed again, fired again, aimed again, fired again, until she'd emptied the magazine into the black silhouette and the slide jutted back toward her.

Fifteen shots, all within two inches of each other.

A gentle push of her thumb released the magazine, and she inserted the second. The mugger's face appeared again, and morphed into a New Orleans gang-banger, then into the black silhouette of an anonymous man grasping the shadow of a little girl. She pushed the visions back down, and ignored the anxiety that bounced up.

The head this time. Rapid fire.

After the initial shot she allowed her intuition to float the gun back into position between shots. Fifteen more, all positioned cleanly into the silhouette's skull.

She retrieved the target and replaced it with a new one. As she watched it sail back down the lane, another face condensed in front of her: Anthony Marchand, smiling and confident in the picture that dominated his company website, meeting her eyes with a mocking smirk. He was the key to all of this. No innocent man refused to talk to the police about his murdered child. No innocent father lawyered up and put off conversations that could help the police find his daughter's killer, like some misguided game of cat and mouse. He was hiding something, and they could follow up all the leads they wanted, but until they figured out what it was, they'd get nowhere. And worse, her failure to find it had cost another life. If she'd insisted on tracking down his work location, if she'd staked out his house to be sure she was there when he arrived home that first night, would she have been able to prevent Layla Madani's death? She'd never know, and she'd find no peace until she was across the table from him, eye to eye, measuring every wince and twitch and breath he took.

She channeled the fear and her demons into anger as she repeated the process of loading and firing, until she ran through all the ammunition she'd brought with her. Ten targets, three hundred shots, all of them exceptionally well grouped.

Except one. One had inexplicably strayed almost six inches from the rest, like a recalcitrant child who refused to hold hands.

Excellent accuracy, she tried to convince herself as she packed up and left. The sort that would win medals at competitions. The sort that brought commendations, and would save lives in the field.

But she couldn't focus on the tight groupings any more than she was able to stack all the arrests she'd made and the criminals she'd put away high enough to counter the loved ones she'd failed to protect. Couldn't put aside her failure to prevent Layla Madani's death. The one stray shot was all that would ever matter, not the perfect three hundred, or three thousand, or even three million. Because that one mistake could mean the difference between someone's life or their death. That's the one that would creep up and sit on her chest, suffocating her as she tried to sleep at night.

CHAPTER TWENTY-SIX

Jo spent Monday morning with Arnett widening their searches. They did thorough sweeps of social media, looking for anything unusual on Facebook or Instagram. They branched out to Anthony Marchand's family—his parents were retired, and they were visiting Anthony's only sibling, a brother, who lived out in Los Angeles. That information came from their housekeeper since the family themselves refused to talk to Jo. Gia's parents were deceased, and she had no siblings. They dug into Don Hayes' business, but couldn't come up with anything suspicious, and Karen's parents both lived in Ohio. Jim Karnegi had no presence on social media, and parents that lived in Nevada.

Arnett pushed himself away from his desk. "We're spinning our wheels."

Jo rubbed the bridge of her nose. "Until we find some new wheels, we're gonna have to spin the ones we've got. Tomorrow we'll have Anthony Marchand here, and—"

Her phone rang. She tapped to answer it. "Christine. What's up?"

"We have a situation. We need to find Gia and Anthony Marchand, now."

Jo bolted upright, and waved Arnett over. "What do you mean? What's happening?"

"I got a call from a long-lost confidential informant of mine, a guy I haven't talked to since I was partnered up. He's a *reformed* dealer who just happens to have other reasons for keeping in touch with his same wide group of friends. He was visiting one of those friends' place of business when Gia Marchand showed up."

"What type of business?"

"The type people go to when they need a new identity. An ID, a new social security number, a passport."

"And your guy decided to drop dime for old time's sake?" Arnett asked.

"You're right to be suspicious, my friend. His explanation was, and I quote, 'I'm not down with child-murdering bitches. Why does she need a passport if she didn't kill her kid? That shit ain't right.' Nonetheless, I figured I should verify. So I quickly did a little look-see, and found that the contents of Gia's personal savings account and an additional million dollars were wire-transferred into an offshore account half an hour ago."

Jo and Arnett sprung up and pulled on their coats. "Do you have any idea where she is now?"

"None whatsoever, unfortunately."

"So we send out a county-wide APB on both the Marchands, and contact Harristown PD directly. Can you take care of that?"

"On it."

Jo and Arnett raced out of HQ, and with the help of their portable beacon light, made fast time out to the Marchand residence. As they approached the house, Gia Marchand's Lexus, with Gia driving and Nicholas in the back, pulled out of the driveway and headed toward them. As she neared, Gia met Jo's eyes, and her face registered a shock of recognition.

As Jo braced herself for a chase, a Harristown PD squad car turned onto the other end of the street, blocking Gia's possible escape route. Gia stopped, put her car in reverse, and did a two-point turn back into her driveway.

Jo and Arnett rolled down their windows to watch and listen as the squad car pulled up behind. The officers got out and cautiously approached the Lexus, hands hovering near their weapons. Gia sat still, both hands visibly displayed on the steering wheel, head turned over her shoulder, watching.

"Exit the vehicle," one of the officers called.

Gia pushed open the door and came out with her hands up. She looked over to Jo and Arnett and called out. "This isn't what it looks like. I need to talk to you."

Jo signaled the officers to continue. Once Gia and Nicholas were secured in the back of the squad car, Arnett asked the officers to bring them to SPDU headquarters, and followed them in. The officers delivered Gia to an interrogation room while Jo and Arnett informed Lopez that they'd caught her in time.

When Jo pushed open the door, Nicholas sat cuddled into her chest like a preschooler, with Gia kissing his head. She'd been crying—two tracks of smudged mascara lined her cheeks. "Please, can you take Nicholas somewhere safe while we talk?"

"We'll find another detective to sit with him." Jo ducked back out with Arnett to make the arrangements.

When they returned, Gia's head jerked up. "I know what this looks like, but I didn't kill Nicole," she said. "My husband did."

*

Jo took a moment to process the dramatic turnaround from the solid, self-contained woman they'd dealt with over the past week. Was this some sort of ruse to shift the blame away? She didn't think so—the tears were real, the emotions frantic, and her tone was a frightening blend of desperation and resignation.

"Anthony killed Nicole?" Jo asked.

She hugged her arms around herself "Yes. And now it's only a matter of time before he kills us."

Jo slipped her phone out of her pocket. "Where's your husband right now?"

"He should be at work."

"He's out on a job, right? Your company wouldn't tell us the location."

"Hanson Paper Products," she said. "In Hartford."

Jo stepped out to put a call through to Lopez. "Can you send out a pair of detectives to bring him in?"

"Not uniforms?" she asked.

"I'd like to do it as quietly as possible until we know for sure what's going on. But if he resists or runs, have them do whatever needs to be done," Jo said.

"Your wish is my command," Lopez replied.

Jo returned to the interrogation room, grabbing a box of Kleenex on the way to the table. "Tell us what happened."

Gia pulled three Kleenex out with quick flicks and wiped her nose. "I don't know what happened."

Jo tried again. "I'm confused, and I need you to help me out. Start at the beginning."

"I don't even know where the beginning is. Anthony has always been controlling, I knew that from the start. But powerful men are, that's how they manage to be successful, and I figured you have to take the good with the bad. So I guess I just didn't see." She covered her eyes with the tissue, and her body wracked with sobs.

Jo shot a look at Arnett, who looked as confused as she felt. She reached over and put a hand on Gia's arm. "I need you to take a few deep breaths with me, okay?"

Gia met her eyes, sat straight up, and nodded her head.

Jo lead her through five cleansing breaths. As she did, she took a moment to consider Gia's accusation. Gia and Nicholas had been alone in the car, without Anthony, and while a large chunk of money had been transferred from the Marchands' joint family account, the account that had been fully cleared out only had Gia's name on it. They'd also only found a fake passport for Gia and one for Nicholas when they searched her, not one for Anthony. That all pointed to her running away *from* Anthony, not running away *with* him. But it was still possible she was planning on meeting up with her husband somewhere, possibly after he finished clearing up important business. He could very well have his own fake passport already with him.

"Okay, let's start again. You acquired a set of false identities, and transferred over one-point-five million dollars into an offshore account. You're trying to disappear."

Gia exhaled a pointed breath through her mouth and nodded, trying to keep control. "Away from Anthony."

Jo leaned back. "You're safe now. We aren't going to let anything happen to you or Nicholas. But we need you to explain what happened to Nicole."

Tears filled Gia's eyes again. "I told you, I don't know. I wasn't there."

"He told you about it after the fact?"

"No, I haven't asked him about it. That would just set him off."

"Then why do you think he killed her?"

She closed her eyes for a long moment, then opened them again. "It started when Nicholas was about four. We had a nanny for Nicholas' first two years. I didn't want one, but Anthony was working hard building up his new company, trying to break away from his family, and he needed his sleep. I said I'd sleep with Nicholas, but he said my place was 'by his side and in his bed, and that's what nannies were for.' After we got rid of the nanny, Nicholas was usually in bed by the time Anthony got home, and the result was he never spent time with Nicholas that wasn't pleasant and controlled. But as Nicholas got older, he wanted to spend more time with his father, and you know how kids are—if they can't get your attention in a good way, negative attention will do just fine."

Jo nodded.

"I don't believe in physical discipline. But he said I 'couldn't control' Nicholas, and started 'spanking' him. With his hand, with a belt, it didn't matter. I didn't like it, but I told myself spankings weren't unheard of, and Nicholas was as much his child as mine."

"But then it escalated," Arnett said.

She nodded, and a tear ran down her face. "About a year ago he completely lost control. Nicholas had gone into his office looking for something, I don't even remember what, and knocked over a mug of coffee on his desk. It went all over his files, and some stupid faux diplomas he'd ordered to give out to the employees at the company he was working with. For some team-building exercises." She waved her hand. "They cost maybe fifty cents each, it's not like they were made of platinum. But he completely lost it. Just picked up his stapler and started beating Nicholas with it. I jumped in and tried to stop him, and he turned on me. I don't remember exactly what happened but I must have pulled Nicholas into me, because when he finally stopped I was huddled over Nicholas, and my back felt like I'd been run over repeatedly by a truck."

"Did you file a report?" Jo asked.

Gia's eyes flashed to her, filled with terror. "Of course not. He stormed off to have more of the documents made, screaming profanity and screeching off down the street. I waited a few minutes to make sure he didn't come back, then took Nicholas to the emergency room."

"The ER doctor didn't report it?" Arnett asked.

She looked off into the far corner of the room. "I told them he'd been climbing a tree, a tall one in our yard he knew he wasn't supposed to climb, and must have hit several branches on the way down. He had a few bumps on his head, and a few bruises on his arms."

"They believed that?" Jo asked.

"Of course not. But they couldn't say for certain it wasn't true, so they let it go at that." She met Jo's eyes again. "I've learned that no matter how much people protest otherwise, they grasp onto any plausible excuse to discount evidence of domestic abuse."

Jo nodded gently. If she had a dollar for every mother or partner or teacher—or even police officer—who'd turned a blind eye because it was easier, she'd be able to afford one of the Harristown mansions.

"And after, he swore up and down it'd never happen again?" Arnett asked.

Gia's eyes flashed to him, the fear now anger. "Oh, no, absolutely not. I don't get gorgeous bouquets of flowers or diamonds from Tiffany. He wasn't repentant and he damned well expected *me* to be if I didn't want worse next time."

A memory came back to Jo. "The day Nicole was murdered. Nicholas had been in a bike accident. That wasn't an accident, was it?"

Gia shook her head, and pulled at the wad of Kleenex. "Anthony shoved him, and his bike slammed into a tree."

"And Karen mentioned something about Nicole breaking her arm a few months ago, and you being so upset about it you hid behind sunglasses?" Jo asked.

"Like I said, people are eager to believe whatever you tell them if it means they don't have to see the bruises on your face. Although Anthony is usually very careful to avoid our faces, or anywhere hard to cover up." She shifted in her chair. "But yes. About six months ago, he started going after Nicole. Up until then, he'd never even spanked her, and I'd managed to convince myself he wouldn't, because she was his little darling and he doted on her."

She paused a long moment, then sat upright. Her eyes bounced between the two of them, now defiant. "I know what you're thinking. Why didn't I leave? Why didn't I protect my children? What sort of horrible mother doesn't protect her son, and then lets the same thing happen to her daughter? But it's not that easy."

"No, it isn't," Jo said.

Gia turned to Arnett, taking his silence for a challenge. "A man like Anthony—you're not his wife or his child. You're possessions, like his car and his boat and his huge house. Set dressing for his ego. There's no way in hell he'd let me walk away, he'd kill me first. He told me in no uncertain terms that he'd arrange a very tragic accident if I even thought about leaving."

"But then he killed Nicole," Jo prodded.

"Yes. And I knew it was only a matter of time. For Nicholas and for me, and for—" She placed a protective hand over her abdomen. "He's careful not to leave marks—my stomach is his favorite place to punch me. I was stupid. I tried to tell myself there were worse things in life than a few beatings, and that I could love Nicholas and Nicole enough for both of us. I told myself if it got too bad, I'd leave. That was delusional. We were always on a collision course and I just couldn't see it until it was too late."

"So you bought yourself a new identity," Arnett said. "But I don't get the part about the million-five. That's just gonna piss him off—even a man who didn't already have murder in his eyes would hunt you down for that."

She leaned forward toward him. "So what should I have done? Left with a few thousand dollars? How far would that have gotten us? I have an art degree, and the only work I've ever done is modeling, and I'm a decade and two children too old for that. The paltry sum I make with my ceramics wouldn't pay our grocery bill. Running from someone rich and powerful takes money. You need to be able to disappear without a trace, and move again at a moment's notice if he gets close. Even a couple hundred thousand wasn't going to give me what I needed."

She was right. Arnett nodded.

She continued. "And, as soon as I disappeared, everyone was going to assume that I killed Nicole. He'd have told you that anyway, so you'd all hunt me down. And I have no way to prove anything to anyone. I never filed a police report against him, and I never told anyone—not even my mother, even though she's gone now—because I was too damned ashamed."

"The emergency room reports. They'll corroborate your story," Jo said.

She snorted out an angry puff of air. "Nicole broke her arm, what does that prove?"

"There's the fall from the tree—"

"Oh no, I'm far too smart for my own good. I took him to the ER over in Springfield where nobody would recognize us, and I used fake names. I don't even remember what names I gave them."

"Nicholas would confirm it," Arnett said.

"Of course he would. And Anthony will hire the best attorneys who'll argue I manipulated Nicholas into lying or brainwashed him, and he'll have to go through hell. And at the end of the day, Anthony will still come for me." She threw up a hand in a stop motion. "No. Disappearing was the only way, and now it's over. As soon as you let us go, I'm a dead woman, and God only knows what will happen to Nicholas." The panic returned to her eyes, and two fresh tears fell down her cheeks.

Jo reached over and grabbed her arm again. "We're not going to let that happen. I promise you."

Gia looked at her like she was a child spinning tales about sugared plums and cotton candy. "I'm sure you'll try."

Jo held her gaze. "That's why we need your help to put him away for Nicole's murder. So, please. What happened that morning with Nicole?"

She mopped her tears with the tissue, and shook her head. "I keep telling you, I don't know."

Jo leaned closer to her. "But you're sure he killed her. Why?"

Her gaze bounced between Jo and Arnett. "Because, who else could have done it? He's come close to killing her several times now already. You told me yourself he was at the school right before recess. Maybe he ran into Nicole when recess started, I don't know. Maybe she tried to follow him and he got upset when she wouldn't listen and he shook her too hard, I don't know."

Prickles of doubt tugged at Jo, and she fought to keep her expression unchanged. "So he didn't say anything to you, or come home with any evidence, anything like that?"

Gia's expression turned sour. "God, no. He put on quite the show. Stormed into the house angry at me, demanding to know why I hadn't managed to get a message through to him at work. Threatened to sue the school for not protecting Nicole adequately. Then he stormed off to his office to talk to his lawyer, and stayed in there the rest of the night. When I went to check on Nicholas before I went to bed, I heard him inside sobbing. He never came to bed, and when I passed him in the hall the next morning on the way out of the shower, he still reeked of Scotch."

"You didn't try to talk to him? He didn't try to comfort you?" Arnett asked.

"I told you, he never apologized after hurting one of us. I was just happy he left me and Nicholas alone, and I was focused on figuring out what to do."

So, not only did Gia not have evidence that Anthony had harmed Nicole, she was only assuming he had. Or, was this all some elaborate attempt to get them to go after Anthony? Could this be some sort of twisted revenge for the affair he was supposedly having?

Jo exchanged a surreptitious look with Arnett, then stood. "We'll need to get all this written up in a statement for you to sign. We'd like to talk to Nicholas briefly if that's okay with you. We'd prefer to talk to him alone, but you do have the right to be present."

"No, that's fine, I understand. You don't want me pressuring him. I have no problem with that."

"Thank you. We'll bring him back in here after," Jo said.

She took a deep breath as she nodded. "What about Anthony?"

"We'll have him in custody shortly." Jo turned as she reached the door, "Oh, one more question. Is Karen Phelps having an affair with your husband?"

Gia's brows shot up. "If she is, she damned well deserves what she'll get."

CHAPTER TWENTY-SEVEN

Jo turned to Arnett once they were out of the room and out of earshot.

"What do you think?" he asked.

"I'm torn, but mostly it fits. Sophie told me she's known for being friendly on a surface level, but doesn't let people into her life—classic abused partner behavior. If she had hurt Nicole herself, she'd have put on a huge show of being distraught about losing her daughter. Maybe she's just using it as a way to get out and get him put in jail, but if so, she's giving us nothing to work with."

"Agreed. But did he actually harm Nicole?"

Jo shifted, and took a deep breath. "That's the million-dollar question. He at least had the opportunity, and it's possible busy teachers and kids wouldn't even notice a known parent talking to one of their own children."

"Or even carrying them. When they're that young they just fall asleep on your shoulder. Would anyone have even noticed if she was dead?"

"Good point."

Arnett rubbed his chin. "So I'm thinking maybe if we lean on him, we might get him to say something we can use—"

Jo's phone rang. She put the call on speaker. "Christine."

"We got him," Lopez said. "They're bringing him into interrogation three right now. But don't get your hopes up—he's in a mood."

"Ah, well. Let's see if we can't turn his day around," Jo said. "Thanks."

She hung up, and followed Arnett down the hall.

As they pushed through the door to interrogation three, the smell of coffee hit Jo like a forklift. The source was a venti Starbucks cup sitting on the gray table in front of Anthony Marchand. His black hair was short and meticulously styled in deceptively casual layers, and his red Armani tie popped from his dark-gray button-down shirt. His taut, chiseled face was handsome, and his eyes flicked over Jo before returning to Arnett. He picked up his drink, and took a languorous sip.

Jo fought the urge to punch him directly in the neck.

Arnett turned to the uniformed officer, whose name tag read 'Melber'. "Did you stop for the Starbucks, or did he sneak it into the squad car?"

The officer's face reddened. "You were gonna give him coffee anyway. What's the harm?"

Arnett shot him a scornful look. "You give that courtesy to everyone, or just the perps with hundreds dripping out of their pockets? Did you at least remember to Mirandize him?"

Melber stiffened and nodded. Arnett made a dismissive gesture toward the door. Melber couldn't leave fast enough.

Jo studied Marchand's face. He was calm, almost smug—not the expression you'd expect from a man whose wife just stole over a million dollars from him. Did he know?

He appraised her in return. "I was under the impression I had a scheduled meeting with you tomorrow, yet you sent officers to embarrass me at a client's site. That puts my reputation, and thus my business, in jeopardy. I call it harassment. Something my lawyer will be taking up with your lieutenant."

"Know what really puts your reputation in jeopardy? Killing your daughter," Arnett said.

Marchand's face paled, then shot through with red. He jutted forward over the table toward Arnett. "How dare you?" he hissed.

"We have security footage putting you on campus right before she was killed." Arnett plucked a piece of fluff from his sleeve. "What'd she do, run up and wrinkle your shirt? Get paint on your expensive tie?"

"I never—" Marchand started, but stopped suddenly, as though a stone had dropped into his throat. He straightened, tugged at his cuffs, and reached for his coffee. "My lawyer is on his way."

"Guess something in his busy schedule cleared out." Arnett smirked. "Lucky you."

Jo leaned back in her chair. "Here's what I find fascinating. Most men would be upset that someone killed their daughter and would rush to give the police all the help they could. But you, you dodge our calls and refuse to talk to us without an attorney present, and make sure to put a whole week between her death and your visit to us, because your work schedule is apparently so busy. Innocent men don't behave like that."

"Who the hell do you think you are?" Marchand's eyes flashed between them. "I showed up to identify her body! Do you think that was easy for me? You'd already talked to my wife, she answered all of your questions. She told me you were out looking for pedophiles! How exactly was I going to help with that? I'm sorry you don't approve of how I mourn, Detective, but I have responsibilities, and I've always dealt with stress by throwing myself into work."

Jo watched the tense set of his jaw, and made a split-second decision. "So why did your wife just transfer well over a million dollars to an offshore account and attempt to flee with your son under new identities?"

Marchand jerked upright, mouth gaping, into his coffee. It toppled and the lid popped off, splashing coffee across the table and down onto his pants. "I need my phone. I need to speak with my wife."

Arnett threw him a box of Kleenex. "Not going to happen. Why would she do that, Anthony?"

He slammed his cuffed fists on the table. "I need to speak with my wife! Now! You have no right to keep me from talking to her!"

Arnett chuckled. "You sure seem pissed off. But I guess I'd be, too, if my wife made a fool of me like that."

Marchand's foot lashed out into the leg of the table. It flew across the room, spraying coffee across the wall and floor.

Jo tackled Marchand, then flipped him face down onto the linoleum and pressed a knee into his back. She leaned over and hissed into his ear. "Nicole trusted you. You're her father—you were supposed to protect her."

She stared down at the side of his face, squashed down into the floor, as it distorted with impotent rage. His muscles tensed under her, a physical mirror of his struggle not to speak.

She pushed off of him. "Get up. Try something like that again and we'll put you in leg chains, too."

He raised himself first to his knees, then back into his chair, refusing to touch the coffee now staining his shirt and pants. "I believe once a suspect asks for his attorney, the interrogation has to stop, Detective. You failed to honor that. This is an illegal interrogation."

"You only said your attorney was on his way, smart guy. You never said you wouldn't speak until he got here," Arnett said, and turned toward the door.

Jo followed him out, catching a glimpse of the newly refreshed rage on Marchand's face as she left.

Arnett turned back to Jo. "Nice try. We almost got him to break."

She shrugged. "No matter what he is, he isn't stupid—"

Her phone interrupted her. Lopez again—and there was no way she'd interrupt an interrogation unless it was important. "Christine, what's up?"

Her voice was urgent. "Eileen Pham is dead."

CHAPTER TWENTY-EIGHT

By the time Jo and Arnett made arrangements for securing both Anthony and Gia Marchand, Marzillo and her team had already arrived at Briar Ridge and were processing the scene. Jo pulled aside the two officers already present, Officer Reyes and the responding officer from Nicole's murder scene. Both men were trying to calm the sobbing assistant principal, Sally Lechliter.

"What are we looking at?" she asked after pulling Reyes out of earshot.

He looked down at his notebook. "According to the assistant principal, Pham walked out of her office, stumbling randomly and looking around like she didn't know where she was. She approached one of the support staff, Riley Pratt, and said something nobody understood, then approached Ms. Lechliter, shielding her eyes and complaining that someone had changed the light settings. She said something else, but Ms. Lechliter couldn't make sense of it. She didn't know what to do, so ran to get her some water from the suite's main bathroom. By the time she got back, Pham had collapsed to the floor, and was in the throes of a seizure. She and Pratt hurried to move chairs and tables out of her way, believing it was best to let the seizure run its course. When she didn't come out of it, they called nine-one-one. By the time the paramedics arrived, she was dead."

"Did she have a medical condition of some sort?" Jo asked.

"Not as far as Ms. Lechliter knows."

Jo turned and looked at the assistant principal. On a good day Sally Lechliter came across like a lamb searching for her mother;

now she looked like she'd been struck by lightning. Blouse untucked and long beaded necklace half over one shoulder, her hands fluttered between her face and a hank of escaped hair from her brown bun. She tucked it up, rubbed her nose, tucked it up again, pulled at her chin, tucked the hair up again, and clasped her neck.

Arnett followed her gaze. "I'm amazed she managed to tell you anything."

"Poor woman. Three deaths in just over a week, and now she's in charge." Jo looked back at Reyes. "We'll talk to her after we check with our techs. Have next of kin been notified?"

"Pham isn't married or in a relationship, and as far as Lechliter knows, all she has is a sister in California. We already called her."

Jo thanked him and turned with Arnett to the stacks of protective gear. Once suited up, they slipped under the crime tape and through the half door that led to the rest of the office suite. Marzillo came to greet them, then shifted over to Eileen Pham's body.

Pham lay face up as though staring at the ceiling, lost in thought, her legs and arms extended flat against the ground. Just like corpse pose, Jo noted ironically. She'd always found the yoga pose's moniker incredibly inaccurate, considering the very small percentage of corpses she'd encountered that were actually posed that way. Eileen's aubergine skirt was slashed with dust from the floor, otherwise her clothes were in perfect condition, blouse tucked and collar crisply folded, as if even in death Eileen Pham refused to be less than professional.

Jo had been heartbroken when she saw Nicole's body, and confused when they'd found Layla Madani's. Now she was both those things, but most of all, she was angry. Three people now dead, and why? So an abusive father could cover his tracks? Or is that just what someone wanted her to believe?

"The ME hasn't arrived yet," Marzillo said. "We've photographed everything and I did a 3D scan, although I doubt we'll

need it. We're processing her office now because from what I can
see and the witness statements, I believe she was poisoned."

"Why?"

"Three things. One, the description of her behavior before
she died. The symptoms don't line up with a stroke or the sort
of seizure an epileptic would have. She wasn't making sense, but
her speech wasn't slurred. She was walking and moving her arms
well. The seizure itself came on after the other symptoms, and
just before death. And, look at this." Marzillo squatted down and
pointed to Eileen's open eyes. "See how dilated her pupils are?
The assistant principal said when she came out she was wild-eyed,
eyes wide and dark, complaining about how bright the light was.
That means they were dilated well before the seizure. And while
her eyes are open now, they were closed when I got here. None
of that is necessarily conclusive, but together it paints a picture
that's more consistent with a drug-induced seizure. Two, nobody's
aware of any history of seizures, and she doesn't have any sort of
medic alert bracelet to indicate a problem of that nature. And,
three, given the circumstances surrounding the death, I guarantee
you the ME would want to do a tox panel even if she did have
such a history."

Jo nodded. Medical examiners looked more closely at surrounding circumstances when deaths were suspicious, particularly
if the victim was in good health and death by natural causes was
less likely.

"And take a look at this." Marzillo stood back up and carefully
entered the principal's office. She pointed to the top of the desk.
"See that smoothie?"

Jo recognized the tumbler with the ill-fitting lid they'd knocked
over during their first visit. It lay on its side, and a channel of green
liquid had oozed from it.

"If you look closely at the edges, you can see the liquid has
started to dry, but only just. So this hasn't been exposed to air for

long, and my guess is she was drinking it just before she died. In fact, if you lean close to her face, you can smell it. And it's not a smell you can mistake."

"We found that out the hard way the other day. Smells like complete ass," Arnett said.

"Well said. And I'm sure it tastes the same, which makes it a perfect vehicle for poison. Depending on the type and amount, you probably wouldn't even notice. And based on the symptoms, I'm guessing a form of atropine."

Something clicked in Jo's memory. "Dilated pupils. Belladonna?" Her voice was skeptical.

Marzillo smiled at her tone. "Sounds dramatic, I know. And not necessarily belladonna, but yes, some form of that same toxin would be my guess. It's not as rare a plant as people think. Lopez's mother has some in her backyard. Didn't even realize it until Lopez told her. Then her mother tried to rip it out, but Lopez wouldn't let her."

"Why in the hell not?" Arnett said.

"I asked her the same thing, and all I could get out of her was a mumbled response about the zombie apocalypse, and how we'd all be glad we knew her when the time came." Marzillo stared at them unblinking.

They sat with that in silence for a moment. Then Jo said, "Good to know. So you'll have that tested, and it sounds like we need to find out as much as we can about that drink."

"Anything else?" Arnett asked.

"Not yet. I'll let you know if we or the ME find anything else."

Jo and Arnett carefully made their way back through the half door and stripped off their protective gear, then headed back into the large entryway. Sally Lechliter was still talking with the officers, but seemed slightly calmer than she had before.

They crossed over to her. She didn't notice them, focused as she was on Officer Reyes, and jumped when Jo spoke to her.

"I'm so sorry," Jo said. "I didn't mean to startle you. Can you walk us through what happened?"

"I don't know. I don't know what happened, it was so strange, like some sort of horror film." She continued on, repeating what Officer Reyes had just told them, gripping her neck again while tears filled her eyes. "But the seizure just kept on, and then she was still, but not in a good way."

"Do you know what she was doing just before it happened?" Jo asked.

"She was in her office, doing some sort of paperwork."

Jo glanced around the suite. "Who has access to her office during the day? Does she keep it locked up when she's not inside?"

Sally shook her head. "There wasn't any real reason to. She was emphatic about having an open-door policy, so unless she or I was in a private meeting, we kept our doors open while we worked. And we were constantly up and down for whatever reason—getting printouts, going to deal with students as needed, whatever."

"So the office was conceivably left open with nobody around?" Arnett asked.

Her face crinkled. "Well, yes, technically there are times when the office is empty for a minute or two, if we're off doing tasks and someone has to go to the bathroom or something. But someone's pretty much always around. We have Riley and Jennifer that work out here, and in the afternoons we have a student volunteer who comes from our sister high school for work study. Between the five of us…"

Jo latched onto a shift in tone. "What? Did you remember something?"

"Well, nothing. It's just that, on Monday mornings Eileen and I do our classroom observations, so we're both out of the office for a couple of hours. But still, Riley and Jennifer should have been here the whole time, and they'd have noticed anything strange."

Jo glanced around again—the space was relatively small, and it would be difficult for anyone to get into the principal's office unnoticed. "Did either of you have any meetings this morning?"

"Of course," she said, tucking the hank of hair into her bun again. "We have our agendas computerized. I can have them printed out for you if you like, or give you a temporary password to access it directly if you'd prefer?"

"Both, if that's possible, thank you," Jo said. "Do you happen to remember who she met with today?"

"I'm sorry, I don't. I was focused on my own work."

Jo didn't get the sense that multitasking was one of her strengths. "And I'm guessing that if an emergency cropped up while you were in a meeting, you wouldn't think twice about leaving a parent alone in your office?"

She shook her head. "No, not at all. But there were no emergencies today that I'm aware of."

"Twice now we've noticed a green smoothie drink in Eileen's office. Do you know what that is?" Jo asked.

Sally's eyes filled with tears. "She was a big believer in nutrition. She always made sure the kids had healthy options in the cafeteria, and that they all got extra modules on eating right and staying healthy. That's one of the reasons she wanted to work at a private school, because she could have more control over what our children were fed."

Jo waited not-so-patiently as Sally finished. "And the smoothie was part of that?"

"Yes. I mean, no, not for the kids. But she had one every day, made it fresh in the morning and brought it here to drink through the day. She said it gave her continuous energy and antioxidants. She'd hold it up when she saw us making pots of coffee. Claimed it was a far better boost than caffeine ever could be. But I'll tell you what, I tried it once, and if that's what it takes to have energy,

I'll need mine in an IV drip, because I brushed my teeth twice and still couldn't get rid of the taste." Her hand flew to her mouth. "Oh, that's a horrible thing to say, isn't it?"

Jo put on a reassuring smile. "No, not at all. I'm sure she knew it wasn't the tastiest thing on the planet."

"Oh, she always claimed you got used to it after a while."

"Who knew she drank these smoothies?" Arnett asked.

"Everyone. She was always preaching about them."

"Just to the people who worked here, or to parents too?"

"Everybody. It was sort of a running joke. Wait." Her brow creased as she put the pieces together. "You think someone tampered with her smoothie?"

"We don't think anything yet. It's possible that the stress of recent events triggered a condition she didn't know she had, or created a new one." The half-truth flowed automatically off Jo's tongue. "One last question. Do you remember seeing Mr. or Mrs. Marchand around the office today?'

"No. In fact, Gia Marchand called in to excuse Nicholas from school today."

"Thank you," Jo said. "Can you get us Eileen's scheduling information as soon as possible? And we'll need the security footage from this morning."

"I'll gather it all for you now," Sally said, hand around her throat again, and skittered off to the east wing.

Jo turned to Arnett and sent a text to Sophie as she spoke. "Time to find out exactly where Anthony and Gia have been all morning."

CHAPTER TWENTY-NINE

Tom Barclay, Anthony Marchand's attorney, had arrived at HQ while Jo and Arnett were at the scene of Eileen's murder. When they returned, he had the answers for their questions ready to go. Yes, Anthony had dropped off the field trip permission slip, but was off campus before recess, and never saw Nicole. He was back at work fifteen minutes later, and security cameras could verify that. That didn't conclusively prove anything, but he did have an airtight alibi for both Layla Madani's and Eileen Pham's death—he was in meetings with no fewer than ten employees for the entirety of both days. No, he would not provide his DNA without a warrant, and no, he wouldn't take a polygraph.

Jo and Arnett refused to release him, despite Barclay's vigorous protests. They had the right to hold him for up to seventy-two hours, and there was no way they were going to release him and put Gia or Nicholas at risk until they had a full grasp of what was going on.

"I was really hoping we'd get him to take a polygraph," Jo said. "Even if he isn't guilty of the murder, we could get some solid evidence of the abuse."

"No doubt that's exactly why he refused," Arnett said.

"Because here's the problem I'm coming up against," Jo said. "Eileen made her smoothie fresh every morning. So if she was poisoned and that was the vehicle for it, Anthony Marchand has a solid alibi for that. We still have to wait for the test results, but it's the safest bet I can see."

"So that makes me think they're messing with us. Maybe the whole domestic abuse story is BS, and the plan was to meet up with Anthony later and leave the country together. Maybe Anthony killed Nicole, but Gia killed Madani and Pham in order to cover it up."

Jo fingered the diamond at her throat. "Except my gut says she's telling the truth. She was terrified, and for the first time, her reaction to Nicole's death makes sense."

"So what are you thinking?"

"Karen. If she's having an affair with him, maybe she'd kill for him. Maybe she's hoping he'll run away with her."

Arnett's eyes turned to steel. "Yeah, well. People who betray their spouses are definitely looking for something. So we pull her in. And I say we tell her that Anthony's already made a statement."

"Make her think he turned on her? Interesting." Jo's fist bounced against her thigh. "So what do we do with Gia in the meantime? Regardless of what else, we have her dead to rights on the forged passports, and she's the dictionary definition of a flight risk. And my gut's been wrong before, but, honestly, I think it's more likely that Nicholas accidentally killed Nicole, and Gia's covering up for him. Maybe we ruled him out too soon, especially given Layla's death. The idea of losing both of her children might be too much for her."

Arnett shook his head. "I don't get that. He's too young to stand trial. Why murder two people to cover it up?"

Jo swept her hair back off her forehead. "Because the stigma would follow him forever? He'd never get out from under it, and nobody would want that life for their child. Add in the mandatory psych evaluations he'd have to take…"

"Okay, yeah, I see your point. It's possible."

"What about asking the judge to send her home with an ankle monitor?" Jo asked. "Then we don't have to separate them. You call ADA Rockney, and I'll get Karen to come pay us a visit."

*

Karen Phelps hunched over in the interrogation room chair, legs crossed and arms tucked into her lap as though trying to make herself even smaller than she already was. She stared up at Jo and Arnett as they entered, her eyes wary and frightened.

Jo decided to start things off on a gentle note. "Thank you for coming."

"I'm not sure how I can help, but I'll do what I can. Do you know how long this is going to take? Molly said she'd watch the kids for me, but she's watching the shop and there's only so long they can be in the store without breaking something."

"We'll be as fast as we can." Jo took a moment to settle herself into the chair across from Karen while Arnett pulled a second one kitty-corner to her.

"It's all over town that you arrested Gia and Anthony. Did they kill Eileen Pham?"

Jo chose her words carefully. "We just finished talking to Anthony. In fact, we'd like to hear what you have to say before we go any further."

Her eyes bounced between them, and her arms pulled tighter around her middle. "What I have to say about what?"

Arnett leaned slightly closer to her. "Word around the school-yard is that you're having an affair with a married man."

Her face blazed red and her mouth dropped open. "Who told you that?"

"Is it true?" Jo asked.

Her mouth snapped shut again, and she shifted in her chair. "I don't see what that has to do with anything."

"When he's under arrest for murder, I'd say it has quite a lot to do with his motivation for possibly killing his child," Arnett said.

She stared at the two of them like they'd suddenly started speaking in tongues. "I don't understand. And I'm not sure I should say anything else."

"That's up to you," Arnett said. "But Anthony has been saying plenty. Now, I don't believe for a second you had anything to do with any of these deaths. But Marchand is desperate, and he's going to say anything he can to get himself off the hook for murder. So we want to give you an opportunity to tell your side of everything."

Her brows knit, but now in bewildered anger. "He said we're having an affair? That's a complete lie. No wonder Gia's been acting strange if he told her that! No way. There's no way I'd do that to her. Why would he say that?"

Jo watched her carefully as Arnett repeated the accusations, trying to get her to slip up—and something wasn't right. She'd been caught, and Jo had seen the guilt on her face. But once she heard Anthony's name that had changed. And her body language was genuine. Indignant expression, eye contact that was firm but not aggressive, no hesitation.

Karen was having an affair—but not with Anthony Marchand.

Jo returned to the beginning, the day Nicole was murdered, and the pieces immediately fell into place.

"How long have you been having an affair with Jim Karnegi?" Jo asked.

Arnett, in a testament to his trust in their partnership, didn't flinch at the abrupt shift.

The color blazed back into Karen's cheeks, her mouth snapped shut, and she looked away, down and to her left. "A little over a month. Oh, God, he's going to kill me. He'll lose his job if people find out."

"Never mind his wife," Jo said, her mind coalescing: his previous firing, his sensitivity to the accusation Gia had made about his flirting, Jim and Karen overseeing the playground, Karen's intense guilt the day Nicole died.

She leaned forward, holding Karen's gaze. "It's time for you tell the truth about the day Nicole was killed."

CHAPTER THIRTY

"We didn't kill her, I swear we didn't," Karen said. "But it was our fault."

"What happened?" Jo asked, gently.

Karen shifted in her chair and stared into the one-way glass. "We were just—we didn't think it would do any harm."

"What would?" Jo asked.

She turned to stare at Jo, pleading with her eyes. "Whenever possible we arranged to work the same recess. It was stupid, and I should have known it. I even told him that, but he laughed and said it would be exciting. And we're at that phase when everything is new and you can't keep your hands off each other, and it all just made it that much sexier."

Jo nodded. "I get it. That thrill adds to the adrenaline."

"Yes, right, exactly. And we didn't really *do* anything. Brushed hands as we walked past each other. A quick peck behind a utility shed when our paths crossed."

"But then?"

"Well, that's it really. Except one peck became two, and…" A tear rolled down her cheek, and she leaned forward into her hands.

"And that became three, and four," Arnett said.

She nodded with her head still in her hands. "He pulled me into him and kissed me, and it probably lasted a couple of minutes. There were no kids nearby when we ducked behind, and we both listened for footsteps if someone came close. But… we weren't actively watching the kids during those couple of minutes."

The anger flashed in Jo, dark and deep, along with a picture of Nicole's distorted face. This woman had been put in charge of watching other people's children, and she'd turned the responsibility into a make-out session like some hormonal teenaged babysitter. How close had Emily or Isabelle come to suffering the same fate? And Karnegi was worse—he was a paid professional, and he should have known better. Is this why he was fired from his previous job?

Jo paused for a moment to get herself back under control. Alienating Karen at this point wasn't going to help anything, so she tried to keep her voice as gentle as possible. "And in those two minutes, someone snatched Nicole."

She looked up, her pleading eyes now bouncing back and forth between Jo and Arnett, tears trailing charcoal lines of mascara down her face. "Harristown is so safe, nothing bad ever happens here! It never occurred to me that something like *this* would happen, that the children would be in any real danger. I was there to tend to scraped knees and break up fights, and make sure the kids went back in the classrooms once the bell rang. A little kiss shouldn't have interfered with that."

Jo tried to be kind. "Nobody ever thinks bad things are going to happen to them. That's how we all manage to get through our days, by pretending that the ugly part of life isn't hovering over us every minute."

Karen wiped beneath her eyes, and Arnett handed her a tissue. "Only it did and it's my fault and Nicole's dead because of me."

After a glance at Jo's face, Arnett jumped in. "Nicole's dead because of the person who killed her, not because of you."

"Somehow I doubt Gia will see it that way," Karen said into the tissue.

"Was it Jim's idea to work the recesses together?" Jo asked.

"At first. But I figured I had to do my volunteer hours anyway, so why not?"

"And who initiated the relationship?" Jo asked.

"He did." She took a deep breath. "I mean, I've been told all my life I'm a flirt, but that's just who I am, I do it with everyone. So I guess in a way you could say I did, but not intentionally. He responded, and took it up a notch. And so I flirted back more, and the next thing I knew, he kissed me."

"You said earlier you'd never do that to a friend," Arnett asked. "But you did know Jim was married, right?"

Her ears reddened and she looked down into the tissue in her hands. "I did know. I'm not proud of it." She looked back up. "But you know what they say, if someone goes looking for it, there's a problem at home. It's not breaking up a marriage if the marriage is already bad. And believe me, his marriage is bad."

Arnett's jaw clenched. "Let me guess. She doesn't make time for him. She's a harpy, and browbeats him. They never have sex anymore, he can't even remember the last time, and a man has needs."

Karen stared up at him, expression mortified. "You don't know her."

"Do *you*?" he asked.

Karen shrank slightly into herself, and Jo watched an insecure child replace the adult woman. How was it possible to be coming up on thirty-five and still be able to fall for these ridiculous lines? There was only one possible answer—because Karen wanted to fall for them. She *needed* to.

"Did he ever tell you why he left his last job?" Jo asked.

Her posture straightened as she adjusted to the more solid ground. "Of course. He wanted to come to Briar Ridge because of its reputation. The quality of the academics, and the possibility of moving up the ranks."

"Did he say why his previous marriage broke up?'

"She didn't want to move out of Rhode Island. She wanted to stay close to her family." Karen saw the look Jo and Arnett exchanged. "What?"

"Jim Karnegi was fired from Mary Dyer Elementary School for inappropriate conduct," Jo said.

That got the reaction Jo wanted. Karen shot upright in her chair, like a rod had been shoved through her spine. "What inappropriate conduct?"

"And his wife left him because he cheated on her." Jo watched closely—would the double whammy be enough to jolt Karen out of her fantasy?

Karen narrowed her eyes. "You're lying."

"Why would we lie about that, Karen? These are facts. We verified them." Jo pulled out her phone. "We can call his ex-wife right now if you want, and you can ask her yourself. And, don't forget, you heard Gia say he came on to her last year."

Karen stared at the phone for a long moment, confusion replacing her disbelief, then transforming into anger. "He played me. He doesn't love me."

Love, in a month? Jo felt a tinge of pity for her. "And because of his past employment history, we need to ask one more time. Have you told us everything that happened the day Nicole died? Was Jim ever out of your sight?"

She gasped a sharp breath, but shook her head vigorously. "No, absolutely not. He may be a jerk, but he's not a killer. I watched him closely the entire time we were at recess because I was looking for the little signals, and trying to find the moments we could sneak out of sight together. I swear it."

"And where were you this morning?" Jo asked.

"After I dropped Katie and Willie off at school, I went back home. I cleaned a bit, then worked on my jewelry."

"And you were alone? No housekeeper or anything that can vouch for you?" Arnett asked.

A defensive flush colored her neck. "I can't afford a housekeeper."

Jo stood up. "Bob, can I speak to you outside for a moment?"

He got up and followed her out, leaving a frightened Karen staring after them.

"Are you thinking what I'm thinking?" he said when they were out of earshot.

"If you're thinking that Karnegi and Karen were at the scene of both Nicole's and Layla Madani's murders together, and really are each other's only alibi, then yes."

"So what, Karnegi abuses kids, that's why he was kicked out of his previous school? And Madani recognized the toy he used to get her over to the dumpster, and so he had to kill her?"

"But why would he need to lure Nicole? He was a teacher, she would have trusted him. And if Madani had recognized the toy, why would she have gone up the pyramid with him?"

"No idea. But I think we need to talk to him again," he said.

Jo checked the time quickly. "Six thirty. He should be finished work for the day. I say we call and tell him Karen's here, and ask him to come join us."

"Do it."

Jo tapped the call into the phone and waited while it rang. It went to voicemail. Jo left a message asking him to call back as soon as he got the message.

"Should we just go to his house? Make some excuse, have Karen wait while we go get him?"

"He may still be at school. I say we call his wife and find out if he's home before we drive all the way over there." She did a quick search for the number, and tapped it in.

"Hello," a woman's voice answered.

"Hello, I'm Detective Josette Fournier of the Oakhurst County SPDU. Is this Rachel Karnegi?"

"Yes. Are you the detectives that were here the other night?"

"We are, yes. We're looking for your husband, and he's not answering his phone. Is he there by chance?" Jo asked.

"I'm sorry, he's not. He flew to Nevada last night because his mother had a stroke."

*

Rachel Karnegi gave the name and number of the hospital where Jim was visiting his mother, along with his flight information. Jo thanked her and hung up.

She dialed again immediately. "First things first. We need to verify his mother's in the hospital."

Within minutes, she'd confirmed that yes, she was, that she had a stroke during the timeframe in question, and that Jim Karnegi was at that moment sitting in the waiting room with his father while his mother was undergoing several tests. The nurse asked if she wanted to speak to him, then called him over.

"Detective." Jim's voice was fatigued, and defeated. "Should I call you back on my own phone? I got your message, but haven't had a chance to return your call yet."

"I'm very sorry to hear about your mother. Do they know yet if she'll recover?"

"They're still running tests. They won't know the full extent of the damage to her brain for a while yet."

"She's in good hands, I'm sure."

"Thank you. But I assume you called because of Eileen Pham's death?"

"I did, in part. I already know you flew out to Nevada last night, so there's just one thing I need to know. You're having an affair, and I need to hear from your mouth who you're having it with."

"Who said I'm having an affair?"

"The woman herself. So now is the time to be forthcoming, because I'm very sure you don't want us to have to start nosing around and asking awkward questions to verify it for ourselves."

He paused for a long moment before answering. "Karen Phelps. But it's nothing serious."

"Does she know that?"

"She knows I'm married and I've never made any suggestion that I'll leave my wife."

"I'd like to hear your version about what happened during recess on the day Nicole died."

His story matched up with Karen's in all important respects, but laid the onus of the neglect onto Karen—she'd been the one to initiate the kisses and pull him behind the buildings, he claimed.

"We also talked to your ex-wife, and she claimed you cheated on her, too. So I have to ask again—was Gia Marchand lying when she said you came on to her?"

Another long pause. "I wouldn't say I came on to her, exactly."

Yeah, right. "The signs of possible distress you saw in Nicholas. Would they be consistent with physical abuse?"

A pause, but a shorter one this time. "They could be. Do you think he was being abused?"

"And you still don't believe Nicholas could have accidentally hurt his sister?"

"Karen and I weren't out of sight of the tetherball court for long enough. It just wasn't possible."

She had him wrong-footed—could she push her luck and try a bluff? "One last question, and before I ask it, I want to let you know that I've talked to your former school. Would you like to tell me why you were fired?"

He let out a deep sigh. "Look, I know sleeping with women who have children in my class isn't smart, and I know sleeping with the assistant principal was even less smart. But if you're going to tell me I'm a sex addict, you can save your breath. I've already called the eight-hundred number. It isn't for me. We're all consenting adults, and each of those women knew I was married."

Jo let out a silent breath of relief as she ended the call. She'd still need to verify when the principal came back from vacation, but that was the answer she was hoping for. Serial cheating might not be a pleasant behavior—his ex-wife could attest to that—but it was a far cry from molesting children.

"Well," Arnett said. "If Marzillo's theory is right, there's no way he poisoned Pham."

"No, although Karen still could have, and we've seen pairs of killers working together before. But we don't have any evidence, and they'll certainly testify to cover one another if necessary." Jo rubbed her forehead, frustrated.

"And if Karen wasn't having an affair with Anthony, Anthony didn't kill Nicole to hide his affair with Karen. So if *he's* the one involved, someone else must have helped him."

"Maybe he's sleeping with someone else?" Jo said. "Either way, I'm not sure what to make of all this, but I'm not sure we can hold Karen here."

Arnett nodded. "I say we send her home for now until we can get something concrete. It's late, we should go home and rest up. By tomorrow we should have something from the ME and have a better sense of whether Pham was actually poisoned, and maybe something on the security tapes will help us pull together enough to charge her or Marchand. And both Marzillo and Lopez should have something new for us."

Jo agreed. On the way home, she picked up a smothered burrito from Fernando's for her dinner. Once home, she took the burrito into the kitchen and ate standing over the counter. Her mother would have a fit if she knew—one of the non-negotiable bastions of civilization as far as Elisabeth Fournier Arpent was concerned was a sit-down dinner with cloth napkins, no television, and slow, deliberate enjoyment of one's food. *You have a beautiful dining room, Josette,* Jo could hear her say, with her signature headshake and the expression that communicated the rest of what she was thinking: *Maybe if you had a husband you'd use it.*

She chastised herself—she wasn't being fair. Since the miscarriage, her mother had made an effort to drop the disappointed-mother dynamic, and Jo had to meet her halfway. Years of learning was hard to erase, but if she didn't try, she'd never make it happen.

As Jo washed out the take-out container and threw it in the recycling bin, her phone rang.

"Janet," she said as she answered it. "Are you still processing? I'd have thought it was a fairly easy scene. Even my inner OCD bows to Pham's organization."

"It was fairly cut and dried, although I did find a notepad you may find interesting; it looks like an on-the-fly daily agenda. I e-mailed you a pic of it, but that's not the interesting information. I'm actually in Springfield right now, visiting a friend of mine."

"You've been spending too much time around Lopez," Jo said in response to Marzillo's long pause. "You're developing a flair for the dramatic."

Jo heard the smile in her voice as she responded. "The ME came to the conclusion I predicted. Eileen's symptoms veer too far away from death due to some natural cause. Given everything else going on, he's ordering a tox screen, and will specifically look for several classes of poisons. However, we both know how long tox screens can take, and I'm not waiting around to let a child killer get away. So I contacted a friend of mine who specializes in food safety tests, and he invited me over to his lab to dust off some old analysis muscles I haven't used in quite a while. He has an HPLC-MS/MS analysis he developed specifically for quantifying atropine and scopolamine with an extremely fast turn-around time for emergency situations—"

"Any chance that translates into English?" Jo laughed.

"It means he has a test that can tell if the toxins in belladonna are present, and in what amounts, and he can do it very quickly. The upshot is, there was enough of those toxins in Eileen Pham's smoothie to kill an entire classroom."

"So she was definitely poisoned," Jo said, nails tapping her granite counter.

"Unless someone wants to argue she hadn't ingested any of it and just happened to manifest the exact symptoms of atropine poisoning by coincidence."

"So someone could have pureed some berries and leaves and just dumped it in there?"

"Pretty much. Pull the lid off, dump it in, replace lid. You probably wouldn't even have to shake it, because Eileen was likely to do that each time before she drank, anyway. The whole thing could literally take fifteen seconds."

"But wouldn't she have noticed? I know the smoothies didn't taste good, but surely a toxin like that would have some sort of detectable taste?"

"Actually, the berries of the plant are sweet, that's why the plant is really dangerous if you have kids. They look pretty and taste good, and it only takes a few to kill you. It takes even less of the leaves or roots to kill you, and while I don't know, I can't imagine that would taste noticeably worse than the other greenery she'd already stuffed in there. But that said, given the amount of the toxins we found, even if she just took one swallow, decided it had gone bad and set the rest aside, it was probably already too late."

"That potent?"

"Maybe not if she took a genteel sip. But if she took a great big swallow, almost certainly. And that's what people normally do with health drinks that taste like you just face-planted in yard waste."

"Any idea how fresh the drink was? Could it have been from the day before?"

"No chance. Even just from the time I took the sample to the time we tested it, it's turned brown and congealed a fair amount."

"Could she have a big jug of it in a common refrigerator or something like that?"

"You'd have to ask the office staff, but I don't think it's relevant. To prevent the components from aging, the contents would have to be processed and placed in an industrially sealed container. As soon as that seal was popped, you'd start seeing degradation, and this was fresh. No way the poison could have been added before this morning."

"Damn." Unless they found a hole in Karnegi's alibi, that put him fully out. "Okay, thanks for doing that. It's above and beyond."

"Purely selfish, I wanted to know if I was right. Also, Lopez asked me to tell you she e-mailed you copies of Eileen Pham's phone records, both her cell phone and her office phone, from the last few days. She's going to take a closer look at it all, but she thought you might want to look it over yourself."

"Thanks. How's Ellie?"

"Okay. I'm about to head out to a late dinner with her, actually."

"You don't sound overly excited about it…"

"Yeah, I mean, she's great, but… not the smartest CPU on the desk. I have to figure out how important that is to me. Anyway, talk to you tomorrow."

As soon as Jo hung up the phone, she pulled up the e-mail from Lopez, downloaded the attachment to her phone, and sent it to her printer. She grabbed her Diet Coke and crossed into her home office.

Normally when she was at a crossroads like this, she and Arnett would go back to the beginning and talk through the logic of all the different suspects and possibilities, bringing their current perspective to the earlier portions of the case. But after their busy few days, Laura deserved an uninterrupted evening with her husband. She briefly considered calling Sophie, but stopped herself—she'd have to redact too much potentially damaging confidential information, and wouldn't have the ability to freely associate the way she needed to.

Her eyes landed on the large whiteboard covering half of her left office wall—it would have to do. She grabbed one of the markers and started jotting down notes as she thought.

This had all started with Nicole Marchand, and so the key most likely rested with her. With the subsequent murder of Layla Madani and Eileen Pham, the team had narrowed down the field of suspects considerably. All that was left were a smattering of people associated with the school.

Anthony Marchand, Gia Marchand, and Karen Phelps were the top possibilities. Except that the more she thought about it, the less sense Gia Marchand made as a suspect. Why kill Layla and Eileen to cover up for killing Nicole if you were just going to vanish anyway? You'd become a suspect at that point, regardless. The point was the same if Anthony was in on the plot to run, too.

Jo didn't like the unanswered questions surrounding Jim's departure from his previous school, and while he couldn't have killed Eileen, she really didn't like the coincidence that he and Karen were at the sight of the first two murders; they could easily be covering for one another. Sophie had said Karen's desperation to remarry was practically a joke—was she desperate enough to cover up her lover's crimes out of some misguided sense of loyalty? He could easily have told her Nicole's death was an accident, and convinced her to help him.

She spent her evening reviewing Briar Ridge's security footage from that morning. Since the day of Nicole's death, Eileen had put a stop to the practice of people leaving through the side exits by locking those doors completely; now the only way into and out of the school involved walking past a security camera. Neither Gia nor Anthony appeared, because Nicholas didn't come to school, so if Gia called Nicholas in sick as a cover and still managed to poison Eileen, she must have sneaked on to campus in some way Jo wasn't aware of. Karen dropped off Katie and Willie; she went into the main building, then came back out five minutes later. Enough time to slip poison into Eileen's drink? Possibly, if everything was busy, and she made an excuse for being inside the main office space. That part probably wouldn't be too hard, but would Eileen have refrained from drinking any of her smoothie between the beginning of the day and when she went into her classroom observation?

Jo pushed her laptop away in frustration. She could sit at her desk coming up with a million theories all day every day, but what she needed was evidence. Nobody moved through the ether without leaving a trace, no matter how careful they were, and that meant she was missing something, or wasn't looking in the right place, or wasn't looking at something from the right angle. She needed to break out of her current thinking in order to find what that something was.

She took a shower, crawled into bed, and fell asleep begging her subconscious to find the crevice she'd been overlooking.

CHAPTER THIRTY-ONE

Jo woke the next morning in a funk. Her sleep was again filled with nightmares, and she'd had no revelations about how to proceed. After starting her espresso, she tried to work up enthusiasm about eating, but her appetite wouldn't cooperate—her brain refused to stop circling the three crime scenes and the lack of viable suspects. Once the coffee was finished, she grabbed a banana and snatched up the records she'd printed the night before, then headed out to HQ an hour and a half early.

She worked her way through the phone records from the morning Eileen died, finding comfort in the busy work of identifying the numbers and looking for patterns. There were very few from Eileen's cell phone, one call to the sister who lived in San Francisco, and one to a drugstore. There were several texts regarding a minor emergency in the cafeteria; one of the refrigerators had died, leaving them with warm milk they couldn't serve the children. Her office phone was slightly more prolific: several phone calls to and from district offices, one to a supply company, likely in an effort to get an emergency delivery of milk, and several internal calls to teachers' offices. Nothing, as best she could tell, that would be related to Nicole Marchand or Layla Madani's deaths.

Jo paged back to the calls from the day before. Another call to her sister. A series of texts regarding a situation with the mobile bleachers in the gym. Four children sent to the principal's office for bad behavior, and two sent to the nurse because they weren't feeling well. The office phone calls looked much the same as the other list, with the addition of six calls to parents. Two of them appeared to correspond to the children who'd gone to the nurse's office—most likely the principal was obligated to report this to the children's guardians. Two of the remaining were unfamiliar to her, and she jotted them down—Renaldo Avila and Cheyenne Rivers—she'd need to review what Lopez had pulled on them.

The other two names were far more interesting. Karen Phelps again, and Molly Hayes. Had Gia signed up for some obligation she'd had to withdraw from like the field trip, and Eileen was hoping Karen or Molly could take it over? Or were the calls related to Nicole and Layla's murders? She made a note to follow up.

Finished with the calls, she flipped to the last page of her printouts, the agenda Eileen had jotted down on her notepad. After the date and several administrative tasks, one item on the list popped out at her: *F/U w/Molly Hayes—missing records.*

Little prickles shot up her spine, and her pulse raced. Most likely F/U meant follow up, which made sense given the call Jo had found to Molly the day before. She wasn't sure how missing records could be related to the deaths, but it felt strange. Surely if there had been some sort of routine issue, there'd be more parents on the list.

She reached for her phone and tapped on Molly's contact number.

"Detective Fournier?" Molly answered after the second ring.

"Yes, hello. I have a quick question I need to ask you. We're going over Principal Pham's phone records from the day before she died, and we noticed she called you. Can you tell us what that call was about?"

The pause before Molly answered was a microsecond longer than it should have been. "Oh, right, of course. She called to verify I'd be able to supervise recess on Thursday."

Jo's pulse sped further—that had nothing to do with missing records, as far as she could tell. "Oh, she lost the sign-in sheet or something?"

"No, otherwise she wouldn't have known I was scheduled for it. I think she was just concerned that with all of the tumult, people might forget."

"Right, that makes sense. It says here the call was five minutes long, did you talk about anything else?"

"Not really. She asked how Gia was doing, and I asked if there had been any progress on Ms. Madani's death, and then we hung up."

"Ah, okay." Jo's mind raced for any other way that missing records could legitimately be involved, but she couldn't come up with anything. "Thanks so much for your help."

"I'm happy to do anything I can." She paused. "I don't suppose you know where Gia is? She called me at six this morning and asked if I could cover her day in the boutique. Of course I said yes, but she wouldn't tell me why, just said she was in a hurry and we'd talk later. I texted her several times and she didn't respond, so I'm starting to worry."

"We talked to her late yesterday and she was fine then."

"Is—I—she can't be a suspect?"

"I'm sorry, Mrs. Hayes, I can't discuss details like that in an ongoing investigation."

"I understand. Please let me know if I can help in any other way."

"I will, thank you." Jo hung up, then stared down at the printout.

Molly Hayes had just lied to her. And where there was a lie, especially for something that seemed harmless, there was always a reason.

She stood and paced the office. The problem was, there was simply no way Molly could have been the killer. She'd been working at the boutique the morning Nicole was murdered, something they'd verified in excruciating detail when they reviewed the boutique's security footage. She'd never been off camera for more than five minutes, and during the critical period of the killing, she hadn't been off camera at all. Same for Layla Madani's murder, and according to both Molly and Karen, she'd covered the store yesterday for Gia. She hadn't had time to check the security footage for yesterday at the store, but even if it turned out she hadn't been there all day, there was no way she could have committed either of the other two murders. Could the missing records situation be totally unrelated, and Molly lied about it because it was something embarrassing or private? Or maybe the security footage had been tampered with? She jotted down a note to have Lopez examine the footage. Maybe Molly was covering up for someone? Were her friendships with Gia and Karen close enough for something like that? Normally you only saw behavior like that for family or—

Her husband.

She pulled up the research Lopez had done on Don Hayes. Her theory shattered instantly—he'd been in court the entire day of Nicole's death, and the lunch break had been an hour after Nicole was killed.

But she kept coming back to the universal truth: people didn't lie for no reason. Molly was hiding something, and Jo needed to ferret out whether it was relevant or not.

She pulled up Lopez's research on Molly and opened several windows on her laptop. She double-checked the basics—Molly had no criminal record, not even a parking ticket. No civil lawsuits against her.

Lopez had noted almost daily cash withdrawals from the Hayes' checking and savings accounts. She'd concluded Molly was a secret shopaholic, but what if they were hiding something else?

Jo grabbed her phone and called Sophie.

"Jo. Is everything okay?"

She reassured Sophie and told her about Lopez's theory. "Does that fit with what you know of her?"

"Huh." Sophie considered. "From all appearances I'd have to say no. When she's with Karen and Gia, she looks like the sister who gets the hand-me-downs. Her clothes aren't designer, and her style is fairly bland. Same thing with purses and shoes, and I've never really noticed the sort of ostentatious jewelry a lot of the Briar Ridge mothers wear. But who knows, maybe she has a secret obsession with Tiffany vases or something."

Jo fingered the diamond at her neck. "Maybe."

"You don't sound convinced. She blows glass for a hobby, doesn't she? That has to be expensive. Maybe it goes to her studio fees or her supplies?"

"All of that's accounted for on her credit card records. I know this sounds strange, but, have you ever seen her behave strangely, like she has a drug habit?"

"Not that I've ever noticed, and I've never heard any talk about it. And believe you me, there're always a few mothers dipping into their kids' Ritalin. But for the most part, booze is the drug of choice for the Briar Ridge set. Do you want me to ask around?"

"If it comes up, sure, but don't go out of your way. It doesn't fully fit, but I'm getting that itchy-finger feeling."

"Itchy-finger feeling?"

"When there's something I'm missing and I'm honing in on it."

"Ah. I have that when the kids are hiding something from me."

Jo smiled. "Useful for that, too. Let me know if you hear anything."

"Will do."

Jo hung up, mind racing. Gambling? Molly could easily slip into the casino in Springfield while Don was at work and lose her money there. She might also be following Gia's playbook, and stashing money in some sort of offshore account, but why?

Jo expanded her search to a fuller range of records. Tax rolls and property records yielded no surprises, and she couldn't find a hint anywhere of an alias for Molly other than her maiden name. Social media was no help, because she didn't have Facebook, or Twitter. And while all three women had a joint Instagram account showcasing the art they sold at the boutique, only Karen and Gia had individual accounts, Molly again did not. Jo sat with that for a moment. It was unusual, but not unheard of, for thirty-somethings to stay away from social media outlets, so she couldn't be sure it meant anything. But one of the reasons to stay away from social media was security concerns—was Molly hiding something? Or *from* something?

She plugged Molly's name into Google, but it turned out to be so common the results were useless. She tried again, adding *Harristown,* and retrieved much more tenable results. The boutique's website came up, as did several articles about the three women as artists. Several more showed Molly involved in local charity work, generally in concert with Gia and Karen. The results petered out after the first page.

But Molly had only lived in Harristown for a few years. Jo plugged Molly's name in again with Quincy, the city she'd lived in before moving to Harristown. The page of results contained repeats of the same article about Molly's glassblowing, posted on a variety of sites.

The prickles started up Jo's spine again—a common tactic for banishing something unsavory into the recesses of Google's search results was flooding the internet with more current, innocuous content.

On the fifth page of results, she found what she was looking for.

Four months before the Hayes family moved to Harristown from Quincy, their babysitter, Delia Cruz, had drowned in their swimming pool.

CHAPTER THIRTY-TWO

Jo called to request a copy of the Delia Cruz investigation file. As she studied it, Arnett appeared across the room, and made his way to his desk.

"Perfect timing, Bob. Come take a look at this," Jo called.

He set a Starbucks cup in front of her and leaned down to stare at her monitor. "What am I looking at?"

"The Hayes' family babysitter drowned in their pool right before they moved to Harristown. They just sent over the report."

He skimmed the documentation, reading snippets aloud as he went. "Donald and Molly Hayes came home from a gala to find their babysitter, Delia Cruz, drowned in their pool. Shauna Hayes was in shock and unable to tell them what happened, except to repeat that 'Delia fell in the pool.' ME determined that the death was accidental, caused by drowning. Delia Cruz's mother insisted it was murder." He looked back up at Jo. "You think this is connected to our murders?"

She walked him through everything she'd found that morning, from the note on the memo to the phone records.

"Missing records could be anything, even just inoculations. And since we know for a fact Molly couldn't have committed these crimes, this seems like a big leap in logic."

"Delia's mother didn't think so."

"Grieving mothers want someone to blame that isn't their kid."

Jo pulled in a deep breath. "Maybe you're right, maybe I'm reaching too far because I'm desperate to catch a scent here.

But it feels strange to me that they left Quincy after another odd death."

"Natural to want to get away from that sort of memory. Especially if the mother is blaming you for it." He shrugged. "But, my face is blue from all the nothing we've come up with otherwise. So I say let's go see what the mother has to say."

*

An hour and a half later, Jo and Arnett pulled up to the Pine Regents apartment complex in Quincy, where Alma Cruz now lived. The brown-and-beige brick facade was fronted by half-dead boxwood hedges and framed by red split-rail fence sections that were probably intended to look quaint. But in their half-fallen state, they only succeeded in highlighting the complex's decay.

They located apartment 2D, and Jo knocked gently on the door.

Alma Cruz looked close to fifty, although Jo knew based on the report they'd read that she'd just turned forty. Her hair was more gray than brown, and deep creases had carved themselves into the skin around her mouth and forehead. She wore black leggings, an oversized brown tunic, and gray slippers.

"Who are you?" Her expression was suspicious, and hostile.

Jo introduced herself and Arnett. "We'd like to talk to you about your daughter."

"I don't talk about my daughter." She stepped back and began to yank the door closed, sending a whiff of cheap gin and unfiltered cigarettes out toward them.

Jo's hand shot out and blocked the door. "Then we'd like to talk to you about Molly Hayes."

The woman's eyes narrowed. She dropped the hand that held the doorknob, then turned and walked into the apartment.

Jo raised her eyebrows at Arnett, and they followed her inside. The door opened into a large room that functioned both as living room and kitchen, divided by a counter swathed in everyday-life detritus—mail, takeout containers, magazines. Alma dropped onto the well-worn blue couch, picked up the remote from the equally crowded coffee table, and clicked off the TV. "You want to know what I think about Molly Hayes? I think that bitch came home early and shoved my Delia into the water. She knew Delia couldn't swim—it annoyed her that Delia couldn't let Shauna play in the pool when she watched her."

Jo raised her eyebrows—Mrs. Cruz liked to cut to the chase. "Why would Mrs. Hayes do that?"

"Because Delia was going to quit that night. She wasn't comfortable there. She told me something strange was going on, and she didn't know what. I think when she quit, Mrs. Hayes lost her temper and tossed her in."

"Strange how?"

"She didn't know exactly. But the week before, she'd left her car keys behind and didn't realize it 'til she got out to her car. She went back to get them but before she could knock, she heard Mr. and Mrs. Hayes fighting about something. She couldn't hear it all, but the father was angry, and saying something to the mother about a therapist, and about how 'things had gotten out of hand and how the problem wasn't going to go away on its own.'" Alma made air quotes around the words, then paused to light up a cigarette.

After a long drag, she continued. "Then Delia knocked and they shut up quick, and it took them a minute to open the door. They watched her, silent, while she got her keys. When she went back to watch Shauna the next time, Mrs. Hayes made a bunch of small talk then finally asked Delia what she'd heard. Delia said 'nothing', but Mrs. Hayes didn't believe her and stared at her like she had X-ray vision. It gave her chills. I told her she needed to quit, right then, because you have to follow your gut on stuff like that, and I didn't want her going back there. But she told me she'd promised to watch Shauna for some important event for Mr. Hayes' law firm and she didn't want to leave them hanging. I think Molly thought Delia heard more than she really did, and killed her because of it."

"Did Delia have any guesses about what things were getting out of hand?"

"No, but she said Mrs. Hayes was paranoid. Very protective. Made my Delia do all kinds of strange things, like she wasn't allowed to take pictures of Shauna, weird things like that. And Delia noticed some tension between Mr. and Mrs. Hayes that had something to do with Shauna's school. They were trying to decide whether to keep her there or not."

"That doesn't sound too strange. Private schools are expensive," Arnett pushed.

"But those two never fought. It was one of the things Delia loved about the job at first, she really looked up to their relationship. I guess because her father and I were always fighting, and it made her feel good to be around people who seemed to always be so happy." She took a sip from a tumbler that Jo would have bet contained some alcoholic drink.

"They never fought, ever?" Jo asked.

She looked at Jo like she was an idiot. "Little disagreements that they laughed about as they were happening, yeah. But Delia always went on about how they never got angry at each other. It made me sick when Delia would talk about it, like they were so much better than us. But they got heated about what school Shauna should be in, sniped at each other and threw dirty looks. That was the first thing that made her uncomfortable."

"That was before the conversation she overheard?"

"Yeah, but not by much. I told her, that's what happens when you idolize people without really knowing them."

"Do you know what school Shauna went to?"

She waved at Jo like she was swatting a fly. "Why would I care? Some fancy one is all I know."

"How did Delia become their babysitter?" Arnett asked.

"One of our neighbors. Their older daughter, Lana, became friends with Delia, and the younger daughter went to the same school as Shauna. Mrs. Hayes actually asked Lana first, but she already had a job, so she recommended Delia."

"And you told the detectives on the case that you believed Mrs. Hayes killed your daughter?"

"I did. They blew me off like I was nuts." She noticed Arnett glance at her tumbler, and leaned forward to thrust a finger toward him. "And no, it's not because of that. I didn't drink back then. I started drinking when Delia died. Have you lost a child?"

"No, ma'am," he replied, avoiding Jo's eye.

She leaned back in the chair, grabbed the tumbler, and took a huge swig. "Then don't judge me."

*

"How much of that do you think is tainted by alcohol and time?" Arnett asked back in the car.

Jo tapped a nail on her phone. "She's bitter, that's for sure. But I think the basic gist is right, because I believe she wasn't drinking before Delia died, so her memories are probably accurate. She seemed pretty clear that Delia heard something that made her believe Molly was unstable."

"My mind keeps going back to Molly's ironclad alibi." He put the keys into the ignition.

"I'll have Lopez check the footage, make sure it wasn't altered somehow. But, we've been thinking this was Anthony and Gia working together, or Anthony and Karen, or Jim and Karen. We need to consider Molly may have been working with someone."

"Her husband has an airtight alibi, too."

"The three women are so tight, maybe it's one of them. Or all three." She shook her head. "Although for the life of me I can't figure out why or what that would look like."

"Or maybe this whole thing is just a coincidence. The detectives were clear they thought it was an accident."

Jo gave him a come-on-now look. "We've both seen detectives make easy choices too quickly. And they may have told her that not because they truly believed it, but because they didn't have evidence to make a charge stick. I'd like to hear what they have to say," Jo said.

He nodded toward the windshield. "Go over there, or call?"

"Call. Too hit-and-miss to catch them in." Jo pulled up the detectives' names—Ruiz and Polansky—and got their contact information from their DA's office. Both phones went to voice-mail, so she left messages asking for a callback at their earliest convenience.

She hung up the phone, then sat, thinking.

"Seat belt." Arnett pointed.

"Sorry." She grabbed it, but didn't buckle it in place.

"What?" Arnett asked, hand poised on the keys in the ignition.

"I keep thinking about how Delia said the Hayeses were arguing about pulling Shauna out of her school. Doesn't that seem coincidental?"

"Not really. Laura wanted to pull our girls out of their school about a hundred times when they were growing up. Every time someone bullied them, or there was a teacher she felt was incompetent, you name it. And it seems like Molly struggled with paranoia, maybe had some sort of anxiety disorder."

Jo ran a search. "From what I can tell, the nearest private elementary school to the house here is St. Bernadette's. I think it might be worth having a conversation with them."

Arnett got his I-don't-understand-but-I-trust-you look and dropped his hand to his lap. "Can't hurt."

She put a call through to St. Bernadette's and asked to speak with Ryan Beckett, listed as principal on the website.

"How can I help you, Detective?" Ryan Beckett asked once Jo had identified herself.

"I'm calling about a student who used to go to your school, Shauna Hayes. Do you remember her or her parents, Molly and Donald Hayes?"

"I remember them well," he answered. "Mrs. Hayes was very involved with her daughter's education, and used to make the most beautiful items to donate to our fundraisers."

"Were there any incidents of any kind, something that made them consider pulling Shauna out of the school?"

His tone was now wary. "No incident I'm aware of."

He stressed the word *incident* a bit too hard. "No incident. Some sort of problem?"

He hesitated.

"We'd very much appreciate it if you'd be forthcoming with us. Lives may depend on it."

"Oh," he hurriedly replied, "I didn't mean to imply anything like that. There was never any problem, exactly. Just that Shauna was always a bit of an enigma. Her kindergarten teacher wondered briefly if she were possibly on the spectrum. But when she approached Mrs. Hayes about it, she didn't respond well. Since it didn't seem to interfere with her performance and there wasn't anything concrete we could point to, we dropped the issue."

"You say Molly didn't respond well. Did she get angry?"

"More defensive. She said she didn't want her teachers stigmatizing Shauna because she was a little quiet. But that's common when a teacher raises these issues. I had a mother just this week break into tears when we told her we suspected her son might be dyslexic, and the father threatened to sue if we even hinted in his file that he might need testing."

"I'm surprised. Wouldn't you want to get your child help as soon as possible if there were an issue?"

"I agree with you, of course, but it's a very human reaction. Nobody wants their child to be anything but perfect."

"But she didn't make threats, anything like that?"

"Oh, no. I think the whole exchange lasted two minutes, and then she acted like nothing happened."

"So you don't think that's why they changed schools?"

"Well, I don't know specifically, but I don't think so. That occurred some months before they left. But it may have combined with the Eric Larson situation. I know during that time quite a few families considered leaving. That's an unavoidable consequence when a child dies on school grounds."

CHAPTER THIRTY-THREE

The world flashed bright white and seemed to spin around Jo. Her hand shot out to the dash in front of her to steady herself. "A child died at your school?"

He cleared his throat and dropped his voice. "Yes. Eric Larson, a kindergartener. A horrible accident. He tried to climb the fence, but fell and hit his head on the corner of one of our portables."

Jo gaped at Arnett—he looked as shocked as she felt. "You're sure it was an accident?"

Beckett paused. "We didn't have any reason to believe it wasn't. Is there?"

"I apologize, Mr. Beckett, I don't mean to alarm you. I just want to be sure I understand."

He sounded relieved. "Ah, I see. Yes, a tragic accident. Our children aren't allowed by those portables during recess, they aren't part of the playground. But the gate had a glitch we didn't know about, a way to lift the post so you could open it. After the accident, many of the kids admitted they knew about it and would sneak back there when nobody was looking. We fixed it immediately, of course."

"I see. I'm so sorry."

"I blame myself. Our parents put their trust in me to keep their children safe, and—well, thankfully the Larsons are very kind people, and refused to place blame on me or the school. But there were a number of other parents who weren't so gracious about it. Several pulled their children out, and I'm sure quite a few more considered it."

"Right. I see. Thank you so much for the information."

"Is there anything else I can help you with?" Beckett asked.

Jo assured him there wasn't, thanked him again, then shot Arnett a dumbfounded expression as she hung up the call. "Too many coincidences."

Arnett ticked off his fingers. "So Molly wasn't stable, she had a temper she hid, and she's paranoid about her child. You think she lost it when the school suggested something was wrong with Shauna, and took it out on the school by killing a student in their protection?"

Jo searched the sky outside the windshield for an answer. "Mothers can be protective, there's no doubt about that. Add in some sort of instability, and that could be a very problematic mix. She must have altered the security camera footage somehow, or I can't see how—"

Jo's phone rang, interrupting her. "It's Sophie. She may have found something out." She tapped on the call. "Sophie. What's up?"

Sophie's voice poured out over the line, jagged and gasping. "Molly took Emily! She kidnapped Emily!"

CHAPTER THIRTY-FOUR

Jo turned to ice. "Back up. Tell me what you're talking about."

"I just got a call from the school. Stephanie Roden saw Molly hurrying off campus with Emily and Shauna, and putting them in her car. She said because of everything that was happening, she wanted to check that everything was okay, so she called me."

Blood pounded through Jo's ears, blunting the edge of Sophie's voice. "How long ago?"

"About twenty minutes. She said she was in the middle of talking to another teacher when she saw, and called me after."

Jo gripped the phone, trying to keep hold of a calm demeanor—Sophie needed her to exude competence and control. "There may be a perfectly reasonable explanation. Have you tried calling her?"

"Of course I did, Jo! She's not answering her phone. What possible explanation could there be? Why would she do this?" Sophie's voice turned husky. "I need you to tell me the truth—did she kill Nicole?"

Of course there was no reasonable explanation. "We'll send out an amber alert right now. We know what car she drives, and all of Oakhurst County will be searching for her within minutes." Jo motioned for Arnett to start the car. "Where are you right now?"

Arnett stuck the mobile siren to the top of the car, and took off down the street.

Sophie choked back a sob. "I'm at home, but I'm on my way out the door to go to the school."

"No, Sophie, I need you to stay put—"

"I have to talk—"

Jo channeled the last piece of calm she had remaining, and put on her authoritative cop voice. "Sophie. I need you to listen to me, and do what I say. Molly might be bringing Emily home to you for some reason, so I need you to be home if that happens." It was a lie, but she needed Sophie to stay put.

"Oh. Oh, I didn't think about that—"

"Make arrangements with Ma to pick up Isabelle. I'll get everything in motion and call you back in a few minutes, okay?"

"Please hurry." The words choked out among her sobs.

Jo hung up, then prayed as she called in the APB.

CHAPTER THIRTY-FIVE

Molly maintained a steady, legal pace, careful not to attract any attention. She'd taken off her license plates before picking up the girls to avoid triggering any cameras that registered plate numbers, but the amber alert would contain a vehicle description, and any matching vehicle with no plates was going to be suspicious. She had a long-term solution for that, but it would be useless unless she reached it safely.

In the back of her Volvo, Emily cried softly but steadily. Molly glanced at her in the rearview mirror. She'd made a mistake taking this one, she should have taken the older sister. This one was emotional, crying, and asking for her mother, even putting on a brave little show of telling Molly that her mother would show up any minute and her aunty was a police woman and Molly would be put in jail forever. Under any other circumstances, her brave little face would have warmed Molly's heart, but now she was too frustrated, and she wasn't sure how to handle it all. Even as a baby, Shauna had almost never cried. She watched people, taking them in, and never complained or whined or fussed. Always in perfect command of her emotions.

Emily's anguish ripped at her heart; the very last thing in the world she ever wanted to do was scare a little child. But what choice did she have? Detective Fournier hadn't sounded convinced by her answers about Principal Pham's call. She'd dig and dig and dig, and it was only a matter of time before she contacted St. Bernadette's and found out the truth.

And she couldn't count on Don anymore, he'd made that clear.

The thought of having to leave Don slammed her heart like a ten-ton truck, and tears streamed down her face. Her love for him threaded in and around every part of her, like the capillaries running through her organs and her muscle tissues—there was no way to rip him out of her life without destroying her. But he'd forced Molly to make the choice.

She looked back at Shauna. The only thing on earth more a part of her than Don was Shauna. She was the fusion of the two of them, their love incarnate, her very soul placed into another body.

Molly took a deep breath—she needed to be strong now. She could no longer trust Don's love, regardless, because you didn't treat someone you loved the way he'd treated her. He knew how she felt—that there was no way she'd let anyone separate her from her daughter. But he kept on and on about a therapist. Like that was even a possibility! A therapist would put her away after she admitted to one murder, let alone five. Therapists were obliged to report things like that, and he knew it. He *knew* it.

"Momma, are you okay?"

Shauna must have seen her shoulders quivering. "I'm fine, baby," she said, trying to sound normal. "Everything's fine."

Shauna returned to the book she was reading. Nancy Drew—Shauna was working her way through the series. Always reading, always learning. The sight tugged at Molly's heart.

"Mommy, I'm hungry," Shauna said, nose still in her book.

Molly's eyes squeezed shut as she tried to stay patient. "I know, honey. Hang on, and I'll have something for you soon."

CHAPTER THIRTY-SIX

The amber alert went out immediately on all channels. Minutes later, Harristown PD arrived at the Hayes house, only to find it empty, and that Molly Hayes' Silver Volvo XC90 was gone.

"The officers are searching the house now," Lopez said. "They found her phone. She left it behind."

"So much for tracking her GPS. What about Donald Hayes? He wasn't with Molly and Shauna when Stephanie Roden saw them," Jo asked.

"Harristown PD sent a car to his law office as well, but they're still en route."

"Right. Hopefully one of the traffic cams will flag her license plate and we'll have her shortly. She can't be far, it's been less than half an hour since she left the school. Can you crack her phone? We need her phone records ASAP. And whatever else we can do to find out if Molly or Donald have any friends or family she might be running to."

"On it," Lopez said as keys clicked in the background. "I know Donald's parents live in Boston, because his father works for the same law office. I'll contact Boston PD and see if we can get someone out there as quickly as possible while I see what I can find on Molly. I'm pretty sure her parents are dead."

"Can you get Gia Marchand and Karen Phelps down to HQ? Between them and Donald, somebody has to know something that can help us track her down."

"On it—hold on. I'm getting another call." Lopez placed her on hold for a long moment, then clicked back on. "The officers at the Hayes house found a note, addressed to you. They're texting you a picture of it."

She thanked Lopez and hung up, then stared at her phone, willing the text to come through. When it did, she pinched the screen to enlarge it, and read it aloud.

> *Detective Fournier—*
>
> *I need to get to safety, and I'm bringing your niece along to ensure I can. When I reach my destination, I'll leave Emily behind, unharmed, to be returned to you. But if you try to intercept me, I'll kill her. If I have to, I'll kill all three of us. But enough people have already died and enough people are suffering, so I'm asking you to do the right thing and let us go start a new life. For all our sakes, especially Emily's.*

A cold whiteness overtook Jo, as though everything was suddenly brighter, louder, slower. No—No, no, no. It was happening again—how did she get back here—there was nothing she could do about it—

Scenes flashed through her head. Marc falling, shot, onto the circular stones of Congo Square. Jack, blood pouring from his head in a dark alley, his mugger's footsteps fading in the distance. Herself, staring at her bedroom wall, doubled up in pain from her miscarriage, sobbing over a faceless child she'd never see.

And now Emily. One more person she loved, in danger because of her, about to die because of her—

"Don't worry, Jo, we'll catch her." Arnett's voice came from far away, tugging at her like someone yelling across a crowded room. "She can't go far without triggering one of the traffic cams. The only shot she has is to get off the highways as soon as possible, so I'll send up alerts through Vermont to Canada, as well."

She watched his hand reach for the radio in seeming slow motion.

Traffic cameras—yes, Molly would likely trigger one. Then squad cars would have to cut off her path, or ambush her, or pursue her in a high-speed chase. Did any of those scenarios give Emily even the smallest chance of survival?

If the note wasn't just a diversion, regardless. Molly had proven to be smart, intuitive, and fast thinking. A woman who'd managed to put belladonna into a smoothie and plunge a teacher over the side of a pyramid without detection wasn't stupid enough to forget details like traffic cameras, or fail to realize that Canada had an extradition treaty with the United States. She wasn't going to do the obvious thing. So what *was* she going to do?

Jo closed her eyes and tried to channel Molly's thinking. Normally she didn't have to even try—she could see, almost feel, what a certain type of person was likely to think or do. At the very least, when she tested out different courses of action, her intuition about the person in question would bounce some options away as wrong. But the harder she focused, the less clear the possibilities became. Why? Because she was too scared and unfocused, too worried about Emily? Or because she still couldn't make sense of what Molly had done and why?

Whatever it was, Jo had to pull herself together and figure it out. Fast.

CHAPTER THIRTY-SEVEN

Ten minutes later, as they pulled into HQ, a text came through from Lopez.

Donald Hayes is here. Karen and Gia are on their way.

Jo erupted from the car as soon as Arnett parked, and flew into the building. She might have no idea how Molly thought or what she'd be likely to do—but her husband did.

"Interrogation one," Goran, another detective, called out when he saw her.

Without breaking stride she veered off toward the room. She blew through the door and crossed directly to where he sat at the gray table, tall frame bent over a steaming cup of coffee. Twenty years of training registered his conservatively cut brown hair, the small scar at the base of his neck, the slight bend in his narrow nose, and the panic in his dark blue eyes.

She leaned down and slammed her hands on the desk opposite him. "Where's my niece?"

Donald Hayes blanched, and his hand shook as he put the coffee cup down. "I don't know, I swear." He turned as Arnett arrived. "I never thought it would come to this."

"Come to what?" Jo spat as Arnett slid a chair beside her.

"I never thought she'd run, and I certainly never thought she'd put a child in danger." His head swung back and forth between the two of them like a pendulum. "When I left for work this morning, everything was fine. As far as I knew, Molly was going to take Shauna to school and then go to her studio."

Jo pushed forward, to within inches of his face. "You expect me to believe you had no idea any of this was going on?"

His mouth popped open and closed like a goldfish dropped on cement. Then his face crumpled, and he gasped for air as he fought back sobs. "No. No, of course not. But I didn't—I didn't—"

Arnett gently put a hand on Jo's back. Her head whipped toward his, but he met her angry glare with a steady, calm headshake. She turned back to the weeping man in front of her, then stared down at the popped veins on the back of her hands.

He was right. She needed to rein it in—if she allowed her connection with Emily to destroy her ability to do effective police work, Emily was as good as dead. Now was not the time to let her feelings overwhelm her, and if she couldn't channel them effectively, she needed to push them down. So she took a deep breath, leaned into the prickling numbness in her limbs, and retreated behind protective walls.

She sat down in the chair and cleared her throat. "Mr. Hayes. Your wife kidnapped my niece—a police detective's family member. Police take it very personally when someone goes after one of their own, and there are currently a county's worth of policemen and women all focused on one thing—rescuing my niece, by whatever means necessary. I'd like to bring all three of them back here safely, but I need your help to do that, and we have no time to waste."

He nodded and wiped his nose with the back of his hand. "I get it. I understand. This has gone far too far, and I don't want anyone else getting hurt. But I don't know how to help. She did this because of me, because I pushed her to the end of her rope. She didn't tell me anything about this."

Jo leaned forward. "I want to believe you're not a part of this. If that's the case, you need to help us. We need to figure out where she's going, now."

His brow creased with concentration. "She's hiding from me too, because I'm the enemy now. So she's not going to go anywhere I know. Not my parents, not our old friends."

"Doesn't matter. We'll need a list of them all."

He nodded, then dictated.

"Where else? Does she have any family?" Jo asked.

"No. Both her parents are dead and she's an only child. Both her parents were only children, too, so no uncles or aunts or cousins."

"Vacation spots she knows well?"

"We usually go to Disneyland or Disney World when we go on vacation, do you think she'd go there?"

Jo doubted it—those weren't the sorts of places you holed up. "We'll alert them both to the possibility. Old friends?"

"I don't know of anybody. She left our old friends behind when we moved, because, well—"

"If she were trying to leave the country, where would she go?" Arnett asked.

He shook his head. "I don't know, we went to the Bahamas on our honeymoon, but you'd need a plane trip for that, right, and a passport?"

The word *passport* hit Jo like a bullet between the eyes. She tapped her phone and put it up to her ear. Lopez answered immediately. "Where are Gia and Karen?" Jo asked.

"Interrogation two and three," she answered.

"Thanks." She hung up, mind racing. She didn't have time to question each of them in turn—they'd have to run individual interrogations after the fact. She gestured to Don. "Come with us."

He followed Jo, and Arnett followed him. She led them to interrogation room two and held up her hand for them to wait.

She poked her head inside and found Karen nervously chewing an acrylic nail. "Come with us, now."

Karen jumped up, and Jo filed them all into interrogation three, the largest of the rooms, where Gia sat staring at the table in front of her. Jo grabbed chairs for Karen and Don, but remained standing.

"Molly is on the run with Shauna, and she kidnapped my niece." She turned to Gia. "So I need the truth, now. The man you got your alternate identities from. Did you tell Molly about him?"

Karen's and Don's heads snapped, shocked, toward Gia. She leaned forward, posture taut as a crossbow. "Absolutely not."

"The three of you are the people who know her best in the world. Where could she be going?" Arnett asked.

They looked at each other, but didn't speak.

Jo paced in front of them. "Brainstorm, it doesn't matter how small. Does she know anybody who'd give her a place to stay? What's on her bucket list? Anything."

"Santa Fe. She always wanted to visit the artist communities there," Karen said.

Gia turned to Don. "Didn't you guys make friends with a couple when you went on that cruise to Mexico? Didn't they say to come visit any time you were around?"

Don nodded. "They live in Montreal. And we went there on vacation once, she's always said she'd like to go back."

"Does she speak French?" Karen asked.

"No," Don said.

"That you know of," Gia said, tone scathing.

Don blanched. "She really hates winter. Mexico would be a much better bet."

"OMG, Mexico!" Karen cried. "*Shawshank Redemption*. She's obsessed with that town Tom Robbins goes to. Says the name over and over whenever Mexico comes up and says she wants to go there."

"Tim Robbins," Gia snapped.

Don nodded. "Zihuantanejo. And they don't really check passports for Americans going into Mexico, right?"

Jo called Lopez and asked her to adjust the alerts.

Arnett pulled something up on his phone. "No way she's getting all the way to Mexico without someone spotting her plates. We'll grab her."

"Except we've had the alert out for nearly an hour and we haven't had a single hit on her plates," Jo said. "We're missing something. She only has the one car, right?"

Don nodded. "I have mine."

Gia stood and crossed to the wall. "Didn't she inherit two cars when her mom died two years ago? And the house?"

"She sold them all," Don said.

"Really? You're sure?" Gia said. "Seems to me she has a hell of a lot of secrets we know nothing about."

Lopez, still on the phone with Jo, overheard, and replied in Jo's ear. "There's no other property in her name, I looked when I did the background check. Does Don have the address?"

Don produced an address in Connecticut, and the room went silent as Jo listened to Lopez's lightning-fast keystrokes.

Lopez grunted a choking laugh. "You have to be kidding me. Yep, Molly sold the house just under two years ago—"

"Damn," Jo spat.

"You didn't let me finish," Lopez said. "She sold it to Delia Cruz, her dead babysitter."

CHAPTER THIRTY-EIGHT

Molly pulled up to her parents' curb and hit the garage door opener. "Shauna, I need both of you to stay in the car. I have the child locks on, but I still need you to watch her."

Shauna nodded, still reading her book.

Molly climbed out of the car and strolled toward the garage, careful to maintain a casual demeanor. Once inside, she got into the Honda Pioneer, backed it out of the driveway and onto the street, then returned to the Volvo. She pulled it into the now-empty slot in the garage, lowered the door behind them, then let Shauna out of the car.

She circled around the car to Emily's side. The girl had been strangely quiet for the last ten or so minutes, eyes watching the road, lips moving like she was singing to herself. Shock, Molly decided, and figured she must be doing some sort of self-soothing. But it was odd, and odd things she didn't understand made her uncomfortable.

Molly opened the door and unbuckled Emily out of Shauna's old car seat, keeping her voice pleasant, but firm. "Come on out."

Emily slid down, then hopped onto the ground. She gazed around the garage, taking it in.

"Shauna, take her hand."

Molly grabbed the car seat and led them into the house, wrinkling her nose against the musty scent. The interior was dim thanks to the blackout curtains on all the windows, installed to make sure neighbors couldn't see into the house. She only managed to come down about once a month, but didn't want them realizing that.

She pointed to the bathroom. "Go potty, and make sure she goes, too."

"I can go on my own," Emily said.

"I'm sure you can, sweetheart. But Shauna needs to watch you."

Emily looked like she was about to burst into tears again, but did as she was told. Molly's shoulders relaxed, and she hurried into the kitchen to assemble the emergency supplies she kept here. As much as she hoped she'd never have to use them, a part of her had always known it would come to this.

But she couldn't stay here for long. Soon all three of their pictures would be plastered all over the news. But there were plenty of places they could hide from the rest of the world, if she was careful. The cash she'd saved up was enough to last them the rest of their lives in a small, idyllic village in Mexico, and she wouldn't have any problem making money there with her glassblowing skills.

She opened the oven door and pulled out the box she'd hidden behind the stacks of pots and pans, which she'd slowly filled with bundles of cash. Then she dug out several brown-paper-wrapped bricks of cash from behind packages of meat and frozen vegetables in the freezer. From the cabinets she pulled down two boxes of protein bars, two boxes of disgustingly sugary cereal, a bag of individually packaged chips, and three eight-packs of bottled water. She surveyed the result—that should be enough so they wouldn't have to stop constantly.

The toilet flushed and the faucet turned on, then off. She smiled—Shauna had always had such good hygiene.

Shauna appeared in the kitchen, clenching Emily's hand.

"Wait here," Molly instructed.

In the master bedroom, Molly pulled two backpacks out of the closet, each packed with several days' clothing for her and Shauna, along with travel-sized toiletries and more bundles of cash. She didn't have anything suitable for Emily, but it didn't matter—Emily would be dropped off at some police station within the next couple of days anyway. She hoisted the larger backpack over her shoulder, and handed the other to Shauna in the hall. "Take this, and Emily, out to Grandma's car. The doors should be unlocked, just get in and put them by your feet."

Back in the kitchen, she plucked three reusable grocery bags off a stack on the counter and shoved in the groceries and cash as she tried to think. She couldn't delay any longer, she had to pick a destination now. But making that decision was like playing some demented game of chess—she was trying to guess what the police were guessing she'd do—and she ended up thinking herself in circles, unsure how to outsmart them.

Most likely the police would assume she was headed toward Canada. It was the logical choice, and Don would likely tell them about the vacation they'd taken in Montreal. So logical, she'd almost decided to go there, regardless. But Mexico had no extradition treaty, the dollar was strong there, and they'd be able to meld and disappear, never to be found again.

But the police knew all that, too. What if they decided Canada was too obvious, and staked out the main highways toward Mexico? Maybe the smart thing was to leave some clues that looked like she was heading to Canada, use her debit card or something, then backtrack the other way? Or do the opposite, make it look like she was going to Mexico, then sneak into Canada? Or maybe she should go somewhere else entirely. California still had communes, didn't it? People who hated authority and police and wanted to be left alone, where she could hide and then move on after the police had given up trying to find her?

She sagged over the counter. Why was this so hard for her? All she needed to do was make a decision, then figure out how to make it work.

She piled the bag handles over her empty shoulder and hefted them up off the counter, taking a moment to adjust to their weight. Then she grabbed her purse and her keys in one hand, the child seat in the other, and left the house, locking the front door behind her.

A piercing scream rang out. "Help!"

CHAPTER THIRTY-NINE

"Who's Delia Cruz?" Gia asked.

Jo turned on Don—all the blood had drawn from his face, and he looked stunned. "I didn't know. I swear I didn't. I thought she'd legitimately sold it."

The tapping keys continued in the background on Jo's phone. "Well, well, well," Lopez said. "Delia Cruz has quite an interesting life for someone who's dead. She owns the house and a car that was previously owned by Molly's mother. She makes regular mortgage payments, although I can't find any employment associated with her social security number. Guess we know where Molly's fun money has been going. I'm also gonna go out on a limb and guess Molly has a lovely passport with her picture and Delia's name."

"Can you get APBs put out for the license plate number on the car, and send out new amber alerts including the alias? And bring Connecticut into it?" Jo asked.

"On it."

"Thanks." Jo hung up and pushed past Arnett toward the door. "We need to get out there. In the meantime, we need the three of you back in separate rooms. If any of you think of anything else, call us immediately."

*

With the aid of the siren, Arnett sped toward Molly's Connecticut house while Jo arranged for the local PD to send undercover cars to catch anyone who attempted to come or go from the location.

As she finished, a call came through from an unknown number. She answered it. "Detective Fournier."

"This is Detective Rosa Ruiz. You left a message for me?"

Their trip to Quincy felt like a distant memory. "Right. I was calling about a case you worked three and a half years ago, the death of a girl named Delia Cruz? I'm not sure if you remember it at all?"

"A young child alone and in shock because her teenaged babysitter drowned in their pool? You don't forget something like that easily. What do you need to know?"

"We just talked with Delia's mother. She seemed pretty convinced that Molly Hayes killed her daughter, and now Molly has kidnapped a little girl, so we believe she was right."

Detective Ruiz sucked in a deep breath. "Well, I'm sorry to hear about the little girl, but I can assure you, there's not even a remote possibility that Molly Hayes killed Delia Cruz. I did a quick look-see when I pulled up the information to be sure I remembered it correctly. The girl was already in rigor when we got there, and there were about a hundred witnesses that saw Molly and Donald leave their fancy gala in Boston less than an hour before. Traffic at that time would take more than twenty minutes to get home. Nowhere near enough time for rigor to set in unless she was dead long before they left."

"Maybe they killed her before they went to the party?"

"Not possible. Delia called both her mother and her best friend from the house an hour after Molly and Donald arrived at the party."

Jo stared straight ahead as the implication landed like a ton of bricks. "Had anyone else been there? Maybe Delia had a boyfriend who came over when he wasn't supposed to, or could someone have broken in?"

"Nope. The little girl said nobody had been there except Delia. And Delia's friends swore up and down she didn't have a boyfriend, and her diary showed the same. No evidence of anyone in the house, no forced entry, no mystery prints that belonged to someone else. If it waddles and quacks, it's a duck. She slipped, fell in the pool, and drowned. I understand why her mother wanted to believe there was more to it, but that's what the evidence shows. It's sad, but accidents happen."

Jo rubbed her eyes, trying to slow the thoughts ping-ponging off each other in her brain. "That's what I needed to know. Thank you so much for your help."

She ended the call and turned to Arnett. He stared at her with an alarmed expression. "Are you okay?"

Jo shook her head. The realization clanged in her head so loudly and so certain she couldn't imagine how she hadn't seen it before.

"Molly and Don didn't kill Delia," she said. "Shauna did."

CHAPTER FORTY

Jo squeezed her eyes shut and rubbed her temples as one piece after the other fell into place. "You just never think of a child being a cold-blooded killer—but it's the only thing that makes sense—"

"Wait, back it up." Arnett held up a hand. "You think Shauna somehow caused Delia's accident?"

Jo shook her head. "No. I mean yes, Shauna caused it, but I don't think it was an accident."

Concern took over Arnett's face, and he laid a hand on her arm. "This was a mistake. With the miscarriage, and now Emily, I should never have—"

Jo jerked her arm away and glared at him. "I'm not having a breakdown, Bob. You know me better than that."

He held her eyes for a minute. "Okay. I'm listening."

"There are too many coincidences here. Two kindergarteners dead at different schools, then in both cases subsequent deaths of people who knew the Hayes family. Five people dead, and the Hayes family is at the center of each one."

"I agree something's going on, but Shauna is a leap. Maybe a family member did it. Shauna could have lied to protect them. Even a hitman makes more sense."

Jo shook her head furiously. "From the beginning our main problem has been it's nearly impossible for some adult to have grabbed and killed little Nicole without being seen by anyone. And we haven't been able to find a remotely plausible motive for why someone would want to hurt her. That's partly why we considered her brother might have killed her accidentally—because nobody would have thought twice about another *child* talking to Nicole, or walking with her. And Nicole knew and trusted Shauna. Their families were together almost daily."

"So you're saying Shauna's a serial killer? A kid psychopath who kills kids?"

Jo tapped the dash with her index finger. "It all fits. Think about what Delia Cruz heard. Molly and Don fighting, and Don saying things had gone too far, and that Molly needed to make an appointment with a therapist. But I don't think the therapist was for Molly—based on what Principal Beckett said, I think he was talking about a therapist for *Shauna*. If she'd been exhibiting strange behavior, he may have been trying to address it for a while, and Molly may have been fighting him. Molly's anxiety and supposed paranoia wasn't the cause of the problem, it was caused *by* the problem—Shauna."

"But then it falls apart. Because we then have the same problem we had with Nicholas. She may have killed Eric and Nicole, and maybe I could even believe Delia. But there's no way a kid killed the adults."

"Are you sure?" Jo closed her eyes again to concentrate as her mind raced. "I tried leaning over the pyramid's railing for that watch. Even if someone had just bumped me hard, I'd have gone tumbling down, no question. A nine-year-old definitely could have sent me over. And I bet a hundred children a day go in and out of the main office suite. Would anyone have even noticed Shauna going into Eileen's office? And with Layla Madani dead, she'd have a substitute teacher. You can put anything over on a sub."

Arnett's face tightened, and he shook his head. "But no, see, that's where you lose me. When I was nine, I didn't know what my principal's schedule was, when they would be out for classroom observation, or what they drank. Kids don't pay attention to that stuff. Do you really think a little nine-year-old knows where to find belladonna and knows how to prep the leaves? Or is devious enough to bring a watch to trick someone into leaning over a treacherous railing? Come on, Jo."

"No, I think you're exactly right. I think Molly helped her."

Arnett's eyes skipped across the dash. "So you're saying they're both psychopaths?"

"I'm saying I think Shauna killed two children, and in both cases, Molly had to do something to make sure nobody figured that out. Delia overheard Molly and Don arguing, and Molly was worried Delia had heard more than she admitted. Don said it had gone too far and it was time for a therapist—I think he knew something was very wrong with Shauna, and was trying to get her help. And I think Molly didn't want to believe her child was anything but perfect. Then Delia shows up acting different and says she can't babysit for them anymore…" Jo raised her eyebrows at Arnett.

He rubbed his chin. "You think Molly decided she couldn't risk Delia saying the wrong thing to someone."

Jo continued. "Stephanie told us Layla had a theory about who the Gunter toy belonged to, and that she was following up. Then boom, she's killed. And I'll bet anything something happened that made Eileen pull up Shauna's files, and she realized something important was missing from them. I remember when my mother transferred me into junior high school here, she had to get my records from my school in New Orleans and bring them in. Schools digitize almost everything now, but I'm sure there are some things they have to keep in hard copy. I bet Molly slipped out whatever it was from the file that showed St. Bernadette's was worried about Shauna's mental state. Or maybe she even managed to tamper with the digital file somehow."

Arnett shook his head. "I still think we're taking a few too many leaps."

"Let's see." Jo nodded, and tapped at her phone. When Lopez answered, Jo asked her to bring the phone into the interrogation room with Don, and record the conversation.

"Okay, go," Lopez said when everything was ready.

"Tell us about Nicole's death," Jo said.

"I don't know the details," Don said. "When I got home that night, I'd already heard about it. Molly tried at first to convince me Shauna wasn't responsible, but when I asked Shauna, she admitted it outright."

Jo shot Arnett a look, and he nodded in return. "Why didn't you tell us Shauna was responsible earlier?" Jo asked, voice barely restrained.

Don paused and sounded confused. "But—you knew. You came in and you knew everything—"

Jo cast her mind back over the conversation—he was right, they'd never specified who they thought was the killer.

"How long have you known that Shauna needs help?" Arnett asked.

Don's voice took on a weary tone. "Years."

"So why the hell didn't you get her any?" Jo snapped.

Arnett flashed her a warning look.

"I tried. Molly wouldn't hear of it. She said all children go through phases with cruel behavior and struggle to learn empathy. She said they grow out of it. I work long days, and her job was to take care of Shauna, and she told me I needed to let her do it—"

"We were in Quincy earlier today," Jo interrupted.

"Then you know about Eric Larson?" he asked, tone flat.

"We do," she said, voice tight.

"We had several play dates with him and another child. Shauna was fascinated by him, and watched him like you'd watch an animal at a zoo. A few months later, Eric turned up dead."

"Nobody suspected Shauna?" Arnett asked.

"I think Eric's mother did, but if she told the police, they didn't take her seriously. Shauna's teachers had already noticed she was a little unusual, and Molly felt that if we kept Shauna at St. Bernadette's it was only a matter of time before they started putting it all together. I told her I wanted Shauna to see a therapist, so they could fix whatever was wrong with her. But she said we'd have to tell the therapist she killed someone, and they'd take Shauna away from us. She said if we moved we could start over, and she'd make sure Shauna understood that what she had done was wrong. I reluctantly agreed, and for three years it seemed like it worked."

"And then she killed Nicole," Jo said.

"And then Molly wanted to move again, but my law firm only has two offices. I told her we'd tried it her way, but now we needed to get Shauna to a therapist. She told me she'd find someone. Then Layla Madani called her saying she remembered seeing the Gunter toy, but couldn't remember if it was Shauna's or Stacey Kemp's. She told her that no, it wasn't Shauna's, then, the next thing I knew, Layla Madani was dead." He choked on the last word.

"How did she manage to kill Layla?" Jo asked.

He shook his head. "I'm not sure. She claimed it must have been an accident, but the way she said it—I knew."

"And Eileen Pham?"

He ran a hand over his face. "That was the end for me. I gave her an ultimatum, told her that if she didn't find a therapist by the end of the week, I'd take Shauna myself. That must have been the last straw. I know it sounds strange, but I love my wife and my daughter, and part of me really wanted to believe there was a way to save our family. But I confronted Molly. She told me she had to do it, because Principal Pham had started going through all of Layla Madani's students' files, and had noticed the progress log from St. Bernadette's was missing. Molly had removed it when we transferred Shauna, because it mentioned concerns with her odd behavior. I just—" He choked on the words again.

"Pham never checked it before then?" Jo asked. "I find that hard to believe, as organized as she was."

Hayes cleared his throat, and sounded sheepish. "You'd be amazed how many things get overlooked when you wave a large donation check around during the application process."

CHAPTER FORTY-ONE

Molly whipped around to see Emily careening down the street, impossibly fast for such a tiny thing, screaming bloody murder at the top of her lungs.

She dropped everything and started to bolt after her, but caught herself. Shauna was already closing the distance, and across the street, a curtain had twitched—an elderly woman, all gray hair and rheumy blue eyes, stared out, alarmed. Best to let the whole thing look like a game of tag between sisters—so she held back as Shauna caught up with Emily, grabbed her around the waist, and hefted her up.

"Help!" Emily screamed again.

Molly plastered on an exasperated expression and called out to them. "Girls! I told you to play quietly! You're going to disturb the neighbors. Now get in the car while I load up the back."

"No—" Emily screeched.

Shauna shoved a hand over Emily's mouth and carried her back to the car. "Sorry, Mommy!"

Molly shook her head in a gesture she hoped was appropriately bemused, picked everything up and carried it all to the Honda. She shoved it all into the trunk, then bent to take Emily from Shauna and secure her into the car seat.

As she buckled Emily in, she leaned close to her ear. "If you try that again," she hissed, "I'll let my daughter kill you slowly with her bare hands, the way she killed Nicole."

Emily's green eyes widened, and she shrunk back in the seat as far away from Molly and Shauna as she could get.

CHAPTER FORTY-TWO

By the time Jo and Arnett screeched to a halt on the curb in front of the Connecticut house, teams of officers had the block locked down.

Two of the cars pulled up behind them, and two plainclothes officers stepped out of one. The tall blond man introduced himself as Pete Turner, and the slightly shorter woman with a tight brown bun as Ellen Weinburg.

He gestured to the house. "We've been here for fifteen minutes. Nobody's come or gone."

A door slammed across the street, and a tall fragile woman with white hair hurried toward them, waving her arms. "Hey! Are you police?"

Jo strode over to her and identified herself and Arnett.

"I knew something was going on. That house gives me the creeps to start with. Nobody's ever there, but once every month or two this woman shows up. She's always alone but today she had kids with her, and one ran down the street screaming at the top of her lungs. The older girl played it off like it was some sort of game, but what game has you run down the street screaming for help?"

"And you didn't call the police?"

She looked uncomfortable. "I should have. But the mother laughed it off, and just packed them up in the car and left. The little girl didn't do anything else, so I figured I was being oversensitive. I should have followed my instincts."

"Can you describe them?"

"The one screaming was about six or seven I think, brown hair and light eyes." She peered at Jo's face. "Button nose like yours, actually."

"And the others?"

"The girl was slightly older, and the mother was in her thirties. Medium height, but dumpy. Both had red-brown hair."

"How long ago was this?"

"About half an hour ago."

"Do you know if anybody else is inside?"

"I don't think so. They came and left all within about fifteen minutes."

"Thank you for your help." Jo turned and walked back to Turner and Weinburg. "No sign that anybody's inside?"

"Not that we've seen."

Jo popped the trunk of the Malibu and grabbed a tactical bulletproof vest. "Then we'll approach. We have other teams that can come in as backup?"

Turner pointed to the other car. "Bringing them in as we speak."

Jo removed her shoulder holster, slipped the vest over her head, and adjusted the straps. "Then let's do this."

Once Arnett was in his vest, Jo pulled her Beretta from the holster. Arnett, Turner and Weinburg did the same with their weapons, and followed her as she moved around the perimeter of the house. A fence prevented them from entering the backyard, so the sweep was quick. Jo pointed to a shrub around the side of the house, next to the gate. "Well, look what we have here."

Arnett leaned slightly forward for a better view. "If I'm not mistaken, based on the crash course we just gave ourselves, that's a belladonna bush."

Jo carefully climbed the stairs to the porch and, standing to the right side of the door, knocked.

Nobody answered, and she couldn't detect any noises inside. She knocked again, and called out, "Oakhurst County SPDU welfare check. Open up."

When nobody responded, Jo pointed to Turner and gestured toward the window near the door. He nodded, pulled out a baton, and smashed out the windowpane. He paused, listened, and then reached through to unbolt the door. Then he opened the screen and flung open the door.

Jo raised her Beretta, then swung around and stepped into the house. She surveyed the empty living room. "Clear."

They moved systematically through the house, ending in the garage.

"Nobody here, but that vehicle looks familiar." Arnett pointed to the silver Volvo.

Jo put her hand on the hood. It was warm, but only just. She circled the car, examining both the outside and inside. "Looks like she was smart enough to swap out her vehicle, and we must have just missed her. I'm not seeing any blood, or any other sign of a struggle, so it seems at least the girls are alright." She tucked her Beretta into her hip holster. "We need a CSI unit out here to go over all this."

One of the other officers appeared in the doorway. "We've got a hit on the Honda Pioneer, heading south out of Hartford on I-ninety-five."

*

As Arnett flew down the highway with the siren clearing the way, Jo liased with the Connecticut State Police. Because of the hostages, they decided just to tail Molly, hopefully staying under her radar, until she had to stop. Jo stared down, calculating possible routes on her phone, her right leg bouncing nonstop as she tried to distract herself from the fear that kept leaking out through her barricades.

"How far do you think she'll be able to go before she stops?" she asked Arnett.

"With two children, it's hard to say, especially one Emily's age. I can't imagine more than a couple of hours without one of them needing a bathroom break."

Jo nodded, stilled her leg, then tapped on Sophie's number.

Her mother answered. "Josette."

"Ma?"

"Yes. Sophie is trying to calm down Isabelle. I told her not to tell the child the truth and to let me take her for the evening, but she's not willing to let Isabelle out of her sight."

Jo couldn't blame her. "I promised her I'd call with an update as soon as I had one. We found Molly, and we have state police following her vehicle. We have a witness who says Emily is unhurt. They're keeping Molly under a close watch until she stops, and then we'll apprehend them. Bob and I have almost caught up to her, so I'll be on site when it happens."

"So, what, this is like an OJ-Simpson-white-Bronco police chase?" she asked.

"Similar, except she doesn't know we're following her."

"What if she gets away?"

"She won't. We have cars ahead of her and cars behind her. We'll see any move she makes."

"And what if she figures out you're following her and runs?"

Trust her mother to hone in on one of the main risks of the plan. "They have unmarked cars and they're trading off every few miles. She won't figure it out."

"Then what happens?" Her voice rose—she was envisioning one of the other main risks.

"When she stops, we'll surround her."

"Then she'll just shoot Emily!"

"We don't believe she has a firearm," Jo said, hoping her mother wouldn't press her too closely on that point—Molly wasn't stupid, she must have some sort of weapon on her. "But of course we'll act as though she does. We'll take every precaution."

Her mother's voice shook. "I don't see how this can end well, Josette."

The quiver rent Jo like an earthquake. Elisabeth Fournier Arpent was never frightened or weak—or at least, she never showed she was. Her mother's unfailing strength had calmed and sustained Jo as a child, and had taught her how to be strong through her own tribulations. To have that surety gone felt like someone had ripped off her limbs—but now her sister and her mother needed her to be the strong one.

She squeezed her eyes shut and summoned every bit of strength she had, forcing her voice to be strong and confident. "Mom. This is what we do, and we're damned good at our jobs. I need you to trust us. We'll bring Emily home to you, safe and sound."

Trust us. Why couldn't she bring herself to say *trust me*?

Her mother paused a moment before responding, but when she did, the quiver was gone from her voice. "I'll let Sophie know you have eyes on Emily. Let us know if there's anything you need from us."

Jo ended the call, then leaned back in her seat and stared out the window, walls crumbling and mind racing. She'd just assured them she'd bring Emily home safely, but how likely was that, really? Every time someone she loved had needed her, she'd failed them. Marc, the boyfriend she'd watched get shot in New Orleans—she hadn't had the strength to tell her father, and force him to let her identify the gang members responsible. Jack, who would most likely have walked away from the drug-addled mugger in Boston if she hadn't prematurely played cop before she'd even entered the academy. And her own baby—she hadn't even been able to protect the child tucked deep within her own womb. Every single one of them, failed by her. If she wanted to save Emily, the best thing she could do was turn around right now and let the real professionals deal with it.

Arnett's voice, gentle but firm, broke through her thoughts. "How can you expect them to trust you if you don't trust yourself?"

She turned to the blur of trees passing her side window. "Don't start thinking you can read minds."

"You're as hard to read as a Broadway marquee. And you know I'm right. What has your therapist been telling you if she's not telling you that? I've lost count of how many murderers and rapists you've caught and put away, and how many commendations you've received. I'll never, if I live to be a thousand, get *this*." He waved a hand toward her.

Her head snapped to him. "Oh, I'm a damned good cop. Except when it involves people I love."

"Nope, sorry, not buying the bullshit. You weren't a cop then. Your teenager boyfriend, what were you, fourteen when you saw him get shot? The fact that you got out of there alive yourself is a testament. And your fiancé? Also before you were a cop, and also not your fault. You and I both know the stats on that—the likelihood one or both of you was getting away from a desperate addict with a gun was nearly non-existent."

"No, because—"

"Save it, I've heard it. And mostly I've figured you had the right to carry them with you however you needed to, cause we all beat ourselves up over something, and for the most part I've watched it strengthen your resolve and make you a better cop. But right now your niece needs you focused, and getting lost in your own head over crap that happened decades ago is just self-indulgent." He turned and met her eyes. "Time to get over it, Jo. Now. You want to honor their memories? Turn your survivor's guilt into a superpower or get the hell out of our way. That little girl needs you."

He turned back to watch the road in front of him.

She did know he was right—if she couldn't put this away, she was a liability. But if she hadn't been able to put it away after all these years, how the hell was she going to be able to put it away now?

CHAPTER FORTY-THREE

Ten minutes later, they pulled within two miles of the cars trailing Molly's Honda. Arnett turned off the siren, and slowed his approach. As they closed the remaining distance, he identified the undercover cars, then stayed as far back from those as possible while keeping them in sight.

They continued on in silence, Jo calculating every variable she could as Connecticut flew past her. Emily's lunch would have been at eleven thirty, and it was now nearly five. Emily would be hungry by now, so there was a possibility that Molly would stop for food. Even a drive-thru would work; actually, it would be a very effective way to intercept her unnoticed. But no, Molly was an attentive mother, she'd have thought about food. She was the type who carried snacks in the car regularly, *just in case*.

A far more likely possibility was that one or both of the girls would have to go to the restroom. For the life of her, Jo couldn't remember how often Emily went to the bathroom, she'd frankly never paid enough attention to that sort of thing. But surely it couldn't be hours, especially since Emily would be scared? They'd left the Connecticut house at least an hour ago, so surely within the next hour she'd have to go again?

She radioed the state trooper in front of them about the possibility.

"A truck stop would be perfect," he responded. "I can't get units out in time for the next one, but I can have a set at the one after that. But, I don't want to get your hopes up. Most likely we won't be able to intercept until she tries to get a hotel for the night."

Jo winced. A hotel was the type of place where a hostage situation could go very, very wrong.

CHAPTER FORTY-FOUR

Molly struggled to keep her focus on the road.

There wasn't anything more she could do. After Emily's escape attempt, she couldn't risk taking any sort of unnecessary detour, so trying to mislead the police was out. If Emily got it in her head to have a screaming fit while Molly tried to use an ATM, the next person might not be so easily fooled into thinking she was just a misbehaving child.

Her new strategy was threefold. One, hope the police were looking in the wrong place. Two, hope it took them long enough to figure out she had another car for her to get to Mexico. And three, in accord with that, get to Mexico as quickly as she could.

Damn you, Don.

Why did he have to push it? Why couldn't he have just helped, rather than insist on taking Shauna to a therapist? Like Shauna would just have to go once a week like some play date and everything would be hunky dory. Like she wouldn't have been instantly ushered into a padded cell in some sort of institution, stigmatized and scarred beyond recognition for the rest of her life.

Okay, sure, Molly had been mistaken when she thought Eric Larson was a one-time thing, and that they'd just teach her killing was wrong. She was fully willing to admit that. But you didn't just give up on your child, even if it took them a bit longer to learn right from wrong than other children. And for three years, all had been well. Sure, she should have done more when she saw that same look in Shauna's eyes while playing with Nicole that she'd had with Eric. But Molly had the stern conversation with Shauna, and Shauna had sworn up and down she'd never hurt Nicole. Was it so wrong that she'd wanted to believe her child?

Regardless, that was in the past, and she knew now that teaching Shauna right from wrong wasn't enough. But it was also her responsibility as Shauna's mother to make sure she had a good life. Shauna might have to stay away from children until she was an adult, maybe even for the rest of her life. But *no way in hell* was she going to spend her life as a drug-stuffed zombie in an asylum.

She straightened her spine and focused on getting to Mexico—which would be easier said than done. Shauna was solid; as long as she had a book to read, she'd be silent for hours. She'd eat protein bars and chips and Lucky Charms with delight, like the whole thing was a vacation filled with treats that she normally didn't get to have. She'd even sleep in the car if Molly needed her to. But Emily wouldn't eat anything, and she wouldn't drink anything. If she kept it up, she'd make herself sick. No way Molly would be able to stop to get her medical attention, and a sick, fussy child would prevent her from being able to get any sleep herself. *Stupid*, she berated herself, again frustrated that she hadn't taken the older girl.

Little sniffles pulled her attention to the back seat. She stared, weighing her options. When she'd taken Emily, she had no intention of hurting her, not for a second. It was a bluff really, something to rattle Detective Fournier, so she'd be distracted and make bad choices. But now, she was realizing, keeping the girl alive wasn't realistic.

She'd already accomplished what she needed to—Fournier would be flustered now, and if they did catch up to her, they wouldn't come in shooting. She didn't actually need Emily alive to keep that charade going; the smart thing would be to kill Emily, dump her in some field where it would take days for someone to find her, and get herself and Shauna across the border as soon as possible.

Yes, it'd be the smart thing to do. But five people were already dead. And she couldn't kill a little girl herself—could she bring herself to allow Shauna to kill right in front of her?

Emily looked up and caught her eye in the rearview mirror.

"I have to go to the bathroom," Emily said.

Molly squeezed her eyes shut—of course she did, and of course Molly hadn't factored in the frequent potty breaks a child that young would need.

That clinched it. There was no way she'd be able to deal with this nonsense the whole trip. The girl had to go.

She looked up at the exit sign. They were a good fifteen minutes away from the sort of open spaces she'd need to hide Emily's body. "You'll have to hold it."

"I've been holding it, and I can't hold it anymore."

"You're a big girl, you can do it. You're just going to have to wait." She flicked her eyes back to the windshield, and refocused on the road.

"Oh, gross!" Shauna squealed. "Mom, she's peeing all over herself! I'm gonna throw up!"

The smell hit her along with Shauna's shriek. "Don't you dare throw up. Just ignore it, and the smell will go away in a minute."

Shauna started to wretch. Molly hit the down button to open the windows, but that just sent the smell of warm urine swirling through the car. Shauna's mouth opened and orange Cheetos vomit doused her seat and the floor in front of her.

Emily started crying again.

Molly felt her own stomach clench. Damn it all to hell—she couldn't spend the next two days in a car that smelled like pee and vomit.

She yanked the wheel of the car and crossed over two lanes, barely making the ramp to a truck stop.

CHAPTER FORTY-FIVE

The unmarked cars in front of Jo and Arnett suddenly swerved across several lanes, heading for the truck stop exit.

"She's pulling off," the trooper's voice crackled over the radio. "We'll keep distance until you advise."

Arnett slowed into the exit and scanned the lot. Large and roughly rectangular, with gas pumps lining the right side while a blocky beige building with sections for restaurants, restrooms, and showers sat at the far end. The unmarked cars split up and curved around either side toward the black Honda, which had parked next to the restrooms. Arnett hung back as close to the entrance of the lot as was possible.

"Looks like a bathroom break?" Jo asked into the radio.

Before the trooper could respond, Molly burst out and rushed around to the passenger rear. Shauna crawled out of the driver's rear with a backpack and met her mother on the other side. Molly said something, Shauna nodded, and Molly handed her the car keys. Molly pulled open the car door, leaned over into it, and pulled Emily out, extended away from her body.

Jo tensed and leaned forward. "What the hell is she doing?"

Arnett held up a hand. "She's fine. That's the universal posture for 'this child just had an accident and I don't want it on me.'"

Rage erupted through Jo—Emily hadn't had an accident in over four years. A soft strangling noise erupted from the back of Jo's throat as she pictured the fear on Emily's face.

As Molly headed for the bathroom, Shauna hit a button on the car remote and the Honda beeped. Then she trailed her mother into the bathroom.

Jo clicked the radio button. "Does the restroom have another way out? Does it open into the attached stores?"

"It shouldn't. I'll send someone out to check the perimeter." A trooper jumped out of the left-most unmarked car and trotted toward the building.

Jo turned to Arnett. "We're not sure how long she'll be. Should we intercept her at the car, or outside the restroom?"

"She'll see us as soon as she comes out, unless we wait and drive up."

"Once she's back inside the car, we're screwed. We'll have next to no way to get Emily away from her."

Arnett nodded. "Outside the entrance is the best way."

Jo clicked the radio button. "We'll intercept as she comes back out. She won't be expecting it, and she doesn't appear to have a weapon, although she may have something in the girl's backpack."

"Once she doesn't have to hold the kid like a football, she may come out with it at the ready," the trooper replied.

"What the hell kind of football did he play?" Arnett grumbled. "But he's right."

Jo bounced a fist on her thigh, then clicked the radio button again. "We'll put one of us to each side of the exit, then two farther out in front. As soon as she comes out, the closest two will step behind her so she can't dive back into the restroom. We'll do the best we can from there."

The trooper acknowledged, then Jo jumped out of the car, one hand hovering near her holster as she and Arnett moved into place.

CHAPTER FORTY-SIX

Molly surveyed the restroom. A small, older woman stood washing her hands at the filthy sinks, and each of the three stalls were empty.

"Shauna, pull down the change station for me, please." She kept her voice pleasant as the woman finished and left.

Shauna lowered the station, and Molly set Emily on it.

"Let me have the backpack. Clean yourself up with the paper towels while I do this."

Shauna tugged several handfuls of towels out of the dispenser, wet them under the faucet, and washed her face. Molly selected two clean shirts and a pair of leggings out of the backpack, then yanked off Emily's top, pants, and underwear and threw them in the trash.

As she pulled a clean shirt over Emily's head, Shauna came over and grabbed the other shirt. "I like her shirt better."

Molly nearly snapped out, *Do as I say now,* but caught herself—it was the first time in Shauna's nine years where Molly had almost turned into her own mother, and a dab of hysteria bubbled up inside her. She couldn't afford to lose control right now, she had to hold it together. "That shirt matches the leggings."

"Does it matter if they match?" Shauna asked.

"Yes, it matters." Molly gathered up the leggings and stabbed one of Emily's legs through.

Two women entered the restroom. "I'm telling you. Something's going down out there."

Molly's head whipped up. Two limp-haired brunettes in dirty clothes shuffled by. The one talking displayed a mouth of rotted teeth.

The second woman flipped a hand at her as she entered the closest stall. "You don't know."

The first woman sniffed, and headed into the second stall. "If you say so. Go ahead and meet up with Johnny, then, but don't blame me when you get busted. I know an unmarked car when I see one."

Molly froze in place as Emily finished wiggling into the leggings on her own. How reliable were these two druggies? Were they being paranoid? There was no way the police could have found her so quickly—was there? Maybe the woman was wrong, or maybe the cops outside had nothing to do with Molly. Maybe they were here for Johnny, looking to catch themselves a dealer. That was probably it.

But she couldn't take that chance.

She ran through her limited options. There was no other exit. If the police were waiting for her, how could she get to the car safely? Could she wait inside, then try to slip out when it was dark? No, for all she knew they had a floodlight trained on the door, and the extra time would just give them a chance to bring in help. Could she wait and leave behind these two ladies, use them as cover, slip by unnoticed? Not with two children.

She was thinking about this wrong—this situation was the whole reason she'd brought Emily along in the first place. She'd use her as a shield to get to the car, then find a way to lose the police once safely inside. For now she just needed to get out of here.

Angry with herself for never getting a gun the way she'd intended, she reached into the backpack and pulled out her switchblade. Then she shifted Emily off the changing table onto her left hip.

"Shauna, grab the backpack and the keys. You're going to need to open up the car."

Shauna picked them up, eying the knife as she did.

"Stay behind me until I tell you to go."

Shauna nodded.

Molly popped the switchblade open and, ignoring Emily's whimper, pointed it down by her leg, obscuring it in the folds of her coat.

CHAPTER FORTY-SEVEN

Once the trooper returned from circling the building, he and a second man pressed themselves up against the wall ten feet on either side of the restroom opening, weapons pointed toward the ground. Jo and Arnett took positions slightly diagonal to the door so they wouldn't be directly in line of sight.

A moment later, Molly stepped out of the opening. She whipped a switchblade up to point at Emily's jugular, and froze in place.

"Aunty Jo!" Emily screamed.

Molly pressed the side of the knife so hard against her neck the skin bulged around it. "Shauna. In front," she said, and Shauna came and stood in front of Molly's legs.

The blinding rage returned, and Jo forced herself to stay in place, her Beretta trained at Molly's head. She met Emily's swollen, terrified eyes. "Everything's going to be fine, baby. But I need you to be very quiet and still for me, okay?"

"Okay," Emily whimpered, without moving.

"Put the knife away, Molly," Arnett called.

Molly stared directly at Jo. "What are you going to do, shoot two children? We both know you're not going to put your niece in danger. So everybody move back, away from the cars, and we'll be on our way."

"Then what do you think's gonna happen?" Arnett asked. "You're gonna just drive away? Wherever you go, the police will be waiting for you. It's over."

"For your sake you'd better hope it isn't over," Molly said, still staring at Jo. "Because if it is, I have no reason to keep Emily alive."

Jo could see Emily shaking with the effort to remain still and not cry.

"You're fine, baby. You're gonna be fine," Jo said.

"Think it through, Molly," Arnett continued. "Shauna's too young to be tried as an adult. She'll receive psychiatric care. There's no reason to do this."

Molly laughed, shrill and fast. "They'll put her away forever, and I'll go to jail. I'll die before I let you take my daughter from me. And if I die, Emily dies too."

Jo's blood pounded, so hot and hard she felt the pulsing in her fingers. As she stared at Molly, calculating any possible shot, the world in her periphery shrank away as though she were staring down a long tunnel. Shauna stood in front of Molly, blocking her legs and abdomen. Emily's body covered most of her chest. Molly's head was exposed, but Emily's head was pulled right next to it, mere inches away.

Jo's mind flashed on the targets she'd shot at the range. One missed shot, just inches off target. Exactly where Emily's head was.

"So you'd rather be dead, and leave Shauna to deal with it all alone?" Arnett called out.

"You can't shoot me without shooting her."

Nausea roiled over Jo. "Your own daughter? Think about what you're doing, Molly. You're using two children, two babies, as shields. Think about that," Jo said.

"Put the guns down, and I won't have to," she answered.

Arnett flashed a glance at Jo, searching for an indication of what she wanted to do. She shook her head almost imperceptibly, and assessed Molly again. Maybe her right shoulder? It was farther, but still only six inches away from Emily, and still too dangerous. Maybe if she shifted her position?

She took a step to her left, and Molly took a step backward, cutting off any change in angle.

"You know I can't let you leave with her," Arnett said.

Molly smiled. "I think it'll be far easier to explain to your boss, and *the press*, why you let us go than why you killed two *children*. Now it's time to stop playing this game." She took a step forward, and started edging back toward the car.

"Freeze!" Arnett shouted.

She took another step.

Jo matched it, her heart racing into overdrive, so fast she couldn't feel the beats any longer. Because it was happening again—just like Marc, just like Jack—someone else she loved, and she couldn't help them, couldn't stop them from dying—

She had zero doubt this woman was insane. If she'd kill her own daughter, she'd never leave Emily alive. How would Jo explain that to Sophie? How would she ever look her mother in the face after she'd told them both she could handle it and they could trust her—

Arnett's comment sliced through the noise in her head: *How can they trust you when you don't trust yourself?*

Trust. This was her last chance, Emily's last chance. Jo had to find that trust.

She pulled her shoulders back, and relaxed her posture, weighing the weapon in her hand. The pounding in her chest stilled.

Molly took another step.

Jo aimed, and fired.

The impact of the bullet yanked Molly's arm down and back, dragging the knife across Emily's neck before it dropped from Molly's hand. Emily fell with Molly, still clasped in her left arm. When they hit the ground, she pushed herself away and bolted toward Jo.

Jo safetied her weapon and slipped it into the holster, then grabbed Emily up into her arms and clung desperately to her.

CHAPTER FORTY-EIGHT

Arnett and Jo separated themselves from the scene while they waited for the local district attorney to assess it. Jo watched, everything running in slow motion, as Molly was rushed to the nearest hospital for emergency surgery, and the paramedics insisted that both Emily and Shauna be taken to the hospital. Because Jo's niece was involved and she was the nearest relative, the DA walked her through the scene with a local union representative quickly, took her statement about the shooting, then released her to deal with Emily at the hospital.

While they waited for Sophie to arrive, Arnett arranged permission from Don Hayes to escort Shauna back to Oakhurst County SPDU headquarters, then they began the requisite paperwork.

Jo held Emily's hand as a doctor who looked and sounded like Mr. Rogers examined her. As soon as the doctor finished, Emily climbed into her lap and wrapped her arms around Jo's neck. The only thing wrong with Emily, the doctor said, was a shallow cut where the knife had slipped during the shooting. He cleaned it, put an antibiotic on it, and cleared her to leave.

That might be all that was wrong with her physically, but Jo understood too well the other scars the day would leave. So she held Emily close and asked if she wanted to talk about it; Emily nodded and launched into a play-by-play of the house and the drive as though she were recounting a trip to Disneyland. She ended with how she was glad she wet herself because it made Molly stop the car so Jo could catch them.

"I was brave, wasn't I, Aunty Jo? Like you." Her eyes peered up, wide and green.

"You sure were, honey. And do you know why?" Jo asked.

"Why?"

"Because Fourniers are made of stern stuff." She rubbed Emily's nose with her own.

Her little brow furrowed. "But I'm not a Fournier, I'm a Belleau."

Jo laughed and stroked her hair. "Oh yes, you are. Half, because your mom's a Fournier."

Emily considered that for a minute, and then smiled. "I guess that's good, then."

"I guess it is." Jo hugged her close, amazed. Maybe it all felt like a movie to her, something not fully real? At the moment it felt unreal to Jo, too, but she knew how it would hit when the shock defrosted.

The curtain flew across its metal rod and Sophie appeared, pushing aside a nurse. "Emily, oh God."

"Mommy!" Emily reached for her mother, and as Sophie scooped her up into her arms, Emily burst into heaving sobs.

Not like a movie, then. Courage wasn't the only Fournier trait Emily had inherited—emotional denial came easy to her, too. Jo would have to talk to Sophie about that.

She stood and smoothed down her blazer. "Sophie, I'm so—"

One of Sophie's hands flew up in a *stop* motion, and she sent a warning glare at Jo. *Not here, not now.* Maybe not ever.

Jo nodded. "Bob's waiting for me, we have some details we have to deal with."

Sophie's eyes squeezed shut as she buried her nose in her daughter's hair. "I'll call you later, once we get home and get settled."

Jo nodded again, and turned to leave. That call was a conversation she'd love to find a way to skip.

She glanced at Emily as she passed, her head tucked into Sophie's neck, her sobs now soft hiccups as Sophie rubbed her back.

CHAPTER FORTY-NINE

As Jo drove back to HQ, she periodically stared back at Shauna, trying to get a read on her.

She knew all the facts about psychopaths, well past the typical descriptions—during her hunt for Martin Scherer eight years earlier, she'd dug into profiling and learned as much as she could about serial killers specifically and psychopaths generally. Psychopathy was chilling enough when the subject was a grown man who killed women. But this… Her mind reeled.

Shauna alternated between staring out the window and reading her book. To all appearances, she was a small, sweet little girl with an angelic face and wide blue eyes, quiet and demure. How was it possible that this innocent-looking slip of a thing had murdered two children with her bare hands? You'd swear up and down she was the sort who'd ask you to have tea with her dollies, or to make a TikTok video with her to the latest hit pop song. You'd never suspect the tea would be full of belladonna, and the dancing was a trick to push you into a swimming pool.

Shauna's face was peaceful, completely untroubled by the events of the day. Before the ambulance had arrived, she'd asked if her mother would be okay, but there were no hysterics, not even any tears, and once she was told her mother would be fine, she asked if she could get her book from the car. When the trooper told her everything had to stay as it was, the look of utter disappointment on her face had been so heartbreaking he'd bought her a book from one of the shops inside. She thanked him, promptly sat on the sidewalk, opened *Diary of a 6th Grade Ninja*, and read until the second ambulance arrived. At the hospital, she plopped onto the exam table, smiled up at the doctor and answered his questions without hesitation. When he finished, he remarked how lucky her parents were to have such a sweet, charming daughter. Shauna had watched him walk away, expression cold and calculating like a diner choosing which lobster she wanted from the tank, and a numbing chill had permeated Jo from head to foot.

Once back at HQ, they brought her directly into an interrogation room where her father was waiting for her. She rushed to give him a hug, then showed him her new book. "It's a little silly, but mostly good," she said.

Jo repeated part of what she'd already told Don when she spoke to him from the hospital. "Under Massachusetts law, your daughter is too young to be charged with any crime. You also have the right to refuse to allow us to speak with her, or to ask that your lawyer be present when we do."

"I understand." He turned toward his daughter and stroked her hair. "Shauna, these detectives are going to ask you some questions. I want you to tell them the truth, okay?"

"Mom said I shouldn't talk to anyone about what happened, that I'd get in trouble."

"I know she did, baby. But she's wrong. We need to tell the truth, okay?"

"And I'm not going to get in trouble?" Her glance flicked to the detectives and back to her father.

"No, baby. You're not going to get in trouble," Don said.

"Okay." She sat in the chair Arnett had pulled over next to her father, facing them.

Jo had spent much of the drive back deciding how to approach the interview. With most children she'd want to establish rapport, to make sure the child was comfortable. But based on what she'd seen over the last couple of hours, she doubted Shauna would be affected by any of that. A direct approach would work better.

"Do you know who killed Nicole Marchand?"

Shauna set her book in her lap and fiddled with the cover. "Yes. I did."

"Why?"

"Because I wanted to." She shrugged.

"Did she do something you didn't like?"

"No." She ran the corner of the book's cover under her index finger's nail.

"How did you do it?" Jo asked.

"I held her down by her neck and covered her mouth with her jacket."

A wave of nausea pushed through Jo—from Shauna's cool demeanor, she could have been describing how she put her shoes on in the morning. "Did you worry someone might see you?"

"No." She met Jo's eyes. "Karen and Mr. Karnegi go behind the sheds to kiss all the time. I just waited until she gave him one of those gross google-eyed looks, and then asked Nicole if she wanted to play with Gunter."

Jo took in a deep breath. Shauna didn't miss much, if anything. "What about Eric? Did you kill him?"

She tilted her head. "Yes. But I don't remember much about it. I just remember watching the blood come out of his head."

Jo pushed down another wave of nausea. "Do you remember what happened with Delia Cruz, your babysitter?"

She shook her head. "A little bit. My mom told me she was going to take me away from her and my dad, and that I should pull her into the swimming pool until she stopped moving."

"Did she tell you anything else?"

"Just that it should be in the deep part."

Jo thought she saw something flit across Shauna's face, and tried to imagine a six-year-old being instructed by a trusted parent to commit murder. "How did that make you feel?"

She shrugged. "It didn't make me feel any way."

Jo swallowed hard, then moved on. "What happened with Ms. Madani?"

Shauna's brows shot up. "That one was *hard*. My mom gave me a really nice watch and told me to throw it out from the landing onto the stones. But I had to be really careful because I had to throw it far but not too far. She made me practice on the stairs for an hour, and I was really stressed out because I wasn't sure I'd be able to get it right at the museum. But I did, while everyone else was eating their lunch." She smiled, proud of herself.

"Then what happened?" Jo asked.

"That part was hard, too. I had to cry, and I don't like to cry. So I stubbed my toe really hard on purpose against a brick wall, and then just pretended I was upset about the watch. I told her I'd borrowed it from my mom when I wasn't supposed to and it slipped off because it was too big for me, and that if I didn't get it back I'd be in big trouble. And then when we got up there and she saw she was going to have to reach for it, at first she told me she couldn't do it, and we'd have to ask the museum to get it. And then I was scared that the plan wouldn't work so I got upset for real, and when she saw how upset I was she said she'd try. And then when she leaned over the railing, I pushed her." She ran her finger over the corner of the pages of the book, making a *thwuuup* sound as she finished speaking.

Jo glanced at Don Hayes, whose expression reflected her own horror. If he'd known about any of this, he was doing an amazing acting job.

"You thought of that yourself?" Arnett asked.

She threw Arnett a skeptical look. "No, my mom did."

"Did your dad help you plan it all out?" Arnett asked.

She didn't even glance at her father. "No, my mom said we shouldn't tell him because he wouldn't like it. But it was for his own good." She nodded, knowingly.

"Did she say why it was good?" Jo asked.

"Because if anybody found out I killed Nicole, I'd get in trouble and have to go away."

"Did your mom sneak into the museum while you were there?" Jo asked.

"No." Shauna looked and sounded confused.

"But you said she told you to throw the watch from the landing. There are a few landings, how did you know which one?"

Her brows cleared and she *thwupped* the book pages again. "Because we went there the day before to decide where to throw it from."

Jo shot Arnett a look, then moved on. "And what about Principal Pham?"

She broke out into a smile. "That was so much easier than Ms. Madani. My mom gave me some stuff to put in her drink. *Super* easy."

Jo's abdomen contracted as the nausea returned—Shauna could have been talking about winning a game of hopscotch. "How did you get it into the drink?"

She shrugged. "I told the substitute teacher I had to go to the bathroom, then I went to the office. My mom told me to go before morning recess because that's when Principal Pham goes into the classrooms."

"How did you know she'd leave her drink in her office?"

Shauna blinked at her. "No food or drink allowed in the classrooms, except bottles of water."

Of course. How stupid of her. "Weren't you worried one of the office staff would see you?"

"They did see me. I had a pass and I said Mr. Walker sent me to drop off the attendance sheet. When I asked to go to the

292   M.M. CHOUINARD

bathroom, I offered to take it." Shauna held her eyes, and smiled a sly, calculated smile. "But it wouldn't have mattered even if I didn't. Nobody pays any attention to kids."

*

"I've dealt with drug kingpins and maniacs who've killed in cold blood, but I don't think I've ever sat across from anyone who terrified me more than that little girl," Arnett said to Jo outside the interrogation room.

Jo nodded. "Something about the innocent package makes it all the more sinister."

Arnett rubbed his chin. "The question is, what do we do from here? We can't prosecute Shauna, and we can't compel her to testify against her mother. And even if Don does testify, he didn't have first-hand knowledge of anything. At least we have Molly for kidnapping."

Jo pulled out her phone and typed in a text while she answered. "I'll have Lopez see if the museum keeps their video for any length of time; hopefully we can catch Molly and Shauna on film the day before Layla died. And, we've got that clear patch of belladonna outside the Connecticut house. With the note she left when she took Emily, she'll have a hard time claiming this had nothing to do with the homicides. But, at the end of the day, I think our greatest shot is the possibility that we can pull Shauna's DNA from the watch or the Gunter toy."

"And yet, at the end of the day, Molly didn't actually kill anyone. So at best we're looking at accessory to murder, and a skilled defense attorney is gonna have a field day with that."

Jo rubbed her eyes. "We'll make it as bulletproof as we can. But my real worry is Shauna."

"Agreed. Even if the department of children and families evaluate her and decide to put her in a psych facility, I don't believe for one second that *that*"—he pointed back to the room—"is something you can rehabilitate."

Jo shared his skepticism. But she needed to believe mental illness could be treated, if only for the sake of her own struggles with trauma. Admittedly, PTSD was very different from psychopathy, but she wanted desperately to believe that some form of medication or therapy was possible. Not now, but maybe in time for Shauna to live a normal life.

The smile on Shauna's face when she talked about her killings flashed through her mind.

She hoped to hell that medication or therapy would be viable in the next few years.

CHAPTER FIFTY

Jo hurried to the museum the next morning as soon as they answered their phone. She and Arnett easily identified Molly and Shauna on the museum's video footage, walking through the galleries the afternoon before Layla Madani's death. Not with the casual, interested stroll of patrons enjoying the exhibits, but with the brisk, analytic posture of someone examining a potential kill site for cameras and opportunities. Jo stared at the footage, staggered by the twisted mother-daughter outing and the premeditated cunning that underlay it all.

Molly woke in the hospital screaming for her daughter. Despite her lawyer's counsel, she refused to stay quiet about the murders. Quite the opposite: she made a full, repeated, loud confession insisting that Shauna had nothing to do with any of the deaths, and they were all Molly's own doing.

"No way," Jo told Assistant District Attorney Rockney. "We have video footage from the boutique that shows she couldn't have committed any of them by her own hand."

"Who cares?" Arnett had objected. "She weaponized her daughter's psychopathic tendencies. This time to protect her daughter, but how long before she does it just because someone looked at her cross-eyed? Let her rot in jail."

"Two reasons," Jo said. "First, any impetus to put Shauna into a psychiatric facility would evaporate. And two—"

The ADA cut in. "Once we try to prosecute for murder one, the defense attorney will produce the footage himself, and undercut our case. If we then try to put on another case for accessory before the fact, he'll argue we're flailing, and it will undermine our credibility."

Frustration twisted Arnett's face. "Yeah, fine."

"Don't worry," Rockney said. "We have a solid case for two consecutive life sentences."

Arnett nodded, only somewhat mollified.

Rockney pointed at Jo. "I need you to go home, and don't come back until you've seen a department-approved therapist to discuss the incident."

"I have an appointment this afternoon." Standard procedure required this for a detective-involved shooting, so she'd co-opted an already scheduled appointment scheduled with Nina.

"Good. Let me know if you need time off."

"Will do."

But the strange thing was, the calm she'd felt after shooting Molly had remained. Shooting another human being always weighed heavily on her, of course. But apart from the gravity of that, she'd been at peace in a way she'd never been before, at least not in conscious memory. It could very well still be some temporary protective device, but over the years she'd developed an awareness of her defense mechanisms, and this felt different. Nina would certainly let her know either way.

But there were several details she needed to deal with first.

*

Jo had a long conversation with Gia, then had Anthony Marchand sent into an interrogation room before they released him from custody. Once he was safely ensconced, she and Arnett joined him.

He stared up at them, his rage barely contained beneath his pasted-on smugness. "Still not going to say anything without my lawyer present."

Jo sat slowly on the chair across from Marchand. Arnett stood in the corner, hands clasping a thick folder.

She tapped the gray laminate table with her index finger for a moment before replying. "Not a problem. I'll do the talking."

She lifted her chin and ran her eyes over his face. "We've heard a fair amount about your anger problem," she finally said.

He sneered at her. "I don't have any—"

She bolted up toward him. "I thought you said you didn't have anything to say?"

He flinched, and leaned as far back in his chair as he could manage.

"As I was saying." She made a show of sitting slowly back down, while holding his eyes. "We've heard about your anger problem, and how you like to take that anger out on your wife and children. Personally and professionally, I have a serious pet peeve about assholes who beat up people weaker than them, especially women and kids. What about you, Detective Arnett?"

Arnett didn't move a muscle. "Couldn't agree more, Detective Fournier."

"So here's what's going to happen. We're going to release you in a few hours. A police escort will take you to your house to allow you to pick up your necessary personal belongings and your vehicle. Then they'll escort you to whatever location, not your house, where you intend to spend the night. With me so far?"

Anthony didn't respond. Jo held his gaze without blinking. Finally, he nodded.

"First thing tomorrow, even before you go into work, you're going to sign up for an anger management program. Then you're going to call me or Detective Arnett with verifiable proof of that enrollment, along with an address for your new residence."

He sneered again. "Or what? You're gonna beat me up? Police brutality?"

"We've done a little digging, and we've found the hospital reports for Nicole and Nicholas." She motioned back to Arnett, who waved the folder he was holding. "If you miss even one of your anger management sessions, or if you take up residence somewhere without reporting that new address to us, or God forbid you give Gia or Nicholas even a dirty look, not only will I prosecute you for their assault and throw you into gen pop with felons who have strong opinions about child abusers, but I'll make sure these reports are sent to every company you do business with."

The blood drained from Marchand's face and a film of sweat popped out on his temples. Jo narrowed her eyes and smiled, relishing his discomfort.

A thought occurred to him. "You can't make those stick and you know it, that's why you're not charging me now. They were too long ago and she didn't file charges at the time. My attorney will walk right through it."

Jo laughed. "Do you really want to take the chance that a jury won't believe it? Or that the companies you do business with won't believe it?"

Rage flashed across his face again, and he stared at the wall.

Jo stood and turned toward Arnett. "Do you have anything to add, Detective?"

Arnett gave a hmm-let's-see head wag. "Well, my wife has a new hobby. Which means for the foreseeable future, I'll have a lot of extra time to just… hang out around town. Might as well drive by your place now and then, just to make sure everything's good. What do you think?"

"That's harassment," Marchand said.

Jo turned back to him. "I'm really glad to see you know the definition of that word. That means we won't have any misunderstanding about behaviors that constitute it, will we?"

She watched him struggle to control his rage. "No, *ma'am*."

"Glad to hear it." She took a step toward him, then bent over the table and whispered. "The next time you need to beat up on someone, Mr. Marchand, you come find me."

She straightened, turned, and strolled out of the interrogation room.

CHAPTER FIFTY-ONE

Gia Marchand pulled her pink cardigan tight around her as she walked the alarm-company techs out of the house and thanked them a final time. She closed and locked the door behind them, then spent the next fifteen minutes following the instructions to reset all of her passwords.

After Molly and Shauna were apprehended, the detectives moved quickly to get her ankle monitor rescinded and all charges against her dropped, something for which she'd be eternally grateful. They sent her home with Nicholas after a conversation.

"We'll hold your husband until tomorrow afternoon," Detective Fournier had said. "That should give you enough time to make arrangements. My suggestion is that you use that time to update your security system—install cameras if you don't have them, get your locks changed, reset all your passwords. Then file a restraining order against him. I'll have a talk with him to make sure he understands his new reality."

Gia had done just that. With suitable 'expedition fees' the alarm company was willing to send out a crew first thing the next morning, and the locksmith came not long after. She watched as they did their work, and while Nicholas caught up on the homework he'd missed.

Now, with them gone and with Nicholas playing in the backyard, she paced through the house, checking and double-checking that the new system secured every room. She was scared, but oddly, she wasn't as scared as she thought she'd be. She'd been terrified of everything for so long—terrified for years of what Anthony would do at any given moment, then terrified that if he could kill Nicole, he could kill her and Nicholas, too. But equally terrified by the prospect of living her life on the run, constantly afraid that Anthony would find them and kill them. Compared to that, what she was facing now felt like a rainy day after a blizzard—unpleasant, but not insurmountable. He'd make life hard for her, she was sure of that. And he could always turn homicidal in the future, but that would be difficult for him since everyone knew the truth about him now. He'd been dragged away from work, there was an official complaint against him with the police, and the entire town's eyes were on him.

Especially Detective Fournier—Gia had seen the look in her eyes when she learned about the beatings, and she was sure Anthony would get a clear look at them, too.

As Gia passed by the living room fireplace, a yellow rectangle caught her eye. She reached in and retrieved it, then brushed off the ash clinging to the back and side. The grief-counselor's business card the police had given her when they'd come to inform her of Nicole's death.

She stared down at it. Funny how it had looked tawdry and aged before, but now, covered with black slashes, the yellow peeped out like rays of a rising sun. She skimmed the name and number, and the print blurred together as her eyes filled with tears.

She sank to the floor, card pressed against her abdomen. Sobs wrenched through her, hunching her over, shaking and choking her. She gasped for breath as the face of her sweet, darling Nicole sheared through her soul.

*

Karen Phelps stared frozen down at her phone, finger hovering over the WhatsApp contact, unsure of what to do.

Shauna had known about her and Jim. Had her philandering on the playground cost Nicole her life? If she'd been fully focused on the kids instead of Jim, would Shauna have had the opportunity to kill little Nicole? If she'd been paying more attention, would she have noticed something not quite right about Shauna, something that put up her warning signs as a mother? When her and Molly's and Gia's kids played together, the three of them had always spent the time chatting to one another, or cooking, or whatever, but always mainly interacting with each other instead of the children. They watched over the kids, sure, but didn't pay close attention to each word said and each expression on their faces. But when she was in the schoolyard, she *should* have been paying that type of attention. She'd agreed to do a job and failed to do it, all because she'd been obsessed with a man.

At thirty-five, it was time for her to face a few things she should have faced long ago. Time to be self-reflective enough to realize that her constant need to have a man in her life was a misguided attempt to replace the love she craved from a father who wasn't capable of giving it. Time to admit that the sort of men who responded to women like that were damaged in their own way, and that any partnership with them was doomed. These weren't hard concepts to grasp—even an armchair psychologist could see it plain as the day was long. The hard part was doing something about it. Changing those destructive behaviors.

She'd never know for sure if she could have prevented Nicole's death. Maybe Shauna would have found another way on another day. Probably she would have. But the fact was, Karen's choices had made it easier, and she'd have to live with that forever.

But she could make different choices, starting today.

She deleted the contact, then went into her phone's drop-down menu and blocked Jim Karnegi's number from her phone.

*

Stephanie Roden eased up to the curb outside the bookstore. She put the car in park and reached for the box of tissues on the passenger seat.

Since Layla's death, she'd cried nearly nonstop. So much so that she'd rubbed her nose and mouth raw, until they were cracked and bleeding. But still the tears kept coming, like a faucet whose threads had been stripped away, and she couldn't even conceive of a day when they'd stop.

She hadn't believed it at first when she'd heard about Shauna— she'd been convinced there must have been some sort of mistake, that Molly must be trying to push blame on Shauna since a child couldn't be prosecuted. But Molly was trying everything she could to take the blame for the murders. And when Stephanie started thinking clearly again, she realized that logistically it had to be true.

And that meant not only had Shauna taken Layla from her, she'd also taken everything Stephanie believed in.

Stephanie had dedicated her life to children, to educating them and nurturing them, to being a positive force for the ones who had nothing good in their lives, to encouraging the ones who got no encouragement elsewhere. To finding something in each of them to celebrate, and teaching them to take pride in whatever strength that happened to be. She had always been guided by her belief that every young soul was beautiful and good and had endless potential.

How could she have been so wrong?

A child that killed other children. And adults. Evil, plain and simple, and there was no redemption for that. No therapy in the world that would fix it.

She'd researched it. They'd test Shauna, and they'd probably require some sort of long-term treatment. But even what that looked like wasn't clear. In-patient, out-patient—it all depended on a myriad mix of 'factors.' And none of it cured psychopathy.

But one factor was certain. Wherever possible, she'd be there to testify to the destruction little Shauna had left in her wake, and to make sure she was never left unsupervised, not even for a minute. Especially over the next two years, until Shauna was eleven, old enough to be tried as an adult in Massachusetts. Whatever psychiatrist or social worker or judge needed to hear from her, she'd be there to speak for Layla. And if Shauna put one foot out of step, Stephanie would be there to call in Detective Fournier and put her away for life.

The door of the bookstore opened and Shauna pushed out, followed by her father, with a plastic bag swinging from her arm.

Stephanie watched as Shauna halted at the curb, waiting for the stoplight to change so she and her father could cross the street. Then she peered up and down the street, and froze as she noticed Stephanie sitting in the car.

Their eyes met.

Stephanie lifted two fingers to her eyes, then pointed them at Shauna.

A chilling smile spread across Shauna's face.

CHAPTER FIFTY-TWO

That evening, Jo pulled up to the curb in front of Sophie's house and turned her engine off. She leaned back against the seat and stared up at the house, unsure and apprehensive about what awaited her inside. Dinner with everyone, including her mother and stepfather, and the first time she'd seen any of them since she passed Emily off to Sophie at the hospital.

Her therapy appointment had taken on a very different tenor from the ones she'd had before. They'd talked about children, and parents, and various forms of love. They talked about mental illness, and the intersection between it and those relationships. And they talked about trust—or rather, how the need for control had so much to do with a lack of trust.

But mostly they talked about Emily. About whether Jo had behaved irresponsibly and ultimately put her in danger.

Had it been wrong to elicit Sophie's help with the investigation? Using sources inside an organization was nothing new, and confidential informants were an important part of police work. Sophie wasn't the first family member a detective had relied on; you used whatever connections you had. But had that really been all there was to it? She'd felt a connection to Sophie during their conversations, felt like Sophie had seen her in a new light, and had, for the first time, seen value in Jo's life choices despite them being so very different from Sophie's. Were Jo's motives tainted by that approval? Had she pulled Sophie in farther than she otherwise would have because she wanted more of that connection?

Ultimately, they'd decided that wasn't the case. She'd gone over every move with Nina, and it boiled down to one thing—that first day at Briar Ridge, when Emily called out to Jo, Molly most likely had seen. Even if she hadn't, the school culture was small, everybody knew everybody, and by looks alone Molly would likely have identified her as Sophie's sister. None of that was Jo's fault, and keeping Sophie at arm's length would have just slowed the investigation. By the time she and Nina finished the discussion, Jo knew it to be true and was at peace with it.

But she doubted Sophie would feel the same way. Jo's involvement had put Emily at risk, and she wasn't sure Sophie could ever forgive her for that.

With a deep breath and a sigh, she forced herself out of the car. She circled around and grabbed the tarte tatin she'd picked up for dessert from the passenger seat, and headed up to Sophie's porch.

Little feet tramped toward the door after Jo rang the bell, and two little faces peeped out of the curtains. Isabelle swung the door open. "Aunty Jo!" both girls cried, and threw themselves at her.

She hugged them back as best she could with the pie in one hand, and laughed. "You know better than to look out the window, Isabelle. Let your mom look out the peephole."

Isabelle rolled her eyes. "Everybody's home and we knew it was you."

"Can I carry the pie?" Emily asked.

"Of course." Jo handed it to her, noting the dark circles under her eyes. "It's your favorite."

The girls ran through into Sophie's dove-gray dining room, set the pie on the credenza, then continued through to the lemon-yellow kitchen. Her mother and Sophie were putting last-minute touches on the food; Elisabeth finished a salad while Sophie sliced roast beef.

"Josette." Her mother wiped her hands on a towel and kissed her cheek. "Can you put the potatoes into that dish for me?"

"Of course." Jo grabbed the pot.

Sophie jutted her chin toward the other side of the house. "Girls, go tell your father and Grandpa Greg that dinner's ready and to help you set the table."

Jo watched them run off together. "How is Emily doing?"

Sophie looked back down at the meat. "She's trying to pretend nothing happened. But she had a nightmare last night, and wet the bed. I got her in for a first appointment with a specialist today, who assured me that she'll probably have a rough few weeks, but that children are resilient and she'll come out of it with our help. We need to keep up routines, give her space to react however she needs to, and show her through our own behavior that everything is okay and she's safe."

Jo fought back tears as she turned the potatoes into a blue bowl. "I'm so sorry."

Sophie put the knife down, and turned to Jo. "Why are *you* sorry?"

"Because—all of it," Jo stumbled.

Jo's mother grabbed her arm. "You saved Emily's life. That crazy woman would have killed her, Jo. You stopped her."

Sophie crossed to Jo, grabbed her by the shoulders, and pulled her into a rib-crushing hug. "You saved my baby. You promised me you'd bring her back home to me, and you did."

Jo stood, dumbfounded, holding her sister's shaking body, uncertain what to say or do in the face of her tears.

Emily and Isabelle ran in. "Grandpa Greg said to ask if there's any food we can carry in," Emily said.

Sophie stepped away from Jo, and, her back to the girls, quickly wiped her eyes. She turned, demeanor completely changed, and transferred the sliced meat to a platter. "Emily, you can take the bread. Isabelle, you can take the salad."

Jo selected a serving spoon for the potatoes and followed the girls into the dining room.

Dinner was sedate. David and Greg kept the conversation light by talking about possible vacations for summer. Sophie and David proposed Disneyland; both girls were excited, even if Isabelle tried to keep up her I'm-older-and-less-interested-in-these-things facade.

As Jo watched the girls argue about which Disney princesses were best, Shauna's face, and Nicole's, flashed through her mind. Each of them so different—Nicole sweet and reserved, Emily ebullient and energetic, Isabelle serious and bright. And Shauna, a psychopath. Even the two sisters, who shared the same parents, the same environment, and much of the same DNA, were so distinct. For the thousandth time she wondered about her own unborn child—but this time she wondered, what if her child had been like Shauna?

A knee-jerk streak of rebellion answered back—*her* child could never be a monster.

But surely Molly would have said the same? In fact, she was still saying it, was still in denial about what was wrong with Shauna. Jo hugged her arms around herself. Having a baby was a huge leap of faith, one you just crossed your fingers and hoped would go well. But so much could go wrong, even short of psychopathy. And while Molly loved her child *too much*, Jo had seen firsthand women who didn't love their children *enough*, and some who didn't love them at all. And it was always possible your children wouldn't love you. There were no guarantees when it came to having a baby.

Just like everything else in life.

Once dinner was finished, Sophie sent the girls off to watch *Frozen 2* while the adults had their coffee. Once brewed, she added a healthy dollop of brandy to everyone's cup, took a large gulp of her own, and sank back in her chair.

"I didn't want the children to hear this," she said. "But I need to know. Did Molly kill Nicole?"

Jo sipped from her cup as she explained everything.

Sophie shook her head, eyes wide. "A nine-year-old serial killer. That's the sort of thing that makes you lose faith in humanity."

At that moment, Jo found it very difficult to argue with that.

"I'm not sure what I find more disturbing," Elisabeth said. "A child who's a cold-blooded murderer, or a mother who uses her child's psychopathic tendency to murder people who got in her way."

David fiddled with his Apple watch. "Either is terrifying. People like that just *out there*, and in my daughter's school."

"It's a side of human nature I think most of us can't really cope with. It takes a special type of person to be able to deal with that darkness day in and day out." Greg lifted his cup, ever so slightly tilted it toward Jo, then drank.

The others nodded and sipped their coffee.

Jo swallowed a gulp of her own, and allowed the warmth to seep through her.

Her phone vibrated on the credenza. Her mother reached over and handed it to her.

Jo froze for a moment before taking it—her mother had a very strict no-phones-at-the-dinner-table policy.

Her mother nodded toward it. "It might be important."

Jo checked the notification—just a text from Matt.

"Is everything okay?" Sophie asked.

Jo stared down at the phone. Normally she'd say, 'It's nothing,' and change the subject, unwilling to assign a label to whatever man she was currently seeing, or to encourage her mother's overbearing interference into her love life.

She cleared her throat. "Just a text from my boyfriend asking about my day."

Silence fell over the table for a long moment as everyone judged how to respond to this new territory. Jo tensed, waiting. Would her mother demand details? Would her sister roll her eyes? Would they cast significant glances at each other and awkwardly change the subject?

Greg drained his cup. "Well, we're just about to cut into dessert. Do you want to ask him to join us?"

Jo nodded and sent the text, amazed to discover she really did.

A LETTER FROM
M.M. CHOUINARD

Thank you so much for reading *The Other Mothers*. I hope you enjoyed reading it as much as I enjoyed writing it, and if you did, then you'll love my other Jo Fournier thrillers, *The Dancing Girls*, *Taken to the Grave*, and *Her Daughter's Cry* and my standalone thriller, *The Vacation*. If you enjoyed the book and have time to leave me a short, honest review on Amazon, Goodreads, or wherever you purchased the book, I'd very much appreciate it. Your reviews help me reach new readers, and that means I get to bring you more books! If you know of friends or family that would enjoy the book, I'd love your recommendation there, too. And if you have a moment to say hi on social media, I love hearing from you!

If you'd like to keep up-to-date with Jo Fournier or any of my other releases, please click the link below to sign up for my newsletter. Your e-mail will never be shared, and I'll only contact you when I have news about a new release.

www.bookouture.com/mm-chouinard

You can also connect with me via my website, Facebook, Goodreads, and Twitter. I'd love to hear from you.

Thank you again, so very much, for your support of my books. It means the world to me!

M.

💻 www.mmchouinard.com

f mmchouinardauthor

g author/show/5998529.M_M_Chouinard

🐦 @m_m_chouinard

ACKNOWLEDGMENTS

Books are nothing without readers, and I'm deeply grateful to every person who takes a chance on one of my books. I'm also deeply thankful to everyone who takes the time to review them or blog about them—your support means the world to me.

I continue to be amazed by all of the talented people at Bookouture who work such magic everyday. Leodora Darlington helped birth this book and Maisie Lawrence took it over to get it toddling out into the world; Alexandra Holmes, Martina Arzu, Jane Eastgate, Nicky Gyopari and Ramesh Kumar all helped edit and produce it; Kim Nash and Noelle Holten tirelessly promoted it; Alex Crow, Rob Chilver and Hannah Deuce helped market it; Ellen Gleeson made the audiobook a reality; and Leodora Darlington, Oliver Rhodes, Jenny Geras, Ruth Tross, Jessie Botterill and Natalie Butlin helmed the ship that transported the product to its readers. So much time, energy, and heart!

Thank you very much to the NWDA Hampshire County Detective Unit and the juvenile court for their help. Any errors/ inaccuracies that exist are my fault entirely.

Thanks also to my writing tribe, who help me in more ways than I have space to list. This includes Erika Anderson-Bolden, Dianna Fernandez-Nichols, Christina Flores, D.K. Dailey, Writers Bloc, and my fellow Bookouture authors.

My husband has made it possible for me to pursue my dreams. I couldn't ask for a better partner and best friend on my path through life. My furbabies keep me warm and happy as I clack away through the night, and never complain when I read scenes out loud to them (take note, husband).

Made in the USA
Middletown, DE
04 September 2021

47639470R00176